Harley's Bootstraps

Lois C. Henderson

 FriesenPress

Suite 300 - 990 Fort St
Victoria, BC, V8V 3K2
Canada

www.friesenpress.com

ISBN
978-1-5255-6874-9 (Hardcover)
978-1-5255-6875-6 (Paperback)
978-1-5255-6876-3 (eBook)

1. FICTION, COMING OF AGE

Distributed to the trade by The Ingram Book Company

Harley's
Bootstraps

Chapter 1

Harley

I was named after a motorcycle. The effort to name me, the youngest of nineteen children, ended in the back alley where Dad parked his bike. With each of my sisters and brothers having a first and second name, thirty-six of the easy names had been used up, as had any inclination to raise solid citizens. I was the last in their line of insipid manufacturing.

After I was born, they closed the shop. With their desire having dried up, Mom and Dad spent their time instead smoking pre-mades in plastic bags from the Indian reserve, watching television, and ripping open Nevada tickets.

With so many brothers and sisters around, no one assumed responsibility for me. I was like our budgie bird. Every once in a while, someone would notice that The Bird needed food or water, but mainly it lived in a state of neglect. Its droppings were piled in a hill beneath its perch, a miniature of the guano islands in South America stuck to a Canadian Tire flyer. Water was at constant low tide, and bits of seed shell were crusted around the edges of the plastic dish that was clipped to the side of the cage. There had been a series of birds, each dying a desiccated death in a crowd, and each replaced by the next bird from Zellers. Turquoise, green, yellow, blue, green, turquoise with black and white. Margie, Scout, Sunshine, Buster, Princess, Yo Bird. Better names than mine. I once heard of a boy named Ryan Danger Boyuk. I think his parents were worse than mine, giving their son the middle name of Danger. Kids aren't jokes, although having nineteen of them seems to me like a pretty big joke. Maybe Harley is a joke name, which makes it worse because it's my first and because I am a girl.

When I was born, Mom drove herself to the Brandon Regional Health Centre, which used to be called The Hospital. She was as big as a house, and after eighteen babies, she waited for no one. Wham, bam, thank you ma'am. Out I came, as quick as shit through a goose, looking just like the first eighteen.

With so many children at home and after nine months of pregnancy, Mom was exhausted. She wanted to stay in the hospital for a few days, just to catch up on her rest, but they sent her home the same day. The hospital is crowded, they said. The bed is needed, they said. When Mom tried to plead her case, the nurse insisted she call Dad and tell him to bring a car seat when he picked her up. Hospital rule. Babies can't leave the hospital rolling around in a car like a pea in a bathtub.

Dad sent the car seat in a taxi. Maybe he was too drunk to drive, although all the years since, I have never seen him hesitate to get behind the wheel, not for any reason. My guess is he was standing proud on the fact that he hadn't attended a single birth of any of his children and wasn't about to start with number nineteen.

Around number eleven, Mom got a visit from a nurse who suggested attendance at a Lamaze class. She went alone to a few classes, but she soon gave up, tired of telling the lie that her husband was sick in bed. Later, she laughed with Dad about the huffy-puffy breathing she had learned and made fun of the pregnant parents. "Parents ain't pregnant," she said. "Women is." When she told that story, there was a silent pause in her eyes. I always thought going to Lamaze classes alone was too alone for Mom.

Mom also told the story of birth number thirteen when she took a tennis ball to the hospital. A few years earlier, the Lamaze nurse had suggested that Mom squeeze a tennis ball during her contractions to distract her from the pain of childbirth. Mom thought a better idea was to squeeze a tennis ball between her knees during sex. When the doctor arrived for rounds, he asked how she was doing. Mom let him know. She fired the tennis ball at him, bouncing it off the side of his head. After that, he referred to her as his little athlete. I think Mom was proud of that because she always ended her story with the words, "Don't mess with a woman in labour." She would know.

Before the babies started coming, Mom and Dad moved from Up North to Brandon, the land of the Manitoba Maple, the most common of maples, growing wild and unchecked. If you see a Manitoba Maple, don't assume it was intentionally planted. It spreads suckers, and even if you cut the tree down, its suckers continue to grow. In a country where the red maple leaf is a symbol of hardiness, strength, bravery, and valour, the Manitoba Maple sheds yellow leaves in autumn. It's a cowardly tree, a nuisance tree, dropping seeds and leaves and sprouting branches everywhere. Just like our family—unattractive and common and a background to everything better about Canada. When Mom and Dad pulled up their roots, nothing changed.

There is an evenness to southwestern Manitoba. Everything has parallel edges, including shabby cedar shakes that line up straight with front yards planted with bluegrass. The bluegrass lines up with the sidewalks, which line up with the roads, which travel in honest lines, echoing the yellow and green of the farmer's efforts and the distant small strips of windbreak trees paid for by the government many years ago. Here and there, the roads make allowances for rivers, meandering interruptions in the great grid, deviations from the norm.

There are no skies in the world like those of the Canadian prairies. The Manitoba licence plates read "Friendly Manitoba," but there is a darker, shady side. In summer, the thunderheads roil and grow and begin to move, their silver linings not a blessing, instead belying the shady intent of their contents. Vertical grey curtains appear on the distant horizon as the sky opens up, indiscriminately dumping rain or hail or hell, or all of the above, before moving on like a tramp that leaves trouble in his wake.

We live in an old bungalow at the corner of Park Avenue and 16th Street in Brandon, across from a do-it-yourself car and pet wash. To protect us from rain and snow, the top half is stuccoed, and the bottom half is covered in cedar shakes. The shakes had once been painted pale blue, and have seen better years. They are moldy and rotten at the bottom, close to the ground, dotted with a few flakes of remaining paint that speak to work that will never be done. Not that we ever notice. The stucco has grey patches where the parging has dropped off, allowing the rain to find it way inside. There is a lilac hedge, overgrown and leggy, that we never prune. Last year's leaves and those of many previous years clog the roots, thin branches trapping plastic bags and paper cups and chocolate bar wrappers. Our neighbours don't complain. They have long given up this battle, a small one in the bigger war of years of fighting parents, kids gone bad, and police visits that deal with both.

I am supposed to go to school every day. School rules. But no one at home cares one way or another, not about whether I go to school or about the school rules. I usually go, sometimes to see my friends or sometimes just to get away from the chaos that is home. Ever since elementary school, I have woken up with an anxious ball of nervous fear residing in my belly. The source of the anxiety isn't discriminatory, moving easily from family crap to school crap and back again. For years, this anxiety has woken me up before dawn. I get out of bed and make coffee for whoever is in the house, but mainly for myself. I like coffee, and have been drinking it since I was eight years old, my morning hours unsupervised by anyone older than me. I didn't smoke back then, but now I pour my coffee and light up, that first cigarette taking the edge off my fear of the day.

There are always little nephews or nieces living in the house; my brothers and sisters and their partners are unable to look after these offshoots. Jail or benders or loss of custody have left a little pile of children growing wild and unchecked, like suckers from a tree. They have potential to be beautiful, but they aren't really wanted. When some of the other eighteen are living in the house, responsibility capitulates to no one. When the house is full of people, there aren't enough dishes for everyone, and even when there are enough dishes, most of them are piled up in the sink. When that's full, the sink is emptied into the dishwasher. The dishwasher is only run when we are out of dishes. Clean dishes are removed from the dishwasher as needed. Dirty dishes are piled up in the sink. Usually, while the little nephews and nieces watch morning cartoons, I manage the dishes situation, emptying dishwashers, emptying sinks, filling cupboards, and putting cereal on the table once I have enough clean bowls. I like the quiet time in the mornings with the kids, their bed-headed little faces bright from a night of sleep.

Last fall, I went to Winnipeg with some friends. I had no money, but that didn't stop me from taking things I wanted. I tried on a patchwork jacket in a dressing room at The Bay, and then put my old, worn, hand-me-down jacket on over the top of it. As I was leaving the store, my new coat hidden from view, a hand grabbed me by the arm. "I'm with Sentinel Security, contracted by The Bay. I would like to talk to you about an item of clothing concealed on your person. Please return to the store so we can clear up this matter." That began a process with the juvenile authorities. The school was notified, as were my parents. I had to meet with a lawyer, provided free by the courts, and was dragged out of school for these meetings. Mom and Dad barely responded. Most of the first eighteen had engaged in similar activities. No biggie, I was no one special.

After that tangle with the law, years of delinquent parenting, and poor attendance at classes, I am not surprised when school authorities finally decide to step in and do something about the situation. They identify me as a young woman at risk of dropping out of school, among other things, and sign me up for the Student Mentorship program. That program culminates with Girls for Tomorrow, a day of scholastic last rites held every year at Red River College in Winnipeg. It's for grade twelve high-school girls from across southern Manitoba, and I am attending along with a couple of other girls from my school. Glad to know I am not the only misfit. Every attendee is carefully chosen, singled out from our peers for serial hooky, suspected use of drugs, alcohol, or sex, liberties with the law, or lack of motivation—activities that are perpetually reflected in our marks and our attitudes. We are those who authorities feel are at risk of not graduating at the end of the school year or of ever achieving our dreams.

Despite being one of the chosen, I don't feel all that risky. The program is meant to prove the school is doing everything it can to save us, but we all know it's a show because at the end of June, they are going to wipe their hands of us. We will be gone from the school, tipped out into the adult world, and replaced by a fresh batch of at-risk kids. To us, Girls for Tomorrow is merely a day of deprivation from cigarettes and friends and known surroundings. Even worse than that, it means forced pairings with grinning, well-intended women, some with lipstick on their teeth, and all with hope in their eyes. Long before that day comes, I have dubbed these women the saviour ladies.

We arrive in yellow school buses, and three loads of potential failures spill out at the entrance to the College. We are then corralled into the gym, no time for a subversive cigarette, and are told to be quiet. Within five minutes, the saviour ladies are standing in one line, us risky ones in another. Two by two, like ark animals, we are about to be paired for the day.

I take my place near the back of the line, shuffling forward like a prisoner in a cafeteria. I have no stripes across my shoulders, but neither do I have the freedom to leave. I glance around at the exits, but they are guarded by cheerful middle-aged women in high-waisted jeans and labels stuck to golf shirts. These labels bear their names in varying degrees of penmanship, all written with the same thick black marker. I try counting backward in each line to see which saviour lady is mine, but they keep moving around, and some are getting more than one of us. It appears that I will be paired with an unhatched chick of a woman with no makeup, solid black flat shoes, and a navy polyester suit. Clearly an escapee from a convent. Then, a lady near the front takes two—deviant ark animals, no doubt—and the saviour chick is matched with a tall, surly girl with half black, half blond hair, a row of piercings along her upper ear, and peeled blue metallic nail polish the same colour as the tattoos on her forearm. For each, my bet is their pairing will be of little value and both will drink heavily tonight, lamenting another wasted day.

As the two lines shorten and pairing becomes imminent, I observe a young woman join the line-up of saviour ladies. She is tall, with square black glasses, long, unbrushed blond hair, scars from piercings in her ears, a tiny silver star in her nose, and bright orange-red lip gloss. She has the pallor of someone who doesn't eat or sleep well. When she is paired with me, she seems distracted, as if I'm not the main event for her day. She doesn't even notice me. I instinctively resent her for that because it means I won't get the opportunity to reject her first, to rock her back on her heels, or to make her try too hard to soothe my beastly soul.

My eyes scan down to her unusual looking jacket, made from patches of green and red and multicoloured silk, worn with the sleeves defiantly rolled back. The fluorescent lighting in the gymnasium, unflattering in almost all other situations, heightens the colours of the silk. The patches appear to be sewn together by hand, with careful, even stitches in contrasting thick threads. A row of buttons rises from her hip, ending at her shoulder. The top button is different from the one below it. I then realize that every button is a different colour, a different shape, and varying in size from the one above and below. The high collar appears as a pedestal on which the saviour lady's head is perched, its jade brilliance a stark contrast to the white of her face. The jacket tucks in around her waist and then flares out, long tails hanging low, almost touching her boot tops. This jacket was no accident. And it makes me think about the jacket I stole last year. I wish I had stolen this one instead.

A massive and worn purse is pulled carelessly across her body, flaps open and zips undone. Her fingernails have no hint of colour, and they are cut so short that no white shows. Her hands seem small, too small for someone so tall, and they are made smaller by her watch. It has a face the size of an open mouth, and it hangs loosely on her arm. Every time it slips around to the inner side of her wrist, she twists it back to where she can see it. When she talks to one of the organizers, I note that there is no lipstick on her teeth. My lady turns to me, her eyes barely acknowledging me, checking me over quickly, passing what I think is a hasty first judgment of me. She looks at her watch, its face more interesting to her than mine. I decide I want to make her see me. I am prepared now to be anything other than what she expects, which seems to be nothing at all. I don't know why, but I want her to acknowledge my existence.

Chapter 2

Meaghan

The dismal weather makes it a bad day to be anyone. The clouds skim the clumpy fields that are bordered with fence posts, their colour darkened by the moisture, piercing the thick fog that shrouds the land. I remember my dad always saying, "Meaghan, the clouds are sleeping when they hang so low to the ground!"

The car heater is barely doing its job, and the dampness from the air seeps into my bones. Steve talked me into buying this car, this Impala, and I hate it. It is practical and mediocre and boring. A grandpa car, painted a dull silver, barely reflecting light, and most certainly not a reflection of the person inside of me.

The weather outside leaves me with an overwhelming sense of melancholy. The gloom sits in my stomach like a hard ball of sadness, heavy and dirty and encumbered, consuming me from the inside. It has been a constant in my life, a depression with which I have always struggled. And neither this weather nor this car does anything to help.

As I drive toward the city, the sky hovers over the refuse of last year's harvest with the sticking, cold wetness that only a day in late March can bring. Shades of tarnished, brassy crop stubble mix badly with the cold grey of the air, their uninspired colours giving an unpleasant feeling of deadness to my world. Nothing is bright; nothing is hopeful; all the colours are dull, reflecting my mood.

I pass a tall recycling box along the side of the highway, the primary blue colour of the plastic oddly out of place against the monotonous natural background. This plastic sentinel also pierces the fog, a beacon of hope for passing environmentalists keeping an eye on the future of the world. It's a big job for a blue box.

When Mom was a child, she would go for rides in the family sedan, hurtling down The Trans-Canada Highway with the windows rolled up tight to keep the highway noise out and the music from the radio in. Her parents smoked Matinees in the front of the car. Mom and her brother and two sisters would fight or sleep in the back seat, or they would sit curled up in the foot well rereading comic books left over from previous road trips. From time to time, the monotony of the highway was broken by the promise of alien Manitoba garbage receptacles sitting on the gravel shoulder of the road. The positions on the highway of those small white globes with round openings for refuse were prefaced by a countdown from ten. When Mom saw the "TEN SECONDS TO TOUCHDOWN" sign announcing that a garbage bin was ahead, she would yell out, "COUNTDOWN!" A group of little heads dutifully popped up, peering through the front window as the entire family banded together to energetically shout out the numbers, backwards from ten, the loud sound breaking the boredom of the trip. It was another lost opportunity, though. The family never stopped to dump their garbage. They just kept it with them.

I can see a Co-op gas station ahead, its red and white signage a throwback to my youth. I should stop for gas, I tell myself, but my bad mood weighs heavily on my pedal foot, and I decide that optimism will get me to the next station. There is something about the straight roads of the prairies that diminish the fear of running out of gas. Besides, if that does happen, the Trans-Canada is the longest highway in the world, and a car parked on the shoulder is visible from a long way off. No privacy for evil deeds. I swill some lukewarm coffee from my black plastic CBC travel mug, the inevitable drip landing on the front of my coat.

The Trans-Canada slows down when it gets to Winnipeg. It jerks into the city, lurching through a brief alias as Portage Avenue, then veering right where it assumes the theatrical name of Broadway, too fancy for its prairie roots. La-di-da. Desperate to reach the lucrative Ontario border, it heads south, then east, picking up and shedding new names as it goes. It was never designed to be scenic, just a grown-up wagon trail that takes you where you need to go.

I drive into the city and turn onto the street where my childhood friend Lydia lives. Nestled in a bend of the Assiniboine River, hers is an abnormal Winnipeg street that deviates from the grid. Large elm trees, refugees from Dutch elm disease, long to embrace each other, branchy fingertips barely touching, protecting the houses and their occupants. This neighbourhood has grown young in recent years, with plastic playhouses and swing sets parked on the front lawns. In March, they are unused, layered instead with the resistant remnants of winter that are slowly melting to reveal the dirt and leaves from last fall. Underneath, the once-proud red plastic has faded to milky pink, bleached by the harsh Manitoba sun. Some houses still drip with Christmas lights and are prefaced with lawns caked with flat, brown and molding leaves, and flat, hard snow gripping the ground. The neighbourhood has the spring smell of a winter's worth of dogs.

I stop on the street, the nose of my car edging past the No Parking Zone sign. I momentarily feel guilty for this, like sneaking nine items into the Eight Items or Less line at the grocery store. I grab my purse and shawl, and cross to Lydia's side of the street.

When she first moved into her house, she outlined a little garden in her front yard with some white, painted rocks. Dead weeds now defiantly poke up through the snow to cover these rocks, suggesting the distinction between the garden and the grass is becoming less obvious. Messy stuff to deal with before she will experience the joys of spring flowers.

I follow the sidewalk through the yard and pause before climbing the front steps to her door. Her house is old, built around 1910 in the style of the day, and although external to the main house, her porch is solidly built, with double-hung windows that allow summer breezes when they are open and that protect from winter gales when they are closed. The porch is filled with comfortable furniture and, in summer, is a fine place for us to catch up on each other's lives and share a bottle of wine. Not today, though. Today is cold and damp, definitely not a porch-sitting kind of day.

I ring her doorbell. Unsure if it works, I also knock on the glass of the porch window. I hear barking deep within the house and Lydia yelling at her dogs to stop barking. She always yells. They always bark. The circle of life goes 'round and 'round. When I think about the inevitability of their communication, a small smile migrates involuntarily onto my face.

I wait for her to open the many locks on the main door of the house, and watch through the glass of the heavy porch door as her dogs push past her, anxious to see who is about to invade their territory. The security façade is a show. I know the spare key to her back door is tucked into the lip of the drainpipe in the back yard. Anyone who knows Lydia knows where she keeps the spare key. The dogs are the real deal, however. Captain is suspicious of strangers, a deterrent to those without access to his otherwise friendly nature. Tennille is a small, brown, yappy Chihuahua who over time has lost most of her teeth. Her breath is rank enough to curl paint. Although Tennille's bark is far worse than her bite, big-black-dog Captain's ensures intruders will likely never hang around long enough to find that out.

When the porch door opens, the dogs welcome me, and Lydia gives me a warm hug. Our worlds collide in the moment of that soft embrace. As I cross the threshold, I can smell the faint sweetness of shisha in the air. It feels good to step into her universe.

Her house is filled with physical reminders of a young life well lived, each an aide-mémoire of where she has been. It is clean and not exactly untidy. A piano sits in the corner of the living room, its bench covered in medical textbooks, bookmarked with post-it notes. An easel sits in the central hall, the same half-finished painting from years ago perched on its ledge. She is too busy studying and working to paint or play. Random piles of possessions live in corners, on chairs, on stairs. They aren't meant to be put away. They just have no other place to go yet. And they surround Lydia as a part of her future. However uncertain their role, she needs them close at hand, each a clue to the next fork in her road. She always tries to pack ten pounds of shit into a five-pound bag. I suppose her days are too short and her nights not long enough to satisfy her quest for living life to its fullest. Those are her terms, not mine, and I have never been sure they will make her a happier person.

I briefly ponder what a driven life would be like. Would it be superior to one that follows a path of lesser resistance, like a spilled cup of coffee?

Her life will be no accident, I know that, although its course cannot be predicted and perhaps never charted.

There is an old chair, legs removed, in the central hall. Captain sleeps in this chair during the day, and Tennille sleeps on top of the back of it. The remnants of dog toys are scattered around the house. Once fluffy stuffed animals, they have had their squeakers chewed out, their stuffing excised, and now resemble bits of dirty rags. A large bin full of dog food sits beside their chair, and a canister filled with dog treats is near the door.

Her purse is open wide, its contents in several locations on the stovetop. There is also junk mail from a pizza place, and third-class mail from a local politician. I resist the urge to shift any of it away from the elements. I don't want Lydia to think I am interfering in the details of her life. But when I spy her stethoscope, its utilitarian rubber tubing and shiny metal contrasting against the useless papers, that is a different story. It calls out to me, and I can't help but rescue it. To me, her stethoscope is a symbol of her hard work, of all her efforts, and it seems too sacrosanct to be casually buried beneath mail she hasn't had time to sort through. While she reaches into the fridge for cold drinks, I reach out and slyly shift it to a more revered location. Out from under the junk mail. My work done, I still feel uneasy. A stovetop means fire to me, and it is no place for unopened mail and the contents of anyone's purse.

Lydia never cooks, relying instead on the generosity of her elderly neighbours to provide her with Ziploc bags of frozen leftovers. Her neighbourhood is an older one, and some of her neighbours have lived in their houses for many, many years. They are mainly widows, their husbands having passed away first, leaving them alone. And lonely. When the young doctor moved to their street, they were naturally curious about her. They knocked on her door, introducing themselves, offering muffins or cookies, gifts of welcome. When she talked of her schedule, of the thirty-hour call shifts at the hospital, of her ongoing exhaustion, and of having no time to shop or cook, the motherly instincts of these old gals kicked in. They started offering her food, like she was a stray cat that had moved into the woodshed. Lydia welcomed these small bags of food as if they were incredible riches, storing them in her otherwise empty freezer. Each bag a meal to be eaten alone, but with gratitude toward the donor.

"Cheers!"

She grins as she hands me a cold beer. We clink our brown bottles and walk to her living room where comfortable chairs await. Captain and Tennille follow us, tails wagging, happy to be a part of whatever is going on. I place my beer well back on the coffee table, away from the edge and away from a naughty dog. Captain loves beer and, given the opportunity, will knock over a beer bottle with his nose, just so he can lick up the spilled contents. He stares at me expectantly, the intelligent eyes of a Portuguese Water Dog reflecting his desire for a beer. I decline his obvious request and shoo him away. He lies down at Lydia's feet. Tennille jumps onto my chair and curls up in my lap. They are happy in their world, as long as it includes Lydia.

She begins telling me about a student mentorship program she is involved in through Red River College. High school girls from southern Manitoba are paired for the day with successful women as mentee and mentor. She had been assigned as a mentor to a young woman.

"Why?" I can't help but ask.

"To be considered a success as a doctor, I need to give back to my community. Apparently, marathon-length shifts, post-call exhaustion, and a zillion dollars in education debt aren't considered giving back; merely the price of admission." Lydia grimaces at the thought of the cost of medical school. "I am hoping the student mentorship day, called Girls for Tomorrow, will fill the expectations of the hospital administration, while only requiring one day of my precious time, other than perhaps a phone call or two from my assigned student down the road. By the way, I was paired with a girl named Harley, if you can believe it! I asked her if she was named after a movie star, but she said she was named after a bike. I cringed inside when she said that. Imagine being named after a motorcycle."

The name conjures up images of chrome and black leather, reminders of good times in my life with Steve. I had been named after one of my father's old girlfriends, so motorcycle naming rights sound pretty good to me. I say nothing to Lydia.

"I have to admit that, when I first met Harley, I barely paid any attention to her, my only goal being to check the Active in Community box on my professional profile. It didn't help that I arrived almost-late at the event, my usual state of arrival at non-work things, and even though we spent the day together, I didn't benefit personally from the experience. Pretty sure she didn't either."

Lydia continues reflecting on Harley and her unpleasant journey to the ripe old age of eighteen. Clearly, these were girls who had not had the opportunity to learn even basic social skills. Whose role models may not have been the best examples. Who might, given their existing circumstances, drop out of their final year of school. Who, given the right mentorship, could have hopes of reaching their dreams. Lydia and Harley had tolerated each other, with Lydia trying to persuade Harley to finish high school, outlining the need for education, of setting personal goals, and encouraging Harley to reach higher. Lydia felt her words had fallen on deaf ears. She tells me how they learned to shake hands in a business situation, how to look someone in the eyes when greeting them, and how Harley could go from being a class-skipping, cigarette-smoking, shoplifting student-at-risk to possibly being a surgical resident at a Winnipeg hospital. I ask Lydia if they connected, and if she will be in contact with Harley again.

"I gave her my cell number at the end of the day. She put it in her phone. She can text me if she wants to get together. Which reminds me, where did I put those forms I have to fill out? Hang on a sec."

And then she disappears upstairs.

Although Lydia sounds cavalier about her involvement with Harley, I know her. She really cares about people, which accounts for her being a doctor. I think back to when she was around the age of seventeen and still living with her parents. She wore the vigour needed to save the world like the blade on a snowplough, the jading effect of inertia not having yet eroded her righteousness. Despite not being old enough to vote, she had researched the three main political parties in Canada, and she had announced her intention to vote NDP when the time came. My vote was thus so easily nullified. Not far from her house were blocks of old apartments where immigrants and drug dealers and single mothers interspersed equitably with university students and disability pension recipients. She occasionally crossed paths with some of the residents, which is how she came to know Mercy.

Mercy had been born in the British Virgin Islands and had arrived in Canada with her mother, who referred to herself as Mercy-Mom. Mercy-Mom had started her life here marginalized by her income, her colour, her gender, her citizenship, and her lack of education. She had then added to this pile, loading on drug and alcohol and physical abuse, and a circle of low-lustre companions. Mercy-Mom was taking five-year-old Mercy, now in kindergarten, along for the ride, including her in the fun of school-night parties, empty fridges, and exposure to the widest range of humanity. That wide range had never been vetted for child-abusers.

One night, Mercy found herself in bed with Mercy-Mom who was drugged and unconscious beside her. An old and whiskery-rough, whisky-tobacco-smelly man, a party invite of the least desirable kind, was pulling at Mercy, dragging her from the bed. The man prodded Mercy along in front of him, down the stairs, and into the crunchy, squeaky snow of the small hours of the winter night. Her pale flowered nightgown, pink and white, hung straight in the still air. Her brown legs and bare feet were absurd against the dirty snow and cold.

The sordid details of her story remained with the two of them, ending several days later on a country road. With all cigarettes gone, the captor locked Mercy in the farmhouse to which he had taken her, and drove into town to buy smokes at the gas station. Mercy, a survivor of the strongest kind, opened the drawn curtains, broke the picture window, and began her journey back to Mercy-Mom, the only safety she knew. Cut, lonely, cold, abused, and afraid, she was found by an RCMP officer.

I try to imagine the sight of Mercy, tears of isolation frozen on her cheeks, walking barefoot in her nightgown down a farm road in Canada in January. Those straight roads had clearly allowed just enough privacy for evil deeds. My head can paint the picture of Mercy's journey, but my heart can't deal with her pain, or the thought that such a little girl should have a need for such bravery.

The story ended as well as it could, with Mercy back with Mercy-Mom, and the bad man in jail for not nearly long enough.

When Lydia first met Mercy about five years later, she was still disadvantaged in all regards. She spoke English with a strange accent, and it was difficult to understand her. Her classmates, unwittingly and with the cavalier cruelness of children, pushed her away, like a mother dog will push away an imperfect pup. Mercy-Mom showed up at the school from time to time, stoned or drunk, yelling at the children and the teachers, thus ensuring that her daughter's isolation was complete from all sides.

Mercy attached herself to Lydia's family. She spent a lot of time at Lydia's house, usually at dinnertime, usually at the end of a month before the welfare cheques arrived. When Mercy-Mom overdosed and was taken to the hospital by ambulance, Mercy was left behind in her apartment, alone and afraid again. She had made herself macaroni and cheese from a box and had microwaved a cup of hot water for tea. Then she called Lydia, who went down the hill to rescue her.

Lydia-the-crusader wanted to make Mercy her special project, to take her to the movies and for walks, and to be a sister to her. Lydia and I talked at length about whether she was prepared to become someone upon whom Mercy could rely or whether she would eventually become another disappointment. We discussed whether this was about helping Mercy or about making Lydia feel good. With Lydia heading to university in a year or two, and leaving Mercy behind, she would be a no-show in Mercy's life, like the fake uncles with whom she had been raised. As it turned out, Lydia was very kind to Mercy, but she never promised her more than her time in any given moment. And so, Mercy came and went in her saviour's life for many years, drawing on Lydia's energy to bolster her fierce and levied independence. Occasionally, she appeared at Lydia's door at dinnertime, her welcome always a warm one. I wondered what was going on in her life at those times. To Lydia, the reasons Mercy needed help didn't matter. Helping Mercy was just the way it was.

"Found them. Do you want another beer?"

With those words, I snap back from my reminiscing about Mercy and plunge into other thoughts about what all that might have to do with Harley. Is this another special project, or the opportunity to reach out and help someone else? It sounds like Harley's life has already been overpromised and underdelivered. My heart dies a small death for the girl, hoping

Lydia won't be yet another no-show in her young life. I'm not being fair to Lydia, I know that, and she hasn't ever shied away from the hard work of life. But I'm not sure she fully understands what it will be like to have to drag someone along with her, to be responsible for the success of someone else, to have someone like Harley rely on her. Lydia travels alone, holds high expectations for herself and those around her, and allows only slight margins for the weaknesses of others. Not that she can't learn, but learning can be a life-long process. Harley seems like an unlikely jumping-off point for such edification.

Chapter 3

Harley

I am oh-so-ready for a hotel party. I don't usually party and have never partied in the city before. But we are celebrating the end of high school, something special, and the start of…well, the start of something. Mainly celebrating the end of something. Four of us from school have chipped in for a hotel room, an unknowing parent's credit card bearing the risk of damages. We barrelled down the Trans-Canada Highway, smoking and listening to music and laughing about our friends left behind in Brandon. We passed traffic carelessly, not because we were careless, but because we were young and inexperienced, a menace at the speed limit, and holy mother of god at show-off speed. I sat in the middle in the back, the most unwanted seat, my shoplifted makeup achieving the creepy look of a tarted-up toddler. A baby beauty queen. There was a whole lot of not-knowing-enough in the car that day, executed to perfection. We arrived at the hotel in early afternoon, laden with backpacks and makeup bags and cases of beer and bottles of wine, ready to do the big smoke, The Peg, in some kind of style.

The small hotel room carries the funk of tobacco and weed and spilled beer and sweaty mattresses, and the strangely comforting smell of dust burning on electric heaters. It is furnished in the style of cheap, with plastic laminate furniture and a clock radio glued to a night table. The imperfect patch on the bathroom door has the spackled and painted shape of a head-hole from a domestic brawl. Thin and faded brown towels folded neatly on wire racks over the bathtub match facecloths folded neatly on the bathroom counter, which itself is dotted with the ochre smudges from neglected cigarettes. Beige curtains hang unevenly, leaving a triangle of light streaming in from a dirty window. A small round table and one chair are shoved in a corner, the chair pad ripped, and the yellowed stuffing oozing out like a tongue with thrush. Party time.

The cardboard from a case of beer is ripped open, and each of us grabs a warm one. We fill the toilet tank with ice and put in as many beers as will fit. Cold beer is definitely better. We talk about our drive in from Brandon, of no more school, of the loser-man at the hotel reception desk, of crushes on boys. We grab another beer from the toilet and talk and laugh about boys both loved and hated, controlling parents and annoying sisters and brothers, and unfair teachers, our memories of whom are still rank with resentment. Two beers down, and time for another cold one. Someone fills the toilet again, this time with two bottles of sweet pink wine. We order pizza. We share a joint and stories of sex and boys, and we tease each other about our most embarrassing moments. We drink wine from Styrofoam coffee cups, eat the pizza, and share personal stories of neglect and varied types of abuse. One friend cries, and another yells in outrage against life in general, but I do neither. After the second bottle of wine is downed, the recycled foam cups are filled from the third bottle, a warm dessert wine, stolen from a parent's liquor cabinet.

In the mental haze created by the booze and pot, I watch my friends. Their humour is poor, and their anger, at first turned inward, suddenly turns toward each other. The clock radio plays unchosen music. I reach over and turn it up, the sound drowning out the high emotions and escalating voices. We smoke another joint, and things get quiet for a while. When I feel the blood drain from my head, I lie on my back on the bed, one foot on the floor, waiting for the dizziness to pass, waiting for the cold sweat on my forehead to dry. The emotional discussion circles around me, but I can't focus on the words. I feel like I am going to be sick. I jam my phone in my back pocket, and leave the room, seeking sanctuary in the cool evening air, which is refreshingly unpoisoned by the developing misery inside. I hear the door click behind me, locking in the anger of my friends and locking me out.

The cold air is like a caress, and I sit down heavily on the flaking yellow parking curb, feeling my blood begin to circulate again and my world begin to level out. I want a cigarette, but I am not sure my stomach does. In any case, I haven't brought any outside with me. I realize that in my haste to leave, access key and smokes are still in the room, tucked safely away in my purse with the gum and Chap Stick. Out here alone, I am just a kid. A sick, drunk, stoned kid. A cold kid, I realize, as I feel the night develop an abusive harshness, its chilly caress squeezing a little too tightly. I want to stand, to raise myself from the curb, to go back to the safety of the hotel room, but my poisoned body feels heavy, too heavy to stand, and I curl up on the pavement, which is by now devoid of any warmth from the hot sun of the day.

Suddenly, a tall woman is crouching down, rubbing my shoulder, smoothing my hair away from my sweat-sticky face. She is pulling at my arm, trying to get me to sit up, talking of cold weather and no jackets and poor thing, and how I need a soft place to rest. With her help, I stand, the heat from her body beginning to wrap itself around me. The temptress of shelter is irresistible, as is the offer of hot coffee and a smoke, and some relief from my drunken, stoned perspective.

I follow her for a long time to another hotel on a side street. We stop briefly at the front desk as cash is exchanged for a key. The woman's long stride, my short shuffle, both sets of footsteps silently moving down the hall, then a quick slide of a card, a small beep, a faint click. We are in.

She guides me to the edge of the bed and urges me to sit. She introduces herself as Barb and removes her sweater from her gangly frame, wrapping it around my shoulders in a kindly gesture. It smells funny, in the way that someone else's clothes smell funny. It makes me think of old aunties, their sweaters worn, day in and day out, becoming a part of the furniture, never washed. We exchange trips to the bathroom, first me, then Barb.

When she comes out, there is only a towel wrapped around her, tucked up under her armpits, a hint of chest hair curling up over the edge of the thinning white terry cloth. With makeup caked on her face, her porous nose and eyes and forehead huge, her feet too wide, her fingers long and knobbly and covered in sparse black hairs, everything that initially felt right for me now clearly feels very wrong. Barb's nails are wide and smooth, but the edges are chipped, and the skin around the nails torn and red. She smiles at me, her painted lips close to her teeth, and sits down on the bed, offering a cigarette and a light. I look at her legs, muscular and hairy, spread casually beneath the towel. Barb drapes her long arm lightly around my shoulder. Too close, and I butt-shuffle to put some space between us. The worm of worry in my head begins to move, heightening my awareness of danger. Barb's long arm has a hand at the end of it, seemingly an entity independent of her false kindnesses, and the bony, hairy fingers grip my shoulder hard, drawing me back in. She shoves me down on the bed and stands, the towel dropping to the floor. Barb becomes Bob, his full regalia on full alert. His bony features, sickly weird with makeup, are twisted with evil intent. The worm lurches. I look to the door, but Bob's lanky body is completely blocking my view and my escape. As I try to move off the bed, he pushes me back down. I do what I can to resist with my arms, hitting him again and again, with no effect. He is too strong, and I am too weak, but I know I need to save myself. Lurch. Lurch. He pulls at my sweater, pulls at my pants, my arms and legs flail in resistance, but I fear my weakness will only slow his inevitable success.

As the youngest of nineteen, I possess a well-developed sense of self-preservation. And despite my young age, I know that being on my back on a bed in a hotel room with a naked stranger is a bad situation. I bite. I scratch. I feel adrenalin pumping through my body. And then I feel strength rising, a strength I didn't know I had. I bring my leg back and drive my heel into the bobbing dick. Bob immediately suspends all movement in mid-air as a look of shock and surprise contorts his face into a weird grimace, and he grabs himself, emits a long and raspy groan, and collapses to the ground in the fetal position. In that brief moment, I jump from the bed and run to the door. When I jerk it open, it snags on the safety catch and slams shut again. I flip the catch, yank the door open, run down the hallway, and escape out the front of the hotel.

I keep running until I am certain Bob isn't behind me. Then I lean briefly against a wall cloaked in darkness, trying to catch my breath and looking for somewhere that will provide me with safety. The "Sunbright

Hotel" blinks its vacancy status on a sign by the road like a giant warning for anyone hoping for sanctuary. Completely disoriented, I focus on a McDonald's restaurant sign a block up the street. I quickly walk the short distance, entering a safer place through neon golden arches.

I instinctively reach into the back pocket of my jeans, relieved that my phone is still there. I call the first number that comes to mind.

Chapter 4

Lydia

"I'm lost."

I can barely make out the small voice on the other end of the line.

"It's Harley."

Now vaguely familiar, the voice is halting, unsure of a welcome.

The early morning call provokes surprise and extreme annoyance. By calling me, Harley has made herself my problem.

I haven't heard from the girl since we spent a day together in late winter. She had also seemed lost then, and she had shown no enthusiasm for the offerings of the day. I had shepherded her through the various opportunities presented by schools, businesses, and government agencies, hoping to see a spark of interest. She had resolutely ignored my enthusiasm, leaving it useless and hanging in mid-air between us, the snub mildly aggressive. As we wandered through the job pavilions, her main focus seemed to be an attendance book. She told me that if she got all her pages stamped at the pavilions, her name would be entered in a draw for a new cellphone. At each booth, she held out her book, expecting and accepting her stamps with little emotion. Stamp entitlement. From time to time, I caught her looking at me, surreptitious glances that betrayed none of what she was thinking. She didn't speak with me unless I addressed her directly, and then her answers were monosyllabic.

Without the burden of conversation with Harley, I observed the other young women in the room. Each expressed her independence from authority in her outward appearance, with the end result that each was almost identical to her peers. Each except for Harley, who seemed to stand apart while wearing the uniform of the uninspired. Clearly unsophisticated, her clothing revealed information about her that she might not otherwise have intentionally disclosed. Short and heavy, with long dark hair parted down the middle, her carelessly assembled outfit was wrinkled and covered in fuzz and hair and the odd bit of seed shell. Her grey runners were foam-clunky with undone laces, her jeans gripping her legs with the unkept promise of sexy. Her cellphone was tucked into her back pocket and her hoody hid her upper half from the world. She had a small grubby purse, a sign of the awkward time of life when girls become women. To carry a purse was a sign of womanhood, yet she had underachieved, carrying no identification cards, no credit cards, no keys, no makeup. Just smokes and gum and a chap stick. She was not really a woman, but a fertile girl. Not really a girl, but an unfledged woman. A lady person in purgatory on an uncelebrated journey with no destination. I had watched as she stopped at a booth, eyes cast down, fingering some papers. She held out her book, which was duly stamped. Proof of attendance obtained. She exists.

"Where are you, Harley?" She isn't answering, but I can hear her breathing.

"Where are you, Harley? I can come and get you." I say the words, but I am tired and the last thing I feel like doing is going out.

"Harley, are you there? Can you hear me?" No answer. Instead, a pregnant silence, the kind of quiet that delivers bad news in the wee hours.

"Harley, I want to come and get you, but you need to tell me where you are."

She starts to speak, her words free, rushing out in an incoherent stream.

"Where are you? Are you okay? Why do you say you are lost?" I try to get her to answer me, but in my haste to understand her situation, I step on my own questions, not leaving her time to answer before asking the next one.

"Harley, I need you to tell me where you are!" I am more insistent, my imagination now filling the silence with the dark places a mind goes during a phone call from the dark.

"I am at Mickey D's, near the Sunbright Hotel."

The voice is of a scared, drunk, and lost kid. We talk briefly, and I manage to drag a few details from her before she ends the call.

Adrenalin rushes through my body as the dogs rush out the door in front of me. It is automatic for them to go with me, unless I am going to work, and I feel safer with them late at night, especially this night. Twenty years earlier, my Volvo 850 had been the top of the line, a luxury model. If not born in Arizona, it had been raised there, and there was no rust, no weather damage. Though old, it still gleams in its boxy whiteness. It had lumbered between my sisters and me, depending on who needed a car at any particular moment, but for now, and probably forever, it is mine. The cassette player, air conditioning, sunroof, wipers, trunk lock, electric windows, and power seats had once been cutting edge, as far as Volvos go, but have all since quit in protest against changing technology or oldness. The AM radio still works, as does the lighter, although I never use it. Years ago, for reasons unknown, the seat had become stuck in one position, well back from the steering wheel, and I have to drive with my hips slung forward and my driving leg stretched to reach the gas pedal. It is awkward and uncomfortable, but I'm pretty much used to it now. I know that people can get used to uncomfortable things.

I open the driver's door and move the ever-present stack of medical journals, textbooks, and papers from the passenger seat. The dogs jump in, and we head off to find a specific set of arches and an unfledged woman named after a motorcycle.

It takes me about a half hour to get to the McDonald's in question, and as soon as I see her, I can tell she is in rough shape, her body and mind stunned from excess. As we drive to my house, Harley's silence fills the car. The dogs are sulking in the back seat, pressing their noses against pre-snotted windows. I am sulking in the front seat. This was not what I signed up for. I don't want this kind of responsibility. I didn't ask for it. I don't know how to handle it. I don't know what to do with Harley or even what the status of the girl's life is. And I don't have enough questions in my head to get the answers to all that I don't know. A loud voice in my head is yelling, why are you taking Harley to your house at all? Isn't there somewhere else you can take her to dump her, to renege on implied promises, to make her someone else's problem?

Instead, I park on my street and usher all passengers inside my house. I go into the kitchen to make coffee and suggest the still-standing Harley make herself comfortable in the living room. When I tell her we need to talk, she continues to look down, avoiding my eyes. The lesson of maintaining eye contact has clearly not been learned.

"Harley, you are in safe hands here." Judging by the smell of her clothing, I draw my own conclusion that she has been drinking and smoking to excess, and she has paid the price for it.

"Do you want to tell me what happened?" I'm not sure if I should be comforting her or taking a patient history.

"Do you want me to help you in some way?" A change of clothes should be first on that list.

Harley doesn't answer, her head down, chubby fingers picking at her cuticles.

"I can't do anything if you don't talk to me, Harley." Go back to questions, Lydia, I tell myself. I want to help her, but I am tired and annoyed by her silence.

"What are you doing in Winnipeg anyway? I thought you said you lived in Brandon." I look at the dogs, who are looking up at Harley. When I first picked her up, Tennille had sidled up to Harley in the car as if to keep her warm. Now she and Captain are keeping their distance, figuring her out, sensing my level of annoyance.

"Do you have any friends or family here?" My questions are blunt, but my voice is soft.

Harley looks up. "No."

With that quiet answer, I feel the air in the room become heavier and the Harley-burden settle in for the long haul. I try again to get some dialogue going, but eventually give up. The girl clearly needs some rest, so I usher Harley upstairs to the second bedroom. We'll talk later, if at all.

Chapter 5

Meaghan

Our vacation is over, and we are heading back to Brandon via Winnipeg. We left the Whiteshell Park just as the sun popped over the horizon. The quiet morning air of early summer is cool in Manitoba, and it grows colder when we are on the bike. I have my arms around Steve, but the wind is making me uncomfortable. It slinks under my helmet and up my sleeves until the cold air joins at the back of my neck. I press my body against Steve's, his broad back blocking the wind, and move my hands down by his lower back to warm them. I feel the heat from the pipes rise and warm my legs. We had spent a week at Falcon Trails Resort, trying to rescue our struggling love, trying to press a reset button—to remove all the hurt caused by careless words and neglect, and to take what was left of Us back to a better time, a time of love and passion.

We love this part of the country. In fact, it was here that one of the world's most famous UFO incidents had taken place. In 1967, an amateur rockhound encountered two unidentified flying objects while in the bush. As he investigated the cigar-shaped vehicles, he received a grid pattern of burns to his chest, the source of the burns was something coming from one of the UFOs. The area was found by investigators to be rife with radiation. A man of honesty and integrity, he never claimed to have seen alien creatures, and for several years afterwards, he was the target of international aviation investigators as well as media attention from various countries.

Years ago, Steve's interest in that story had taken us to the Falcon Lake area for numerous long weekends, but in more recent years, we opted for the log cabins, hot tubs, and hikes through the forest. On this trip, wood ticks had infested the area, and we spent much of our time picking the insidious bugs off our clothing and checking each other at the end of each day for ticks that had found their way onto our skin. After one particular day of hiking, I counted four hundred ticks on me alone. Having that many ticks on us had left us feeling creepy skin-crawly and edgy. We were happy to see the end of our vacation and keen to get back to Brandon.

The return trip by motorcycle had started, as always, with thin coffee, waking-up sex, hot showers, and the ritual of jeans, T-shirts and socks, riding boots and chaps, jackets and goggles, and finally gloves and the shiny-shiny helmet. It's all part of an important, lumpy process that culminates in swinging my leg over the seat. Now that we are out on the road, old rock 'n' roll is blaring over the satellite radio, leaving a brief pounding beat in the open spaces behind us. I welcome the peace that always overtakes me when all my senses are satisfied by the cool air, the music, the distinctive rumble of a Harley, the smell of coniferous forest or hay fields or cattle, and black leather, the morning sun bright, and the fog hovering over the cool fields as we head along the highway. The entire process takes us to the edge of freedom and the sense of no tomorrow that can only come from riding a motorcycle.

I feel my cellphone buzzing deep within my jacket. There might be no tomorrow, but the buzzing is insistent, so there is definitely a today.

We pull into a strip mall on the west side of Winnipeg. Nothing open yet, but later in the day, Candy's Bar, featuring exotic topless dancers, and The Bible Store, with its evangelical banner blazing in white and orange plastic, will have their daily battle for the souls of their patrons. A closer look, however, reveals that The Bible Store has closed down and the premises are for lease. God has apparently lost this round.

I take my phone from inside my jacket and see that Lydia has called five times. I return her call, and she tells me everything that has happened.

Chapter 6

Harley

It is early afternoon when I wake up hard from a deep, paralyzing sleep. I am still somewhat disoriented, and it takes a few seconds to appreciate my surroundings. Looking around the bedroom, I notice that the walls are painted pale blue and have alcove ceilings. Lacy white grandma curtains hang around the window, through which I can see the stretching branches of elm trees grope the bright blue of the sky. There is a screen on the window, and several holes have been mended with dirty tape, the edges curled up. Last fall's houseflies, having died sometime during the winter months, litter the inside of the windowsill. A new addition quietly buzzes.

I feel my consciousness rise up, along with the stomach pit-squeezing sensation that comes with the realization of what brought me to this bed. I think of the ride into Winnipeg, of the hotel party, but mainly I think of Barb-Bob, of what might have happened. The bed feels safe, and I don't want to ever leave it. Then I realize that I slept in my hoody and jeans and socks. Ugh. The sheets have a claustrophobic hold on the length of my clothed body, and I toss them off.

Suddenly, I hear movement heading my way. Multiple feet racing up the stairs. And then Lydia's dogs jump onto the bed. I remember Captain and Tennille from the previous night, but their enthusiasm for me at this point in the morning far outweighs mine for them as they jump on the bed, licking my face and wagging their tails. I feel for my cellphone, which is still in its usual place, jammed into the back pocket of the jeans that hadn't delivered. My best jeans, worn for the party that celebrated the start of nothing new, the party that had ended so badly. I check for messages, but there are none. My friends are probably still asleep in the hotel room or on their way back to Brandon without me. Either way, no one has tried to contact me.

I walk downstairs, meeting Lydia in the hallway. As we go into the kitchen, neither of us knows what to say, and the awkwardness of our nothing-in-commonness rises like a wall between us.

Lydia pours coffee from the carafe, reheating it in the microwave. We sit at the table, adding sugar and cream, and stirring the coffee clouds in circles. She asks how I slept— "Okay," if I wanted a shower— "Maybe later," or something to eat— "Sure," and if I liked dogs— "Yeah." Small talk stirred in circles. Then comes the question she really wants to ask.

"What happened last night?"

It takes a second cup of coffee and some food before I begin to open up, but even then, I don't share much. I simply say that my night had been a bad one and things hadn't exactly gone as planned. There isn't much else to say anyway because my memory is still clouded on the edges, with the unknown filling any blank spaces.

She nods, smiles, and changes the subject. "And what about school?"

That perks me up a teensy bit, and I explain that I finished high school, my graduation initially in doubt, but the certificate eventually awarded. Hooray for Girls for Tomorrow. Then I admit I that have no job and am not registered for university or college anywhere.

When Lydia asks what's next, I hesitate. There is nothing next.

We drive back to the hotel where I had partied with my friends. The only person in the room, however, is a chambermaid who is busy cleaning floors and changing sheets. When I see my purse and bags on the maid's cart, as forgotten as I am, I grab my things with little emotion. Lydia then takes me back to the Sunbright Hotel, but there is no record of a Barb-Bob. The look on the face of the excuse for a concierge confirms the likelihood of another pocketed cash transaction that is unrecorded in any ledger.

Home again, home again, jiggety-jig. Lydia parks the car, and we go into the house. I head straight upstairs to the bedroom in which I had slept the previous night. My room, I tell myself. Until Lydia says otherwise. Fingers crossed.

Chapter 7

Lydia

I stand in my kitchen, my feet planted firmly on the ground, but still feeling like my world has just shifted a little. There is now a Harley in my house. I remove two of my precious Ziploc meals from the freezer, bags full of pot roast slices, mushroom gravy, and baby carrots. Later, these will be dinner for two.

When Harley comes downstairs again, her hair is combed and her face is washed. I motion to the living room and tell Harley once again to make herself at home. Harley does exactly that by turning on the television. I study surgical procedures as she nurses her hangover, and the rest of the afternoon passes without conversation. Dinner is duly microwaved; an awkward evening is also on the menu. Harley watches television, and I alternate between studying, online shopping, and texting my friends about the stranger in my house.

In the morning, I wake early because I have to report to the hospital at 6:00. I take a moment to sit on the edge of my bed and reflect on the events of the previous day. I have no answer for what to do with Harley, the at-risk young woman in my spare room. I also feel like I have no choices. I get up, shower, and throw on jeans and a T-shirt. I will change into scrubs at the hospital.

My usual routine includes making a quick coffee, letting the dogs out for their business, then feeding them. But as I hurry downstairs, toothbrush in hand, I smell coffee. I pause for an instant, wondering if I left the pot on overnight. When I enter the kitchen, I am met by Harley, who has made coffee. She says the dogs whined at the back door, so she accommodated their early morning needs by putting them outside. She watches my face carefully, looking for confirmation that this is okay. Now back inside, the dogs, their bellies already full, wag their tails as they greet me enthusiastically. Harley prattles on about having to get little ones ready in the morning in Brandon. She thinks maybe dogs are a bit like little kids, and she adds something about always having to get up early at home and having had too much sleep the day before. I am pleasantly surprised by this unexpected behaviour, and say as much to Harley. If you can catch a dog doing something good and reward it, the behaviour will be repeated. I don't say that last bit to Harley, though.

When I get home from work that night, dinner is already prepared and the kitchen clean. Harley spent the day watching television, taking the dogs for a walk, and searching the cupboards for something to make for dinner.

The next morning, the coffee is made, the dogs have been out, and they have been fed. That night, dinner is prepared, and both the kitchen and bathroom are clean.

And so, it continues throughout the summer. Meals are cooked; the house is cleaned; the unfledged woman and I coexist, speaking of nothing deep, sharing little of ourselves, each of us making the other's life that little bit easier. Neither of us speak of changing the arrangement, for to speak of it would mean acknowledging that easy isn't always the best.

Chapter 8

Harley

Lydia has already left for the hospital, and I have the house and the dogs to myself. I pour coffee into a cup, reheat it in the microwave, and move to my favourite place in her house.

Her front porch is a mass of deep cushions, soft, fluffy blankets, crazy floral patterns, and fluttery sheer curtains. There is weird stuff from around the world, including a sculpture of a whole bunch of people joined together that is carved from a single piece of ebony. Lydia says she got it from Tanzania, and it means unity and continuity. There is also a mask of a Spanish missionary that she bought in Bolivia. The face is white, and the hair is real human hair, and the teeth look real, too. Lydia says not all the people in Bolivia were happy about the missionaries. She also has a painting from when she climbed Kilimanjaro that shows the Maasai jumping dancers with the mountain in the background. Lydia explained there wasn't too much air at the top of that mountain, and it was hard to breathe. A water pipe sits on the coffee table, with fruit tobacco in a carved box beside it. There is a lot of other interesting stuff, too, such as fashion magazines and newspapers and books on doctory stuff.

When I am alone, I sit here in the mornings, sipping my coffee and thinking about nothing much. I haven't achieved anything all summer, which is normal for me. I haven't done anything with my life at all, really, other than barely get through high school. Sometimes I feel like a fake, sitting in this porch of someone who has done so much. I certainly didn't expect to be where I am now, living in Winnipeg, in my saviour lady's house, on this porch. Sometimes I don't even know why I am here at all. But I still like sitting on the porch.

I will admit that I feel a sense of peace, a liquid coating of calm flowing over me each morning when I wake up. Lydia has no expectations of me, but has given me access to everything she has. At first, we didn't talk much at all, but now we talk more, like we are kind of friends. If I ever need help, I'm pretty sure she will be there for me because she has already proven that. I don't have any friends of my own, but sometimes see Lydia's friends or boyfriends when they come to the house, although I don't say much to them. And communications from my family and friends in Brandon are sparse, to say the least. No surprise that neglect from family can travel the miles effortlessly.

There is no place for stress here on her porch. I have healed. I know I have healed. I feel the healing so deep in the core of my body, although strangely, I don't know from what I have healed. That same sense of no longer being wounded and having no raw edges has also given me an unrecognizable energy and a desire to do something else. I still don't know what is next, but there grows within me, next to the scars from the healing, the seedling of knowledge that there is, in fact, something next.

As I look out into the street, I see moms and dads and children coming out of their houses, and I realize that summer is over and school has started again. I think back to the first days of school for me, of the dread and the uncertainty that comes with the return from summer break. So much can happen from June to September. Friendships change, people move away, and alliances form. My ties to any group were always tenuous. I lived my life on the outskirts, on the fringe of any crowd, and I knew that my group membership was precarious. I could have easily been replaced. All it took for me to become redundant was someone new to town, or someone who had spent the summer losing weight, or who had a new boyfriend. The fall was always a time for people to join. They joined groups; they joined skating; they joined school sports teams. They joined with boys; they joined the band; they banded in cliques. Unfortunately, Mom and Dad had abdicated on the parenting job and didn't encourage me to join anything. Left to my own devices, I went along with their languor.

When I was eight, I wanted to join skating. Mom had no problem with that, only wanting to know how much it would cost. She told me that if I wanted to skate, I should simply go and join. I walked the half mile to the arena, a long journey alone on short legs, and despite being worn and weary when I arrived, I managed to open the heavy door that was twice as tall as me. The large, echoing building was full of the strange mustiness of warm air that I expected to be cold. I stood quietly for a moment before following the voices, the sound of which was both exciting and terrifying. As I approached the outside of the rink, I noticed that the boards were an unfinished dull and dark grey, but when I stood on my tiptoes and peered over the boards, I saw that inside, they were freshly painted white.

At the far end of the ice was a small group of girls, their bodies covered in skin-tone tights that were lighter than my summer-tanned skin and that contrasted starkly with their bright pink leotards, patterned sweaters, striped legwarmers, and leathery white and shiny metal skates. A smiling lady was laughing with them, and they followed her as she skated in circles. On the ice. On Mars. They may as well have been in outer space. I had no way of crossing over the boards, from the grey to the white, of entering their special little world. Worse, on the bleachers above the skaters was a group of moms, chatting and drinking cups of coffee from thermoses. I knew Mom wouldn't have liked that. I left and walked home. Mom didn't ask, but I simply told her the arena had been closed. And that was the end of that.

Lydia has been studying for some kind of test, and combined with her schedule that rotates from days to nights and sometimes requires that she stay at the hospital when she is on call, I rarely see her and have no idea when she will be around. She doesn't really seem like a person who would go to work from 9:00 a.m. to 5:00 p.m., although I don't know anybody who has ever done that so am not sure what that kind of person would look like. I want to talk to her about my what-next, but she is busy and tired and always doing something. While she's at work or studying at home, I watch television, just like Mom and Dad.

Seeing the little kids leaving for school this morning makes me miss my nephews and nieces, but it also gets me thinking about what I am going to do and what I haven't done so far. I saw a lot of different jobs at the Girls for Tomorrow conference, and I almost took some information papers on becoming a personal counsellor. I didn't know what that was, but it hadn't sounded too hard. When I saw Lydia eyeing me, I quickly put the papers down. Back then, I hadn't wanted to get caught participating in anything with enthusiasm, other than changing Lydia's impression of me. I also hadn't wanted to take any papers home for Mom to find. She got pretty agitated about people who tried to be better than she was.

I have never known anyone like Lydia. She isn't simple. She is complicated. She has more clothes than anyone I know. She has more clothes than all the clothes of all the people I know put together. She is put together. She studies hard. She hardly ever stops. She barely watches television, loves rare steak, and she drinks cheap beer, great wine, and single malt whisky. She listens to country music and smokes fruit tobacco. She runs every day with the twins, as she calls them—Captain running beside her and Tennille tucked into her top. She returns home from her runs all sweaty and satisfied, and carrying a bag of doggie doo doo. Regardless of the poop 'n scoop bylaws, she recycles used plastic grocery bags to accommodate moral compliance.

Lydia had a couple of short interludes with internet boyfriends this summer. Neither of them was serious. She doesn't have time for that. Each started out glossy and new, pink cheeks freshly shaved, and their hair slicked back. They wore new, expensive jeans, arrived straight from the gym, offered dinners and movies and tickets to the theatre, gifted flowers, loved her dogs, and sold themselves. These boyfriends were clearance-bin men, however, who had been returned by past girlfriends or wives for defects or damage. There weren't obvious defects, and they didn't write into their dating profile that they were narcissistic, or drank too much, or were seriously depressed, or were serial philanderers. In their glowing self-assessments, they left out the parts about not being able to hold a job, working so much they didn't have time for anyone, or their brooding anger sessions. Lydia told me that she chooses her boyfriends by height, weight, and whether they can cook. She says the rest of the profile is loosely based on the truth, the kind of truth that stretches to its most ridiculous extremes. You can't lie about height or weight, and she will quickly be able to tell if they can put dinner on the table. She knows the truth about the rest of it is up to her to discover. Those boyfriends eventually showed their true selves—unkempt heaps of misery, clothed in sweatpants with untended whiskers and unmasked back fat, whose preferred modus operandi was lounging in front of the television or boozing out with the boys. Personal reinvention was clearly too much darn work for them, with backsliding the inevitable result of their sloth. When they began to reveal some previously undisclosed reality, they were shown the door. Stat. She didn't have the time to fix them. Lydia left their belongings in used plastic grocery bags on a fence post in her back yard and texted them to let them know. She isn't devious in her dating goals. Ultimately, she just wants a healthy relationship, a friend and a partner, and she has not yet lost her optimism that the newest polished man has more than a weak veneer or that she has discovered a needle in a haystack.

The third internet boyfriend is tall-ish, not overweight, and can make spaghetti and barbeque a steak. He meets all the criteria. His name is Eugene, and he doesn't like using a nickname. She said she tried calling his name out loud, but each time she experienced an internal wince, so she solved that problem by avoiding ever using his name. Eugene is over at the house quite a bit, and he ignores me when he is there. I just listen, and say nothing when he talks. He played hockey at some fancy southern college when he was younger, at least until his coach, and consequently the college administration, found out about the time he cold-cocked an opposition player during the postgame handshake lineup. After that, it seems he spent most of his games warming the bench. His dreams of playing pro hockey ended because of his lack of control and the risk of the college being sued. Eventually, he graduated with a degree in geology. Lydia sometimes calls him a rock knocker. Rock Knocker. A strong man's name that is way better than Eugene. And way better than the middle name of Danger, but who am I to talk? He worked for a year logging diamond drill core and collecting blast samples from a tiny mine in northern Saskatchewan until deciding to go back to school to study library science. Unable to find a job that involved putting books about rocks back on shelves, he landed a job with the Manitoba Ministry of Agriculture and was recently promoted to a larger cubicle. His internet profile, however, interpreted all that as him being a postgraduate-educated star athlete on the fast track in his organization. All Lydia knows or cares about is that he is tall, isn't fat, and can cook. I don't know why she doesn't just put his plastic bag on the fence post, but I guess she still has hope. Or is just too tired from her schedule to dump him. That's her business, but I don't like him.

Lydia has been dating Eugene for a few weeks. Her current residency rotation and studying for a big exam means her schedule is a particularly busy one, and she doesn't have a lot of time to examine her relationships. He does all the usual, flowers and restaurants and blah blah blah, and I think he is just a diversion for her. When he is at the house, he eats like a pig. I heard him explain to her how, as an athlete, he always has to eat a lot to fuel his energy requirements. He's not playing hockey now, though, because he says he is focusing instead on his career and has no time for such games. He could have been a professional hockey player, but he chose an education instead, and now he is using his education for the betterment of mankind. Or some such bullshit, if you ask me.

Lydia is smart, and she should see all this, but she doesn't get it. I have spent my life around losers, and I know one when I see one.

Chapter 9

Lydia

Eugene is still around. So far, he has outlasted the other internet boyfriends. No fencepost bag yet for him. My current rotation at the hospital has been hectic and my hours long. When I get home, he comes over to the house. We watch sports on television with Harley, which isn't my choice, walk the dogs, which isn't his choice, or go for a coffee, which works for us both. The rest of what works for us both is being figured out as we go along.

A few weeks ago, we went together to the Palomino Club, and I could feel his eyes on me the whole time I was dancing with my friends. I got the sense that he only went with me so he could keep an eye on me. He didn't even want to dance, but I didn't care because I was too busy having fun with everyone else.

What little spare time I have is mostly filled with Eugene. Sometimes I feel like I am getting boxed in by him, that I am being molded or manipulated. But when he senses my edginess, he makes a joke, and I laugh, and all is forgiven. He is so smart and so sure of himself, and he has an acidic wit, and I do like being in his company. Twice when I felt deeply that he was wrong for me, I told him I wanted to slow things down, perhaps not see him for a while, but he was persistent and I continued to see him, partly because I wanted some fun and partly because I had hope for my future. Even now, there are times when I'm not really sure why I keep going out with him.

Lately, he has taken an interest in my friends and family, asking a lot of questions about them. He wants to know details, how I met them, what we have done together. He seems especially interested in old boyfriends—a jealous streak, I think. In his own comical way and without being critical, he accurately points out many of their flaws. I can't help but laugh when he does that because it tells me he is particularly observant. Of course, I know about these failings in those close to me, but nobody is perfect, and I accept and love my friends and family for who they are. And thanks to Eugene, I can now appreciate their flaws from a humorous perspective. Harley never says a word when he is around, and he always makes fun of her for that. I should defend her, I suppose, but I feel worn out from work and studying. Besides, what is really wrong with a bit of joking? And I prefer to assume it is joking.

One night this week I had a depressing experience at work. I was on a day-shift emergency rotation at the Health Sciences Centre in Winnipeg. It was a Saturday morning and the hallway was full of patients on beds, in chairs, and in wheelchairs. There was the usual collection of drunks, victims of stabbings and beatings, and other remnants from the night before. Among that motley crew was a mentally challenged young woman who screamed and cried from a cut on her foot. She said she had stepped on a pair of scissors. In my experience, that meant a careless caretaker, someone who should have picked up the scissors. Her constant wails throughout the morning put everyone on edge. She wasn't my patient, but I wished that someone would stitch her up and shut her up.

It was almost a relief to be called to triage. I didn't know why I was called, but it was nice to get away from the screaming. On my way there, I passed a bed in the hallway. A small child was walking around on it, her little feet perilously close to the edge of the mattress. She teetered left, she teetered right, and I reached out and steadied her. She should have been in a bed with sides. An elderly woman sat in a chair beside the bed, watching me. I wondered if she was the caretaker, the one designated to keep the girl safe. Perhaps another careless caretaker? When I asked the woman if she was with the little girl, she nodded. I told her she needed to watch out for the little one, that she was going to fall onto the hospital floor if she wasn't looked after. On edge from the stress of the morning, I overly explained that hospital floors are waxed to a high sheen that is meant to repel blood and other bodily fluids. They aren't meant to repel people. The old woman's eyes narrowed and hardened. She asked me if her granddaughter would be seen soon by a doctor, stubbornly refusing to acknowledge my warning. The woman's words were slurred, her eyes unfocused. She had been drinking heavily. A remnant from the night before.

When I looked at the child's chart, it was clear that an attentive admitting clerk had understood the need for as much information as possible. She had questioned the grandmother carefully, recording the sad history for all to read. Mary was almost four years old, and she was here with her grandmother because the dad wasn't around, and the mom was in jail. She had been brought in for a toothache, and the initial assessment was that some or all of her teeth would have to be pulled. The hospital was just waiting for confirmation from a dentist. I thought it likely she had never even seen a dentist before, let alone a toothbrush. Mary was thin, pale, malnourished, and her face had the dark fingerprints of exhaustion under her eyes. I put the chart back and stood quietly in front of her. I was supposed to be in triage, but first I needed to do something for Mary.

When I moved in to get a closer look at her, I could smell a putrid odour coming from her head. Her teeth were decaying in her mouth, and there was something else. Mary had the worst infestation of lice I had ever seen, a condition that had gone untreated for much too long. Her hair was matted; the matting was interspersed with living lice, their abandoned skins and shit, eggs and eggshells thick and rotting on her scalp. Worse, because she had been scratching to ease the itching from the bites, the skin was broken in many places, and the scalp was badly infected. Antibiotics would be required. It was no wonder Mary looked so tired. There's no way she could have slept with hundreds of lice biting her head, running around on her scalp, and laying eggs. The egg hatches; the little girl scratches. Feeling lousy.

Because Grandma was struggling to stay awake and couldn't be trusted to keep the child safe in that hallway, I picked Mary up and took her to a nurse. She needed an attentive caretaker and perhaps a referral to Children's Aid. The nurse would make sure she got the treatment she needed, without additional injury from a fall from a bed.

By Mary's standards, I have never faced adversity. At age three, her grandma was all but passed out drunk in the hallway of a hospital, and she was living with a metropolis of head lice and a mouth full of rotting pain. There was not even a loving family member in sight. We could cure her lice, but we could not cure her life. The sadness and hopelessness of Mary's life went home with me that night.

When I shared my experience with Eugene, his face softened, and he listened intently as I told him how sad it had made me to see such a little child so dreadfully disadvantaged. My eyes teared up, and he stroked my hand as he comforted me with words. I felt cared about. Then he told me it wasn't fair that I had to work with such people. I was too upset to fully grasp which people he meant, and I let the moment pass.

Not just the moment, but time in general.

I have started a new rotation at the hospital that allows me to spend more time at home with those I love. For the next six weeks, I'm rostered for day shifts only, with no call shifts that can stretch to thirty hours.

When I first brought Harley to my house, we had talked little and shared nothing, but an impersonal camaraderie slowly began to develop, and over the summer and early fall, a friendship evolved. There are eight years between our ages. Eight is not enough for me to be a mother figure, and so a sisterhood of the improbable emerged. I knew her days or nights were long while I was at work, but she picked up the groceries and cooked, cleaned the house, looked after the dogs, and looked after me. She had originally been withdrawn, a victim of some degree of post-traumatic stress disorder of the Barb-Bob kind, and possibly also of a different kind, but she had slowly challenged its power over her, exercising the strength of the resilient. She cost me nothing but her food, and I felt less stressed and more in control with her around.

Several weeks ago, Harley had tried to talk to me about her what-next, but I was too tired to talk with her about it. Then a few days ago, when she brought it up again, I was ready for her and bluntly laid out my view.

"There will be no what-next, at least not until you take some additional high school courses and upgrade your marks. Barely passing high school isn't enough to achieve your dreams."

And that's when it occurred to me that I had never asked Harley what her dreams were.

"By the way, what do you want to be, Harley?" I asked more gently.

"I want to be a writer."

Life zigged when I expected a zag.

Thinking about Harley's what-next that night took me back a few years to when I sat on a beach outside a cottage on Lake Manitoba. I was in heaven. Not dead-in-heaven, just totally in heaven. It had been the warmest evening of the season so far, and there wasn't a midge or a blackfly or a mosquito anywhere around. The lovely Tennille was in my arms, warm and silky-soft, smelling like all the places that small dogs roam. Captain was wandering the shoreline, content with his own company. The hint of a breeze delivered the nostalgia of lilacs that bloom in spring as the full moon reflected on the lake, and the waves splashed onto the shore as if to the beat of their own drummer. The shore of Lake Manitoba is a great big event, wide and flat and sandy and going on forever like long, bronzed arms.

I sat there at the Lake just long enough to read the last twenty pages of a book a friend had given me about love and fulfilment. My friend had read it and signed the inside cover, as had the friend who gave it to her. When I finally finished it, I also signed the inside cover with the intention of passing it on to someone who needed that kind of book in their life. Instead, I put it aside and completely forgot about it.

Harley saying that she wanted to be a writer reminded me of a passage in that book that says "… grab onto the ankles of happiness and do not let go until it drags you face first out of the dirt." I love that passage. Happiness is hard work; negativity is the easy stuff. Grabbing onto anything and getting dragged through the dirt requires effort, but the alternative is to stay in the dirt. I believe that if we grab hold of what we want and look for the positive, it will be there. Like magic. As it always has been.

The next morning, I dug out the book from where it had been residing in the pile of books at the bottom of my stairs. I took it upstairs to the second bedroom and left it for Harley to discover.

When I spoke to Meaghan a couple of weeks ago, she and Steve had just gotten back from another bike trip, this time to the Badlands in South Dakota. She said it had been extremely warm for that time of year and that she loved how the formations of the Badlands, in their uniquely deformed and crusty way, had reached up and around them.

"Is something wrong?" she suddenly asked.

"No," I lied, unconvincingly.

She paused and then continued chatting, saying how much she loved playing music while they rode, and how rock music reminded her of the wide-eyed days of her youth.

"Remember those days, Lydia? When we believed nothing bad would ever happen to us? Well, those days are gone. I think we need to be aware of the truly wonderful moments in our lives, to catalogue them, to remember them, to keep them close. Dark days will come, they always do, and we need to have an arsenal of the good stuff when we need it."

I wasn't sure if she was saying that for my benefit or for hers.

Regardless, those words resonated with me. They pushed me to search for the true moments that open my heart, that make it bigger, that allow me to draw this world into me, and make me feel connected to all that I see and hear, smell and feel, and truly love. And the more I do that, the more I realize those things don't happen to me when I am complaining about something or someone. I always thought that venting made me feel better, but it actually makes me feel worse. When I vent, I search for others to validate how truly awful it was that sometime, someone did something that made me feel some way other-than-happy. I am not so naïve that I live my life looking through rose-coloured glasses, but I don't usually go digging through garbage looking for the worst bits, and on the rare occasions that I do, I don't drag everyone else down with me. I try instead to barely acknowledge the ugly stuff, then I go riding, face first in the dirt, looking for something that will make me truly happy. I wish I could make Eugene see things the way I do now.

With my residency taking on a more predictable schedule and Harley looking after the home front, I have more time for Eugene. I have realized he can be extremely negative, constantly criticizing people he observes remotely, people who have no impact on his life, people going about their daily lives, unaware of Eugene and his carping. His ongoing criticism of others makes me think more about negative people. I don't like negative people. At all. In fact, I am quite negative about negative people. Does thinking negative thoughts about negative people make a positive in the same way that two wrongs make a right?

In any case, that's why I lied to Meaghan. I didn't want to admit to her—and perhaps to myself—that I have a hard time with Eugene's dark moods, his unwarranted criticism. In that regard, we are a bad fit. But, for now, I have chosen to ignore his propensity for railing against the world and look for the good in him. I have found some things about him that I really like, and I hold out hope there is more to discover.

Chapter 10

Harley

"Harley's grades are a direct reflection on her attitude toward school and schoolwork. There is room for improvement with her overall attitude and dedication to school."

"Harley will need to obtain guidance throughout the remainder of the school year from both home and school."

"This grade is a direct reflection of Harley's work ethic. She does not complete in-class assignments, and she could do much better in class if she applied herself to her schoolwork."

"In order to help Harley with her work ethic, I suggest spending time with her each night going over her homework."

These comments and others littered my report cards year after year. I knew that some kids dreaded the day report cards were issued, worried about low grades and resulting parental reprimand. But it was like any other day to me. Teachers shouldn't have bothered because neither Mom nor Dad ever read them, and those carefully crafted summaries of my work ethic were left unappreciated. Each comment was a variation on the same old theme—I had a bad attitude; I never did any work; I needed help at home. One thing I knew was that nobody at home was going to make sure I did homework or that I was even up in the morning in time for school. Nobody at home made sure I ate or went to bed at a decent time. At my house, we killed our budgies through neglect.

I carried the reports around in my backpack for a week or so, until the school started asking for the copy with the parental signature. Even then, true to form, I avoided returning a signed copy. Eventually I carefully signed them myself, a process of which my teachers were probably aware. Don't ask, don't tell. If you lined up my report cards from all the years, Mom's signature had improved as I advanced through the grades. All requests for parent-teacher interviews were ignored. If asked, I answered that Mom and Dad were busy that night. Whatever night.

I started each year with the best of intentions. The school would hand out supplies to students of need, of which I was one. I would snap paper into a recycled binder, and carefully label dividers with my best writing, the same writing I would use for signing report cards. I would take notes in class, and underline headings with a ruler and red pen. I kept my red plaid pencil case with three holes and a zipper in my McKenzie Seed binder. There was a red ribbon blazed across the front of it, and my name was written in thick black marker below the ribbon. I wanted to do well. I tried to do well. I had no idea how to do well.

In order to set out my textbooks on the kitchen table and get down to work, I had to first relocate dinner plates and coffee cups, beer cans, junk mail, overflowing ashtrays and empty cigarette bags, screwdrivers, salt and pepper shakers, bottle caps, used napkins, and bags from junk food. The television was loud in the next room, doing its best to distract me.

I started to read, but I got sleepy. I started to write, but the plot from CSI: New York invaded my head. Then other distractions came into play. Dad would come to the table and sit, the snap of a beer can opening like the snap of a binder closing. He would drink a beer, or three, then start yelling at Mom in the next room. She yelled back, and it was on. When Mom moved into the kitchen, I packed up and moved into the living room. As they fought and argued and drank and smoked, the air heavy with old battles, I watched television. They continued smoking and drinking until one or both staggered to bed. The next morning when I got up and went to school, the air in the house was as quiet and light as the empty beer cans that filled the table.

Sometimes it was worse than arguing, and I ran for cover. Mom screamed and cried, Dad bellowing like a bull moose and swinging wildly, staggering around the kitchen chairs, knocking them over. That's when I went to the back room where my little nieces and nephews slept, their soft sleeping faces and open mouths oblivious to the antics of Grandma and Grandpa. I curled up in the big bed with them and tried to sleep. A big puppy in a bed with little puppies, but all of us were vulnerable. Out of sight, out of mind. It was a time for imagination, a movie with audio but no visual. I could picture them at the table, in the kitchen, in the living room, a spreading plague, their fights boring repeats of past battles. Same shit, different night. He said, she said. You always, you never. I hate. Spent the money. Bastard. Bitch. Drank your life away. Takes one to know one. I know you are but what am I. Around and around went their words, never resolving anything.

Eventually I fell asleep, the wary sleep of the weak. I woke early, made coffee, and fed the little ones their cereal and milk, or cereal and juice if there was no milk. Sometimes they had cereal and water. While they watched TV and ate their breakfast, I got myself ready for school. Then it was hugs and kisses. I checked that they had their lunches, and I told them I would see them after school. I turned them out into the world each morning, feeling loved and cared for. Like I never had been. With the warriors sleeping it off down the hall, I had a few minutes to myself. Should I go to school or stay home?

If I did go to school, it was often without a pen or a textbook. Something was always missing in my life. I wasn't a good bet for project work and had to be assigned to groups by the teachers. When the other members of the group heard my name called, their groans reverberated around the room. They knew I wouldn't do my share, but I would still get credit for their work. It wasn't fair. They resented me and my work ethic and my attitude, and they felt I should get more help at home. They had planning meetings where the work was divvied up. Those meetings were in the library or at someone's house. We never met at my house, though. I never offered. Sometimes a self-important, self-appointed group leader complained to the teacher that I didn't do any work and that I shouldn't get the same grades as everyone else. The teacher explained back that our group was a team and part of working as a team was for everyone to learn to motivate others. Really? The chances of a straw boss motivating me were slim, about as slim as the chance of Mom or Dad attending a parent-teacher interview.

I liked to write stories. We didn't have a computer at our house. We didn't have a spaceship either—both in the same category of unobtainable. If I needed to use one, I had to go to the library at school. I didn't need a computer to write stories, though, and at night, if the war ended early or if one of the combatants had fallen asleep before the battle call, I sat in my room and wrote stories, by flashlight, on the pages in the back of my binder. I used the top bunk of one of the two sets of bunk beds in the room. I used to share that bedroom with some of my sisters, but after they left, I shared the room with the little ones, who curled up together in the bottom bunks. When I had shared a room with my sisters, the floor was always covered in clothes, towels and shoes, half-sorted piles of clean clothes mixed in with piles of dirty laundry, dressers covered in makeup and cans of pop and costume jewellery, blow-dryers and cans of hairspray and dried orange peels. Sometimes in the morning, however, I would wake to find Mom snoring, somehow having managed to climb the vertical ladder to the other top bunk, drunk and in the dark. Perhaps she felt safer higher up, where it was harder for Dad to get at her. Sometimes I found her asleep in my bed.

I eked my way through school as an underachiever. It suited me more when I got to high school and could skip classes or entire days. Halfway through each year of high school, the warning letters would begin, advising my parents that if I continued on that trend, I would not have sufficient attendance to complete my year. I, however, continued on that trend, and I did complete my years. False threats.

I had a series of part-time jobs while I was in school. I started out babysitting for other families. Imagine the money I would have earned if I had been paid for babysitting my nieces and nephews! My jobs progressed to delivering flyers once a week. From there, I did a stint at Tim Hortons. It is one of the Canadian rites of passage that all young people must work part-time at Timmies at least once in their lives. Each store has its own story to tell. Some franchises are wonderful, staffed by kindly mothers and students, and patronized by customers in search of caffeine, electricians and hydro workers on their breaks, crusty retirees meeting with cronies to while away their days, and internet daters meeting for the first time. Some Timmies are safe places; others, not so much. Like the one where I worked.

Mine was frequented by a bike gang, the parking lot filled with motorcycles and drug deals, the restaurant filled with grizzled grey beards and profanity. Boston Cream donuts were served during scuffling-booted fights and late-night stabbings. A sign advising that no smoking was allowed within nine metres of the entrance, as per government regulations, was posted outside. The other patrons entering the restaurant had to walk through the chains, leather, and dirty denim gauntlet of bikers, who ignored the sign, smoking right outside the door like infected scabs around an open sore. At my store, the drive-thru lineups were long, snaking out into traffic, coffee drinkers avoiding contact with the contagious. You can't cure a bike gang with hand sanitizer, and nothing good ever came from contact with them. The general public knew this and stayed locked in their cars, responding only to a metal box that bleated, "Good morning, Tim Hortons, how may I help you?" Help me? Keep me safe. Large double-double. If police cruisers passed by on the highway with sirens blaring, the bikers would joke "Your ride is here" as if that wasn't within the realm of possibility.

My Timmies was a highway store, open all day, every day, except Christmas Day. I usually worked the second shift from four in the afternoon until midnight. I liked those hours. Rules said I was allowed to drink all the coffee and eat all the stale donuts I wanted for free. I ate stale donuts if the boss was there and as much of anything I wanted if the boss wasn't around, and bosses only work the first shift. I put in only a couple of shifts per week, but it was enough to keep me in money for smokes. I ate a lot, and I rarely went to school the morning after I worked. When my shift was over, I either got a ride with the parents of one of the other girls or caught a cab or, sometimes, I walked if it wasn't too cold. There was a scary loneliness to a midnight walk on my own, and the sound of distant footsteps or an approaching car would send my senses into overload, my heart pounding, and my adrenalin flowing. Fight or flight. Both bad choices. Walking alone was a bad choice. My purse was filled with a name badge, a greasy visor, and the jingle of a few tipped coins. There wasn't much worth stealing.

All in all, it was an okay job, and nothing really happened while I worked there. Except for one thing. I met Orval at Timmies.

Chapter 11

Meaghan

I am thinking about Lydia's relationship with Eugene, and my intuition tells me something is wrong. I know from a bad experience that it is important to listen to intuition, and there are consequences to ignoring it.

Steve and I lived in Chile for two years. He worked for one of the big Canadian banks, and they had an office in Santiago. He was transferred there for international experience, and I was not able to obtain a work visa. It was a big deal, this move to Chile. I knew I was leaving so much behind me, but Steve really wanted to take on this position, and he assured me it was only a temporary relocation. After much discussion, I reluctantly agreed to go. Once we arrived in Santiago and without the structure of my life in Manitoba, the job, friends, and family, I had to work hard, harder than ever, to be happy. Instead of working, I had managed to fill my days doing volunteer work, playing tennis, and ordering around the maids and window cleaners.

It was then time to return to Canada. The bank gave Steve a promotion back in Brandon. The moving van was arranged, the flights booked, and the farewell parties lined up. I spent any free time getting rid of or selling things I didn't need or want back home, including all my electrical appliances.

It was a sunny, cool morning, and I was playing tennis with my friends at a posh club in Santiago. My friends were the wives and girlfriends of other Canadian expatriates, all bored and trying to fill their days. They had left jobs behind in Canada, keen to experience living in another country, or like me, supporting their partners in the advancement of their careers. For the most part, they would eventually return to Canada, as I did, and resume their lives. The South American hiatus would be as if it had never happened. At the end of our match, I told the others I wasn't going to our usual morning coffee gathering at the mall because I had to stop at a large department store on my drive home. I explained that I wanted to check appliance prices so I could attach appropriate price tags to the appliances I was selling.

I was busy, and the to-do list was long. Rather than go home and change first, I decided to run into the store in my tennis outfit. Because the mall was already busy and the lot packed with cars, I couldn't be bothered looking for a parking spot close to the door. Instead, I skirted the lot and quickly parked the red Peugeot wagon in the empty nether regions. We had bought the car upon our arrival in Chile, and it would be sold with the rest of our belongings before we moved back to Canada. In my tennis shoes and short white skirt, I made quick tracks into the store. I wrote down the prices I needed and hurried back to the car.

From a distance, I could see that, although there were many empty spots near where I had parked, there was a new-looking, black, half-ton Ford parked right beside my car. My red wagon and the black truck were alone, side by side. A flash of intuition told me that was weird. I ignored the flash. As I approached my car, a man, well-dressed, clean, and handsome, entered the space between the driver's side of my car and the passenger side of his truck. My intuition again told me something was wrong. Again, I ignored it. I stood back behind my vehicle and kept a safe distance between us.

He removed his leather jacket and carefully folded it. He opened the passenger door of his truck, placed the jacket on the seat, and closed the door. He then walked between the vehicles toward me. As he passed the rear of my vehicle, he stopped. He listened. He looked. He then told me that I had air hissing from my tire. I looked, and yes, the tire was flat. He asked if he could help me change my tire.

At that point, my spider senses were going crazy, but still I told myself I should trust the man who had offered to help me change a flat tire. Instead of listening to my inner smart person, I listened to my inner lazy person, and I agreed to let him help me.

I opened the gate at the back of the wagon. The jack was under a black floor mat, encased in Styrofoam packaging, a broad elastic band holding it together. It was still new, never having been used. I removed it and handed it to him, telling him I didn't know how to use it. He asked if I had a manual, as he wasn't familiar with the type of jack that came with the Peugeot. I kept my distance from him and indicated that he could get into the car to get the manual from the glovebox. He opened the driver's door of the Peugeot, leaning across to the glove compartment and got out the manual. He read it quickly, then proceeded to set up the jack and change the tire. From my perspective and past experiences in my youth with old cars and worn tires, that process all took far too long, and I kept my purse, and my person, well away from him. I was relieved when he was done and thanked him for all his help.

When he moved toward the front of the vehicles, I opened my driver's door and got into the car. My heart was pounding. I didn't trust this man who had outwardly seemed like a pretty good guy. As I slid into the seat, three things happened simultaneously. I closed the door and locked it, the man appeared at my door and leered through the window, and I felt a tremendous pain in my rear end. When I reached beneath me and yanked hard at the source of the pain, I was shocked to see a three-inch, triple-pronged fishing hook in my hand.

When I looked at him, he was smiling at me and asked what was wrong. I showed him the hook. He laughed and asked if I needed him to drive me to the hospital. I immediately started the car and backed out of the parking spot.

I will never know if he wanted my car, my purse, me, or all of the above. All I know is that he must have placed the hook on my seat when he retrieved the manual from the glovebox and that his intent was malicious evil. I drove away, leaving the handsome, smiling Satan in my wake.

When I had the flat tire repaired, the mechanics found four holes in it. They had all been made by a three-inch hook.

I should have been safe in that wide-open, busy area in a wealthy part of town. The man looked normal, and we were in a very public place. Yet, my spider senses told me something was wrong. I should have listened. I should have walked away. Blink.

The Devil was there and so was his hook, and by ignoring my intuition, I'd nibbled at the bait. I had learned my lesson from that experience, and I now listen to my intuition. It was telling me that there was something wrong with Lydia's relationship with Eugene.

Lydia and I have been friends since childhood. As we got older and university or jobs separated us, we had periods of time in which we communicated frequently and other times when we didn't. I usually never worried about the times we didn't talk, knowing that our friendship didn't require constant maintenance. I haven't heard much from her lately though, and for some reason, this current silence has a palpable quality to it, something bigger than the lack of sound or the passing of months. This is my intuition talking to me. It seems there is no gulf as wide as this one, between close friends who have chosen not to share, for whatever reason, and I worry that Lydia is avoiding me. My intuition isn't enough for me to intrude when I'm not invited, but I have a niggling feeling that I need to connect with her, but can't. When I call, she rarely answers. And she never calls me. The few times we do talk, the conversation isn't about how she feels, but about what she did. And she never asks about me. When we do speak, she doesn't talk about her friends, and only talks about Eugene. The conversations are mainly superficial. The dogs are fine. Harley is fine. Eugene is great. Work is fine. She offers no free information, making further discussion difficult. I feel shut out, outcast, cast off, offside. A friend knows. I nibble at the bait. Something is wrong.

I feel us sliding down the slippery slope of a failing friendship, with Lydia sliding faster than me. This is different. Lydia has a lot on her plate these days, but she has always overextended herself. She has, however, always included me as a part of her support network. This time, I feel she is isolating herself from me, keeping something important to herself. I reach out, my fingertips barely touching her, but I'm not close enough to grasp her, to hold her, to slow her descent into what might be a bad place. If I can't reach out to her, if I can't get her attention, then I don't know who can. Lydia has always talked freely about herself, her friends, her work, her boyfriends, and her opinions of the world. She still talks, but as someone who knows her so well, I feel there is something she isn't telling me. I sense her becoming smaller, a little version of herself, but perhaps it's only my perspective, seen from my own slide as I watch her hurtle away. Or maybe it is me that is doing the hurtling. Whichever, the distance grows. I know that as those we love live their lives on precarious perches, as they enter tunnels where the only exit is a long way off in a pinprick of light at the end of darkness, we all become smaller. Sometimes we need to be small to pass through such a tiny pinprick. I also know that I need to contact her, to connect with her, to grasp her, and to grow her big again.

The truth, of course, is that I need her. Through my bouts of sadness, diagnosed later as depression, Lydia has been one of my greatest supports. But how can we help each other if we both keep getting smaller? I need to become the biggest, strongest person possible if she needs my help. Otherwise, if I can't reach her, I will be lost, and I will shrink away. My intuition makes me worry for her, but I also know how much I need my friend.

I grow from the people around me. When it is their strength that is reflected, I feel their energy and sidle closer to gather up the scraps. When it is their weakness that is reflected, I sense their need for me to be strong. My own power requires the presence of others in my life. It doesn't exist alone. I have had some weak people in my life, and I have spent a lifetime growing strong in the presence of such flawed souls. Bailers. Capitulators. They don't show up. They buy tickets and don't go. They are the bodies behind the empty seats. Promises, schmomises. They say one thing and do another. They say they will and don't. I have to poke and prod, the sharp end of the carrot forcing action when none was forthcoming. No carrot dangling for me. You can tell the worth of a person by their actions, not their words. Git 'er done. Disappoint me, please, for I will grow stronger. I have to grow stronger because the alternative is to become so small that in one quick moment I will disappear completely. Pfttt. Gone. What will I become, at that moment, when the last of my power is sucked out of me, squandered by those who pave the proverbial road of good intentions, but who fall by the wayside, never arriving at their destination? I need Lydia. My childhood friend who saw me grow from small to big.

Some days I have no power. I wake up in the morning, and I put on my glasses and look around. There is no strength. I look within, but there is only my own visceral solitude. On those days, I have no direction, no purpose, and I flounder, a time wastrel, jerking from one minute to the next. On those days, I am a zilch, putting one foot in front of the other, as slowly I move toward the end of the day. Like another zed-word. Zombie. I need the souls of the weak and the excesses of the strong to bolster me. On those days, I don't recognize myself, don't know myself. Who is this person in my body? Where is my goal, my energy, my desire? But, unfortunately, I am what I am.

I have inserted discipline in my depressed life. Some days this is easy, but there are days and weeks where finding the energy to dig deep, to be productive, to move forward and not backward, is a Herculean feat. There should be recognition for people who gather up their sadness and blow it out the door, even if it is only for that day or that minute. This is the mental health equivalent of breaking the sound barrier or running a four-minute mile. Mach busters. Marathon runners. These small but miraculous achievements are unnoticed and certainly unheralded. I make lists of lists, each accomplishment marked off with a flourish, the top of the check mark flying into other words on the list like a banner. There are days where I need these energetic check marks to keep me sane. I have done something; therefore, I am someone. It isn't enough to simply be me because on those days, I don't know who I am. I measure my worth with my actions, not my words. The more check marks, the more worthy I become. Apparently.

Who sets these rules?

Chapter 12

Lydia

Something is wrong. I don't know what I did.

Last night, Eugene and I went out for dinner to celebrate our six-month anniversary. I know it is such a kid thing to do, but any excuse for a party is a good excuse. I had been anticipating the evening, charting out the process of getting dressed, followed by a romantic dinner, and ending with candles, music, and slow and tender sex. I prepared a hot bubble bath and poured myself a cold glass of white wine. I lit candles and put some country music on the stereo. I relaxed in the fragrant heat, reading non-fine literature as my stress seeped into the water. The trite-but-true lyrics of the music invaded my focus, and I closed my eyes and enjoyed the simple words of love and heartbreak, of cheating and hard times, of women-done-wrong-by and the men-what-done-it, of years in prison, and missing loved ones.

Relaxed and happy, I took my time doing my hair and applying makeup. My hair was a fierce mass of curls, and I finished my makeup with a slash of bright red lipstick. My dress was short and hugged my curves, and my fist-sized earrings hung to my shoulders in sparkles. Stiletto heels completed my look. I thought about the word stiletto and why a weapon would be associated with the naming of a shoe. I dabbed some Poison behind each ear and touched some to my wrists. I felt beautiful, inside and out, and I was ready to be loved. I didn't know where things were going with Eugene.

I liked him. He was funny and handsome, but he also had a manipulative, controlling aspect to his personality. I had begun to spend more and more of my time with him and less with my friends and family. I wanted to be in love. In my deepest places, in the late-night times of awakeness, when I was most truthful with myself, I knew I was weary of the hard work I was doing to be the most important person in someone else's world. With Eugene, it seemed that I was still doing the hard work. I didn't know where our relationship would end up, but for tonight, at least, we would have a romantic evening.

I went downstairs. Harley was curled up on the sofa like a big puppy, and I twirled around in front of her, asking her for an opinion. She told me I looked beautiful and asked where I was going. I said I was going out for the evening with Eugene, and in jest, suggested that she needn't wait up for me. She gave my joke a half smile, but it was followed quickly by a scowl at the thought of Eugene. I ignored her non-vocal input. She wasn't my mother, and my relationship with Eugene wasn't her business. Little brat. Mind your own beeswax.

The dogs started barking, and I heard someone in the kitchen. I had given Eugene a key, and he had let himself in. Captain and Tennille knew him, and although Captain tolerated him, Tennille never stopped barking when Eugene was in the house. She was three and a half pounds of fury, and she let him know what she thought of him. Harley never said a word to Eugene, and Tennille never shut up. What a pair. Yin-Yang.

When he walked into the living room, I turned toward him. I waited for the once-over glance of approval and for his pleasure to register on his face in a smile. I saw the once-over, followed by a shadow that crossed his eyes. No smile. No kiss. No hello hug. No confirmation of the effort I had made. I felt my inside beauty shrink. I looked at him, a question mark in my eyes, but he had nothing for me. I grabbed my purse, said goodbye to Harley, and we headed out the front door, Tennille's barking a background melody to our departure.

As we walked to his sports car, my mind mulled over the anticipated series of events. Get dressed up, enjoy a romantic dinner, have languid intimacy. His uncommunicative sulk wasn't anywhere in my charted process, and I felt resentful. My time was valuable, and my reaction to his self-indulgence was rising inside me. I wanted to turn to him, to grab his face, to ask him, "What's wrong?" I wanted the pall over the evening to be gone. Instead, I held my tongue while I folded myself into his car. If anyone had been watching, they would have seen me prove that the graceful and dignified insertion of the female body into a small car, while wearing a tight dress and high heels designed to draw considerable attention to long slender legs, truly was an art form. Unobserved, I slammed my door shut. Eugene continued his silence. The road ahead was unclear.

I felt anger flow from my core, outward to my skin, and began to form words in my head. Don't say it, don't say it, don't say it. Too late.

"Do you have a problem?"

He turned toward me, his hands gripping the steering wheel. Completely absent were the sparkle in his eyes and the hint of deprecating humour on his lips. Eugene clearly had a problem.

"You slut. Is this how you dressed for all the past men in your life, you whore?" Then he pulled out from the curb with such speed and aggression that I wasn't sure we would reach our destination intact.

I continued looking at him, but I didn't recognize his face. I didn't recognize his voice. I didn't know this man. His eyes were narrowed, and there were red spots high on his cheeks.

"Pardon?" I knew he knew that I had heard him, and I didn't really want to hear those words again, but I was having trouble connecting them to him, to me, to our evening. The air took on an unreal quality. I felt like I was floating on a cushion of anger. Fury had filled the car, and I opened the window a crack to let some danger out. "What do you mean?" I persisted, still not fully understanding my situation. For the rest of the drive, none of my questions, neither the spoken nor the unspoken ones, were answered.

Finally, he roared into the gravel parking lot, the car grinding to a halt in a spot out of sight and too far from the front door of the restaurant. I got out of the car, wanting nothing more than to grab a cab and go home. We walked together toward the front door of the restaurant, not touching or looking at each other. I slowed my pace.

"I am going to skip tonight," I told him. "I think I will just go home." I didn't know what he would say, but I no longer wanted to sit across from him for two hours over candles and wine.

Without warning, I felt something hit me on the right side of my head, and I fell sideways. My shoulder hit the ground first and then the rest of me. Momentum slid me away from him, my bare arms and the left side of my face ploughing through the gravel. What happened? Stupid question. I knew what had happened, but I couldn't comprehend that it had happened to me. Then his hands were around my neck, squeezing and shaking me. My head bounced, up and down, up and down. Then, it stopped. I tried to look, but from my position on the ground, I could only see Eugene's back. He was walking to his car, keys in hand, yelling profanities about my whoreness. I lay there, hurt in body and in mind, and I listened as he drove away, the sound of gravel in the parking lot spraying over other patron's cars. I was alone.

I sat up and looked at my shoulder. It had long, red scrapes with small black stones imbedded in the blood and roughened skin. I touched it, and the fresh pain was raw. I reached up to my face, and it felt like my shoulder looked. I tried to pry some of the little stones loose, but my fingernails were too short, and it hurt too much. I moved my arm around. Superficial damage only. No dislocations. Nothing broken.

Finally on my feet, I walked defiantly, still wearing my stiletto heels, back through the parking lot and toward the restaurant. There were two cabs parked on the street, their drivers the only spectators to the drama. One of them had already started driving toward me.

"Are you okay?" he asked gently, as he got out and came around to open a door for me.

Tears were my only response as I folded myself, for the second time in a half hour, into the taxi, grace and dignity the last things on my mind. My inner beauty was gone. My outer beauty was gone. What the fuck?

Walking in the front door at the house, I slam it hard and fasten the safety chains and deadbolts. No company expected or welcomed for the rest of the evening. The dogs leap to their feet, happy to see me. Harley's head follows them, clearly surprised by my early return. She sees my face first, and then her eyes drop to my shoulder. Her expression softens for the first time in all the months I had known her. My eyes fill with tears. I need sympathy. I need care. Without words, Harley's fiercely protective hand is around my waist as she guides me into the living room. She helps me sit on the sofa. She removes my shoes. She takes off my earrings. She lifts my curls from the sticky blood on my face and winces at my pain. The room isn't cold, but I am shivering, so Harley covers me with a soft blanket, my own warmth filling the space between the wool and my legs. She leaves the room for barely a minute before returning with a package of makeup wipes, a metal mixing bowl filled with warm water, and tears in her eyes. She carefully begins to wipe my face, her hands scraping the stones from my wounds, her calm scraping the outrage from my soul. Everything hurts as she does this. My face hurts. My heart hurts. Sticks and stones. I try to talk to her, to tell her what had happened, but the unfledged woman shushes me.

"Later," she says.

Chapter 13

Meaghan

I wake this morning feeling small. The fine cotton and down duvet rests like a warm hug around me, but at the same time, it is a restraining embrace that keeps me in bed and away from the world. I know that the moment of waking will be my best moment of the day, that today will be a day of slowly crawling through the minutes, time pouring in front of me like cold molasses, and I will smile and nod and make check marks, small indicators of success.

There are lots of days like this right now. Depression overcomes me when I least expect it, not always with a reason behind its arrival. I am groggy from the dream-filled, hard sleep that is aided by sleeping pills, and I reach across the bed to touch Steve, to feel his strength, to inject myself with the power of him. But the bed is empty, and he has gone. Dammit. He has taken his love and his strength with him to live his day without me. I want him beside me, to turn to me and hold me. Tonight, he will return, and I will grow bigger again.

Almost more than I can manage, I force myself through my list. Read the newspaper. Check. Personal hygiene. Check. Each mark a small success, propelling me through my day. I am barely able to harvest the low-hanging fruit of my life, the easy, daily necessities, while the epic tasks remain unstarted or unfinished. If I can manage enough check marks in a day, perhaps I will have enough momentum to challenge my status quo, this feeling of inertia and sadness. How many are enough? Eat less. Exercise more. Drink less. Love more. I need to leverage my tasks, to make myself too big to fit in the tunnel. My power is lost, and only I can find it again. Not today, though. Maybe tomorrow.

What's next on my list? Get cleaned up, the daily process of personal hygiene. Standing in the bathroom, I ignore the sleeping pills in the cabinet. Prescribed by my doctor for wakeful nights, they are the devil on my shoulder, beckoning me to take the easy way. No pain, no gain, but I hold out hope that tomorrow will be better, and I shut the cupboard door. No drinking during the day. No drinking when I am alone. I've been there before, and I need to stay away from false solace. That would be a slippery slope indeed. Instead, I will myself to stand up straight and slowly prepare myself for battle. Moisturizer, foundation, concealer, powder, bronzer, blush, eyeshadow, eyeliner, mascara, eyebrows brushed to perfection, lipstick, watch, earrings, bracelets, rings, and necklaces. The armour grows stronger, and my small person hides safely behind the façade. Only I know. I layer it on thick. I am protected. I can be anyone I want, anyone but me. Except I really want to be me.

I miss Lydia. We haven't talked for awhile, and it seems she is gone to me. I feel our friendship requires an uncomfortable dialogue that I don't have the bravado to restart. I want her energy to fill my cracks, to patch my foundation, to help me regain my structural strength, but I am afraid to call her. I am afraid to have my fear confirmed. I am afraid that Lydia is permanently out of my life, that I must continue on my way without her. It is always like this during depression. Temporary setbacks seem permanent. Alone. Lonely. These are the same to me. I don't have the luxury of differentiating between these two states. I would turn to Steve, but he seems mentally absent, even when he is near. How do I reach out to her, across the painful silence, my confidence shattered, not knowing if there will be a hand on the other side? Woulda-shoulda-coulda, but I don't, and so my demons are mine alone. She was always so good at separating them for me, her practical mind helping me sort the burdens into boxes, to be opened when I was strong enough to deal with them. To deal with them one at a time. Without her help, the demons rush at me, overwhelming me, pinning me in place. Some are small, some are big, but they all seem too big for me today. Help me, please.

But there is no help for me today, so I must find my own strength from actions, not words. Check. Check. Check.

It has been more than a year since the unexpected general staff assembly advised me and almost two thousand other breadwinners of the pending kill-and-cut pork plant shutdown. It would be an orderly shutdown, a slow death, with no parties to celebrate people moving on to new jobs. A cakeless shutdown. Since the announcement, a slow shuffle of cardboard boxes has left the building, each box filled with framed photos of children or pets or partners, lunch bags and Tupperware containers and a fork brought from home. The detritus that comes with a parting of the ways is like posters left behind on bedroom walls by renters. Those small pieces of a workday hung without meaning, although the pictures had been great for conversation when we were all working. How are the kids? Great. Child B started university this fall. Yours? Child A is in soccer this summer. Grandkids? Smart little devils, must take after someone other than me. Heh heh. Eventually, the last of the workers left the plant, replaced by three shifts of rent-a-cops to protect the building and equipment from those of us who had once been responsible for its energy and success.

Melancholy had always been a struggle, but its grip is fierce right now. I began my slow decline months ago, in sync with the final plant closure. At first, groups of us would gather for lunch, chatting about our government benefits and how fabulous it was to finally get caught up on all the tasks at home. We ordered carefully, eating the specials of the day and leaving a ten-percent tip. We sat at our tables past one o'clock, laughing about the freedom of not having to punch a clock, but inside, we all wished we could. We didn't choose this life of leisure, and our unemployment benefit cheques would run out soon enough. The brighter, harder working of our group eventually left our lunch gatherings, taking on new jobs and other companies, picking up their cardboard box of work and life balance and proudly carrying it to their next cubicle or office. The rest of us glowered inside, jealous, wondering why them, why not me? I don't know why I wasn't one of the chosen ones, the fair-haired child invited to move on to a new company.

My telephone rings, and my heart leaps. Perhaps I am not forgotten; perhaps I am too big to fit in the tunnel. I answer, tentatively, my voice sounding like that of someone else. Someone less sure than I am. Than I was. It could be a prospective employer, someone who needs me, but I am expecting it to be someone for Steve or someone selling something.

It is none of those things. It is Harley, the young girl who is staying with Lydia. Her words somersault from the telephone, not making any sense to me. I try to back her up, to make her start again, because I think I hear her saying that Lydia has a problem, that she needs me to come to Winnipeg. I feel my adrenalin kick in, and my weighty self-concern lift. Action. What can I do?

There is no need for check marks right now. I am required in this world.

I drive to Winnipeg with my head spinning, going over everything Harley had told me.

When Harley first started talking, her words spilled over each other. It had been hard for me to understand her at first, her relief at having someone with whom to share Lydia's problem coursing through the wire like the centre line on the Trans-Canada Highway. From the little I know of Harley, she has had a lifetime of experience in dealing with adult problems, and she quickly settled into the tale of the events of the night before.

Lydia had arrived home early from her date with Eugene, bruised and bleeding and in shock. Harley had done what she could to cleanse Lydia's wounds and make her feel safe and cared for. She had seen the results of domestic violence at her parent's home, and she knew that Lydia's physical needs were small. However, the full-scale affront on her emotions by Eugene's attack would take longer to heal than the gravel rash. Lydia was used to doing the healing of others, but not of having to heal herself.

They had sat watching television as the calm after the storm filled the room. It was a small calm, and it struggled to fill the small room in which they sat. Sensing sadness, Captain and Tennille did not leave Lydia's side. Physical size doesn't count when it comes to emotional support, and the strength of the Chihuahua equalled that of the big, black dog. Lydia had slowly relaxed, her shock dissolving into the sofa, into the warmth of the blankets, her tensed muscles softening their hold now that they were no longer required to support Lydia. Harley and the dogs had taken over that responsibility.

They had all drifted into the strange kind of sleep that only happens in front of the television. Temporary, stolen, guilty. It wasn't clear who the caretakers were as they slumbered on, a small, safe knot of security in what was a big, bad world. Many tiny threads make a strong rope, and as they slept, the rope grew in power and the knot tightened. Peace and quiet had settled in for the night.

Suddenly, Lydia and Harley bolted awake as the dogs scrabbled to their feet, barking and racing for the front door. Something had disturbed them, and they were barking and growling in the dark hallway, relentless in their bravery. Confused and still waking up, Lydia flicked on the lights in the porch. Eugene stood in front of her, not moving, as the dogs continued their tirade. His face was a reflection of his mind, distorted and crazy. Lydia didn't caution them to stop. She had observed the broken glass beneath his feet. He had a key for the back door, but had chosen to break his way through the front window, undoing locks as he entered, his intent to cause damage, to violate her home. The ugliness of his anger hit her hard, like another physical blow, and it took a quick moment for Lydia to realize that she was in danger. He looked larger than he actually was. Like his online dating statistics. She heard Harley's voice behind her. Lydia quickly turned as Harley took her cellphone from the back pocket of her jeans, dialling 911. Eugene took a step forward, a knife in his hand, and Captain's barking and growling escalated. Harley gave the address of the house, yelling over the din of the dogs and Eugene's shouts to quiet them. They didn't obey. They didn't care.

When Eugene moved toward Lydia, Captain lunged at him, sinking his teeth into the intruder's forearm, wrenching Eugene's arm. The knife clattered to the floor. Fearlessly and ferociously, the big dog then attacked Eugene's upper thigh. Eugene's distorted features heightened by pain, he backed into the door. Feeling for the knob behind him, he tried to open it as Captain continued to snarl and bite at his hands. Eugene's leg was bleeding badly, and his hands were useless in defending himself. Eventually he managed to turn the knob, his hand slipping in his own blood. Captain continued his attack, biting and ripping at Eugene, leaping higher, trying for his neck. The instinct of an animal. Eugene pulled the door open and turned to escape, but he only managed to fall down the front steps when Captain jumped on his back. Wailing sirens and flashing lights announced the arrival of a police cruiser. When Lydia called Captain, he backed away from Eugene, his barking and growling continuing even as he returned to the house.

The officers checked on Lydia and Harley and even Captain. All was well. Harley didn't notice if they even checked on Eugene. One policeman asked them questions and took their statements while the other stood watch over the cowering figure in the back of the cruiser. Eugene looked small and weak, his anger spent. Was it his rage and hatred that had made him large? Lydia locked her door, a token gesture as she stepped around the broken glass. She made a mental note to leave a recycled grocery bag on the fence post out back. Too bad the cops took the knife. She would have put that in the bag, too.

I arrive at the house shortly before lunch and am greeted by the sound of locks being undone, dogs barking, and Harley yelling at them to be quiet. I see the broken glass in the door, but none on the floor. Someone has cleaned up, mopped up, patched up. Thank god for someone. Thank god for Harley. Who needs me?

Chapter 14

Harley

I hadn't heard from Orval for a long time, since when I worked at Tim Hortons. In fact, I haven't heard from anyone in Brandon at all. Mom and Dad seem content to let me wander Winnipeg on my own. No surprises there. They have my cellphone number, but they need nothing from me and never call. My friends have moved on to new people, confirming what I have always known. I can easily be replaced.

So, it was a complete surprise when Orval did call and said he was in Winnipeg. He told me he had asked around until someone gave him my cellphone number, and he was sorry it took such a long time to get in touch. He hoped I didn't mind him calling out of the blue now and then he asked if we could meet for a coffee. We decided to get together this morning at Tim Hortons on Portage Avenue, a few blocks away from Lydia's house. From where I am living. Home? He loves Timmies, and I like being there when he is. I think he just wants to catch up, but the urgency to his voice suggests something more, and as I leave the house for our rendezvous, I wonder what this meeting is all about.

Orval is eighty-one years old and walks with a cane. One of his feet moves a bit sideways, and he has to shuffle it along, urging it forward like a shy child. It is the result of a motorcycle accident many years ago in South Dakota that forced him to spend a month in hospital with his broken ankle pinned and suspended. It did heal, but then age began taking its toll, and old hurts reinvented themselves in new ways. Most of his hair is gone now, except for a few greys hanging around the back of his neck and in his ears and nose. His eyebrows consist of long white hairs that charge off in all kinds of wrong directions, and his face is covered with the liver spots of the aged. His eyes and teeth are light brown, the same colour as the spots on his face. He sees everything. Everything.

We had spent, over time and many cigarettes, countless hours chatting about ourselves, our lives, and our thoughts. I felt his reluctance to share, to open up, but as unlikely a friend to this old man as I was, over time we came to trust each other. I liked Orval and his stories and his honesty. He had lived his life quietly and peacefully. He had lived in a manner to which I could not relate.

Before he retired, he was the manager of a hardware store in Brandon. He was a great manager, but he didn't own the store, and his efforts had made someone else rich. He had enough for his own needs and bore no resentment toward the owner. The store made money year after year, and Orval never failed to receive an annual bonus and Christmas turkey from his employer.

He grew up an only child on a farm near Minitonas, on land that gave little back. Eventually, he moved to the city as a young man, hoping to find a wife and a life. He never did find a woman, and he contented himself with his work, his curling league in wintertime, and his motorcycle in the summer. He started his career with the hardware store as a yard ape, hauling lumber and concrete slabs and wire fencing to waiting half tons, stopping for a smoke and a chat if things weren't too busy. Over the years, he learned the business, but more importantly, he learned the needs of the customers and loved anticipating their needs and suggesting something new. He had a way about him that people responded to, a nice manner, a kind and helpful smile. Orval genuinely liked people and made friends easily. Each Tuesday he volunteered at Helping Hands soup kitchen, dishing out meals to hungry folks. He made his annual donations to the women's shelter and the Humane society. He was quick to pay for a coffee or drop a dollar into a cold hand in the winter.

He lived in a small house not too far from the store and walked to work, taking what he called his daily constitutional if time and weather permitted. If it didn't, he drove his old pick-up truck the short distance. He wore the store uniform with pride, each day fastening his badge to his red shirt, with his name right over the words Store Manager. On days off, he liked to go to the store and check on the business and then head down to Timmies for a visit with whomever was there. After he retired, he went to that coffee shop every day. He knew all the workers there, and they all knew his name and how he took his coffee. They never had to ask; they simply poured when they saw him come through the door. He liked that. It made him feel special and a part of a small community of coffee-drinkers. He might have liked to change his order to a hot chocolate or a cup of tea from time to time, but they never gave him the chance. So, he quietly drank his coffee and didn't rock the boat. That was his way.

Sometimes, when he couldn't sleep at night, he would go to Timmies for a coffee and the company of others. The old ladies served his coffee in the daytime, but on the evening shifts, they were replaced by young girls or boys who were eager to earn a few bucks for their own clothes or meals or whatever their needs were. He chatted them up and always sat at the table nearest the till so he could talk with them when the store wasn't busy. The night crowd was mixed, with transport drivers having a quick bite to eat before their last leg home, sleepy-looking travellers needing a jolt of caffeine to keep awake on the highway, and bikers hanging around in groups. Harley saved crossword puzzles from copies of *The Brandon Sun* left in the store and kept them in the back for him. He would sit and work the puzzles, occasionally asking the girls for help. They were so young, though, and he knew they'd never have the answers because it takes a lifetime to find the answers. At his age, he knew that, but he liked to ask anyway. Sometimes they filled his cup for free. He would've paid, but he wouldn't say no either.

In the wintertime, if he had an early draw, he would stop in for a coffee after his curling game. Sometimes his friends would go too, but they usually had family waiting at home or dogs to let out or a favourite show to watch. Goddammit, he was lonely most of the time, but he always managed to fill his hours.

He had a few favourites at Timmies, ones he talked to more often than others. And, of course, he liked to look at the pretty ones, although seriously, nobody looks pretty in a hair net. He talked to me a lot, probably because I had a soft spot for those who sat alone, neglected by the world, and definitely because I always asked if he wanted his coffee warmed up.

"I won't say no," was his stock standard reply.

I didn't consider myself one of the pretty ones and, apparently, neither did the pretty ones. I really wanted to fit in with them, but they wouldn't let me, and I soon gave up trying. I had never been any good at the whole 'join' thing, and I decided I didn't want to start with that lot. I was never sure that it was my choice, though.

Orval, however, was always nice to me, and I often wondered if he was trying to make up for me being on the outer edge of the group. One day, he casually remarked, "You have a nice smile."

"When I feel like it," became my stock standard reply.

After that, when I went out on my breaks for a smoke by myself, Orval occasionally did, too, probably for his own company as well as for mine. And, after a while, it got so that every time I told him I was going for a break, he would take his smokes and his bum foot and shuffle around to the back of the store to join me. A group of two. Our own little group. We shared our stories, fifteen minutes at a time, while smoking seven-minute cigarettes. Neither of us complained about our lives. I didn't mind listening to the small details of his disappointing life, and he always looked forward to seeing me. Slowly, but surely, our friendship grew.

Then, in the late spring, I disappeared from work and from Brandon without a word. If he'd even asked about me at Timmies, they likely just said that when I hadn't shown up for a few shifts, they'd taken me off the work schedule. I didn't worry about that, but I did worry about not saying anything to him. Ever since then, anytime I went past a Tim Hortons, I realized that I missed his company. I often wondered if he missed mine.

I am waiting for him when he walks into the coffee shop, and he spots me right away. His face brightens, and he coaxes his shy leg along at a faster pace. He is glad to see me. I note that he looks natty today, with a belt on his trousers and a tie around his neck. Nothing matches, but he is well past the age where he cares about things like that. He has made an effort, and, as he shuffles toward me, I wonder what his mission is.

I stand as Orval approaches the table and put out my hand in greeting. He brushes my hand away and reaches forward to hug me, quickly pulling me toward him. I feel whiskers hiding from the razor in the deep recesses of his face, and old, dry lips puckered and hard against my cheek. I also smell umpteen cups of coffee. He pats my back twice. Enough of this nonsense, his hand says. He rests his cane against the bench seat and eases his uncooperative body down. I head off to get him a coffee. I don't have to ask; I remember what he drinks and that he won't say no. When I get back to the table, he gives me a liver-coloured smile.

True to our Canadian culture, we talk about the weather. Unseasonably cold. Too much rain. Farmers won't like it much. Heard on the radio it would be a cold summer too. All light and fluffy conversation. Before long, however, we begin to probe each other's recent events as the boundaries of the politeness of strangers slowly melt away into the cautious familiarity of acquaintances, ending up just shy of the soul-baring of the friends we had become.

Over smokes in Brandon, I had told him about the shoplifting and the Girls for Tomorrow, and so now I update him on what I have been doing. I tell him about my time in Winnipeg and the strange and lonely young doctor. I tell him about how I ended up at Lydia's place and that I have decided to become a writer. I tell him about my stories, and I can feel my enthusiasm rise as I talk about how much I love to write. Orval is curious, asking me how I plan to become a writer. He says he doesn't know much about it. I tell him I have been writing when I have time, but I don't know too much about it either. I tell him I might have to go to school to learn more about it. It seems like a lifetime of events have happened since I last saw him. Orval doesn't seem surprised by any of it. He says that after almost a lifetime of events himself, nothing surprises him anymore. Almost a lifetime. Ain't that the truth. He pauses for a moment. His smile fades and then it comes back. He sits up straight and looks intently at me, the signal that he has something important to say.

He has been to see the specialist in the city and received news he didn't want to hear. Who would? His cancer, the commonplace cancer, cancer of the prostate, has metastasized and taken over his body. Beneath his wrinkly skin, the insidious cancer is pulsing, growing, beating, unseen but deadly. The doctor laid it out in plain words. It is time to get his affairs in order.

I try not to let it show, but inside, I am both shaken and saddened. I know that old people get sick, but I haven't had any experience with death. I don't know many people and have never known anyone who was dying. My outside face remains composed as we talk about his past treatments, what the doctors and Orval are hoping for, how useless their hope is, and how nothing has quelled the Big C. The telling of folks is just one more stage of his disease, and so here he is. He pushes his cup, half empty of warmish coffee, toward me. In shock, I struggle to stand but eventually make my way to the counter and come back with two more. We sip coffee and talk about the crying shame. Then a silence floats down over us as we wordlessly empty our cups.

After a while, Orval clears his throat and begins to speak again. His words come out slowly, and he watches my face as he delivers each one. There is a deliberateness to his speech, like he has rehearsed this. Over the years, he has saved a bit, a big bit, actually, and he has no kids and doesn't know anyone else who needs money. He is leaving some to charities in Brandon. Some to the Helping Hands soup kitchen, some to the YWCA, and some to the Humane Society. He wants to help those who can't help themselves, but he probably doesn't have enough money to make a big difference to any of them. He hasn't made a big difference at all in his life, although he did what he could, and he wants to give his money to someone who could make a difference, if only they are given the chance.

I finally realize what he is saying. When Orval dies, he is leaving the rest of his bit, a big bit, really, to me.

Chapter 15

Lydia

I am being cautious with my life now. I might have been weary of the hard work it takes to be someone special to someone else, but being alone has to be better than being in a relationship based on size and culinary ability. I go to work and then I go home. I don't feel much like being a part of anyone's life, and I know I have withdrawn into myself. I don't have any energy.

Harley was a huge support to me during the crisis with Eugene and since then has taken on a stronger role in the house. She is in touch with me throughout the day, checking to see how I am doing and sending me a lifeline if I need it, or if she thinks I need it. Sometimes I do and then I appreciate her concern. She has been told by some old guy she knew in Brandon that he will leave her money when he dies. Of course, I'm skeptical that he is only trying to use her, but I say nothing. It all seems super weird and sketchy to me, but she needs to pin her hopes on something, and if she does get the money, it will be her big chance to make a step change and to have a real opportunity to become the person she wants to be, the Harley of her dreams. I still think she needs to get a better grip on who that Harley is, but at least now she actually has a possibility of growing into that person.

She has got me thinking, though, about who is the Lydia of my dreams. Why am I waiting for someone to come along to make me into the best me I can be when I already have everything I need to be that person? I don't need a Eugene or an Orval, but what I do need is to start making better decisions for myself. I am floating, anchored at one end by my work at the hospital, a place that demands everything of me, and tethered at the other end by my home, a place that demands nothing of me. Forward and backward, no left, no right. I have gone through my life with my everything laid out for me, no effort required. I took piano lessons as a child, but the piano, as I grew older and abandoned my lessons, gathered dust. I painted and drew, but as I grew older and other interests took up my time and ambition, my paints dried up. Wanna be a doctor, Lydia? I have the brains and the money. No decision required. Wanna be a concert pianist? Sorry, too busy being a doctor. No time. No energy. I do think there is something more for me, but I am too busy being tired and too tired of being busy. I need to stick a wrench in the spokes and stop this wheel for a minute. Wanna be an artist? Sorry, too busy being a doctor, and thinking about being a concert pianist. I don't even know what I want to want. I can't focus. I'm good at everything, but the problem is, I am not great at anything…well, maybe at being a doctor. Am I a jack of all trades or too lazy to try really hard to be great at anything else? My life demands everything of me, so I demand nothing of my life. This isn't really a problem, I know. Harley is too young and too unspoiled to appreciate this dilemma of the over-advantaged. I need to talk with Meaghan.

Meaghan has been my best friend for a long time, a sandbox friend, one that simply is, that requires no effort. I know this because I have made no effort. I ignore her and expect her to be there for me. She always is. Some people say that the best kind of friends are those who, after a long absence, you continue on with as if there was never any time apart. This, of course, is bullshit. Who makes this stuff up? The best kinds of friends are those who don't have long absences, who don't desert their friends when it is convenient for them to do so. Meaghan is always there, and I don't have to make apologies, although I know I should. I don't deserve her.

She answers the phone when I call and sounds happy that I am going to visit her for a weekend. Steve is away, but she would love to see me. When I add that Harley wants to come too and notice a hint of hesitation in Meaghan's voice, I explain that Harley hasn't been back to Brandon for a very long time and wants to try and catch up with some people. My guess is that Harley doesn't actually know what she is going back to or why. In fact, I think she is afraid to face her old life. I think she is in the process of reinvention, and she doesn't want to get drawn back into whatever she came from. I think this is going to be an interesting trip.

As we pack the old Volvo, I throw in a case of beer, a few bottles of wine, and a bottle of scotch. The dogs jump in. They don't know where they are going, only that they are going. They trust there will be a destination. We pick up road coffees and head down Portage, backwards on the Trans-Canada Highway, heading west. There used to be a tape deck in the car, but it failed years ago, so my music is played from my phone. Classic country plays as we drive, Harley making fun of the music while I appreciate the simple reflections on life that are contained in the words. The straightness of the road is like an arrow. Bullseye.

I stop at the house of Harley's parents. It is a small and shabby one-storey with blue paint flecked away and roofing tiles peeled up on the south side of the house. There is evidence of someone having had potted plants on the step, but that could have been years ago. The screens of the storm door are ripped, like someone has been pushed through them.

Harley opens the car door slowly, if one can do such a thing. She leaves her bag in the car and asks me to wait. Her slumped shoulders and weary walk indicate that she is in no hurry to get where she is going. When she arrives, Harley pulls the outside door open and knocks on the inside door. When the door finally opens, I can't see who is there. I watch her back as her hands move around and her shoulders tense. Whoever she is talking to has a lot to say.

After only a few minutes, Harley turns abruptly and heads to the car. Her head is bowed, and I can't read her face. I look toward the house, but there is no one standing in the doorway. Both doors are closed. As she slides into the car, she asks if she can hang out with Meaghan and me for the weekend. She has no other way back to Winnipeg. I nod. Then I wait. She says nothing. I wait longer.

Finally, she says, "Mom is drunk. Dad is drunk. I can't go back to that, Lydia. I want more."

My Harley-burden doesn't seem like one anymore. I reach out to her and give her shoulder a little squeeze.

"Buckle up, Harley," I say, as I bring the old Volvo to life and steer her out from the curb.

Meaghan's house is only a few blocks, but a million miles, from Harley's previous life.

When we knock on the door, awkward with our arms filled with the weekend booze, Meaghan answers almost immediately. Captain and Tennille are anxious to see Meaghan and rush ahead of us, Captain's enthusiasm almost knocking us over. Meaghan greets them warmly, running her hand over Captain's back, then picking up Tennille, holding her in her arms like a baby. Meaghan doesn't seem surprised to see Harley, and I am relieved. She looks great, her hair and makeup done, her jewellery perfectly matching her clothes. As we enter her home, I see that everything is in place. Only today's newspaper sits in the large wicker basket placed by the door. Of course, yesterday's newspaper will have gone to the recycling bin. Everything has a place, and everything should be in its place. The floors and furniture are gleaming. She really has her life together, and I feel relief and gratitude for her friendship. I know she has had some hard times since the plant closed, but she seems to have embraced her new reality. I feel a twinge of envy.

She hugs me, a big hug that feels like she will never let me go. The hug could theoretically last forever, but she finally pulls away and gives Harley a quick embrace. Meaghan gives me a searching look, her eyes asking if Harley is okay. I make a small grimace and shrug my shoulders. I don't know. Harley asks if she can use the washroom. I know where the washroom is, but Harley doesn't, and Meaghan indicates the general direction. Meaghan and I walk to the kitchen. When Harley joins us, Meaghan asks Harley what she wants to drink. Harley just wants a soft drink. It is no surprise to me that Harley isn't drinking today, and I can tell that Meaghan has already tuned in to the reason for Harley's mood. She always was the intuitive one. Harley takes her drink and heads off to watch television in another room. She knows we have things to talk about without her, and I imagine that she prefers to be on her own after her most recent encounter. I watch her go, her aura heavy and lumbering as it moves with her.

Meaghan sets two huge wineglasses and a bottle of red on the table, the crystal of the glasses reflecting clearly in the glass tabletop. Apparently, we are in for a time of reflection, that special time when old friends slowly squeeze the past for relevance, easing it into the present, setting the course for the future. We re-establish our joint biography. We have been friends for a long time, and I joke to her that we might need two bottles at least. Laughing, I retrieve a second bottle from the kitchen, one of the ones I had brought with me, and set it on the table between us, a physical confirmation that I am ready to talk, to share, and to listen. The dogs have settled in. They know this routine and are content to simply be flies on the walls. Dogs on the carpets.

We talk about Harley before the wine is even poured. She is a safe third party that allows us to begin to share our thoughts, a centre from which we will begin the deep dive, the details and emotions of our own lives to be bared, shared, dissected, and reassembled. The end goal of such talks is never clear, but good friends always know when the goal has been achieved. I know we have to start from a point of chaos and, unfortunately for Harley, she is it.

Meaghan then pours the wine and toasts our friendship. I lift my glass and smile a guilty smile at her, feeling the cringy-stomach feeling of my bad-friend acknowledgement. I drink to our friendship. Fake it 'til you feel it. Our glasses touch, ever so lightly. A butterfly kiss. For the first time since I arrived, I look into Meaghan's eyes and see panic residing in my good friend. I put my own baggage to one side and prepare to listen.

Alone after the others have gone to bed, I absorb the truth of misperception. What appears certain rarely is. I have always viewed Meaghan through the filter of my own life, and she has always seemed clearer, purer than me. Everything has a place, and everything should be in its place. This seems a good, and unattainable, way to live, and I have long admired her for her ability to do a mental and emotional quick-tidy. It appears that she has been sweeping her problems under the rug, though, and it seems obvious now that she needs my help.

She talked to me about her struggles after being laid off from the plant, about her friends that have moved on to newer, better positions, about how she has become more and more isolated. She talked about Steve and how she had relied on him, leaned on him until the burden became too much for even his broad shoulders, and he stepped back, watching her slide, unable to help. He began to spend more time at work, more time in the city, more time with his friends. And, as he withdrew from her, she leaned harder, desperate for his strength. Even when he was at home with her, he found a less-travelled route to a quieter room, a room without her. She wore him out with her anguish, her lack of focus, her lack of fulfilment. No longer one, they became two, each unable to be there for the other. Eventually he said he wanted to get his head together and then moved in with a friend, leaving her alone.

I have known both of them for a very long time. I met him when he and Meaghan first started dating, in their first year of university, and they have both been a part of my life ever since. I feel terribly sad that my friends have worn each other out and wonder if this is normal. Can two people who have consumed each other regenerate? I saw their love in their younger days, and I want it to be possible that it could become again what it once was. What I do know for sure is that Meaghan needs me as her friend. This is no time to fake it.

I wake up earlier than the previous evening's conversation and amount of wine should permit. Although my body resists the early hour, my head is full of thoughts and ideas. The house is silent, all other occupants sound asleep. Whether it is a peaceful sleep for either of them, I have no way of knowing, but I am in no hurry to stir them to the day. I quietly make my way to the kitchen table, and wait as the world outside gently slides from darkness to light.

When Meaghan finally joins me, we talk about her future over coffee and aspirin. I really feel my friend is in danger from herself and needs new hope. My words became a soft blanket, circling Meaghan, wrapping her up, making her feel secure, drawing her closer. I feel the words before I say them. I try to keep them inside, to not have them layer complications on my life. I talk about the great coffee and my headache. The words would be heard, however, and it is another voice, a small but persistent voice, that speaks over the mental din I am creating.

"Come stay in Winnipeg with us, Meaghan. You can catch your breath, look for work in Winnipeg, take some time to sort things out with Steve." Words said that can't be unsaid.

I suck in hard, trying to inhale the words, but they remain out there, life changing and powerful. The words of a friend. I can feel her struggle, her resistance to giving up, her uncertainty in her previous ability to always manage. I can sense her reluctance to lean on anyone after Steve has crumbled all too easily, too quickly, right when she needed him most. I can tell he broke her heart, her spirit, her resolve. I also suspect that if she does come to Winnipeg with me, it will be the harder of her choices.

Meaghan is quiet for a while, her head down, avoiding eye contact. Her shame at failure is palpable, and when she finally raises her head, her face is quivering, her mouth squared with uncried tears, her eyes deep with gratitude.

Harley walks in a few minutes later, looking for a mug and a cup of coffee, the significance of earlier moments unknown to her. She asks me if I will give her a ride a bit later on. She wants to spend the afternoon at the hospital visiting Orval. He isn't doing so well. Meaghan seems to be doing better, though. The see-saw of life.

Meaghan spends the rest of the day packing. She makes detailed lists, washes and irons and folds, checking items off as they go into the suitcase. I watch her growing stronger, more focused, as the activity of packing consumes her time. And because I know she needs this time of small details to understand the change she is about to make, I decide to spend the afternoon studying a medical text. I always have at least one in my car. I wonder if, through helping my friend, I am helping myself as well.

Chapter 16

Meaghan

After arriving in Winnipeg, things have begun to move quickly for me. Harley has unexpectedly become a friend, albeit a quiet one who demands nothing, but who moves about the house, patching us up as required. I like her. Despite being younger than me, she exudes wisdom and calm with an old soul, a soul that has aged faster than Harley herself. Perhaps her soul had started out at a suitable age, one befitting her years, but because she has been overexposed to a grown-up world, it, too, has grown up, learning to accept its reality and to expect little, helping Harley survive in her world of neglect. That soul will remain old as Harley catches up to it, and it will provide clarity to her.

Steve called last week. He said that he isn't good for me, that he is responsible for my sadness and my aloneness, and that it would be best for me if we each went our own way. Permanently. He snuck that last word in there quietly as if it didn't carry the weight of ten years together. I thought he was a better man, that he would have had the courage to bow out of our relationship more gracefully, acknowledging his own share of our failure. But he used me and my weaknesses to make himself palatable to the world's perception of him. I am in no mood to care one way or the other. All I know is that he wasn't big enough to help me when I needed him, and so, perhaps, he is right.

When I told Lydia and Harley about the call from Steve, Lydia called him a coward for ending a relationship over the telephone. Harley's old soul spoke up, summarizing my true feelings in two words. "Fuck him." I agree with her and don't really feel that there is any room for manoeuvring around those words. There is so much to be learned from the bravado of youth. "Fuck him," I tell myself, silently at first and then out loud, albeit in a whisper. There is a lot of power in those two words, a lot of emotion in those seven letters, seven letters that demark the moment between living in the past and living for the future. It is time to move on.

To be honest, I had been expecting a permanent end to the Us. I had also expected to be completely devastated by it, but I wasn't, maybe because it had been a slow death, starting with the Us becoming us, and then finally you and me, and then only me. And it did seem odd to me that during the first few months I spent in Winnipeg I began to rely more on myself. Nevertheless, the soft sounds of my friends' voices and the chatter and drama of their daily lives filtering through my isolation, all served to pad my bones and strengthen my resolve, thereby helping me to grow my backbone and stand up straight. Words are powerful, and Harley had the most powerful of them all. "Fuck him." The words from which I would leverage myself, the short syllables and letters on which I would gain traction.

I have an interview for a manager's job at the airport. I've had a few interviews so far, but not for anything that felt right for me. Apparently also nothing that felt right for any interviewers because I have had no offers. Maybe this time. I have made a list of information that I want them to know about me, the good stuff. The things that will make them want me and keep me. I can be a list, which is better, more extensive, than a check mark. A list has a future. I hope I remember to check the list.

I guess I am like a home that has been on the real estate market for too long. Not a new home. There must be something wrong with me, or I would have been sold already. There isn't anything wrong with me, at least not that I can see. In fact, I feel better and stronger than I have in a very long time. I am ready to be sold. I simply need the right buyer. I am not a fixer-upper anymore. I had hoped that leaving the smaller city of Brandon would open up my horizons, but I look straight ahead, over the Winnipeg landscape, and I see nothing coming my way. Perhaps today will be different, and the interviewers will sense that I have said, "Fuck him." They will sense I am gaining traction, and that they had better grab me, their best opportunity, while they can.

I am still making to-do lists, tiny manifestos to which I cling, declarations of my daily intentions. I still measure my worth by my actions, but there is less desperation in the check marks, fewer inane items. For example, I haven't entered daily hygiene as an action for some time now. There is also less effort required in general. I don't need tomorrow's list as a reason to get through today, to keep passing the open windows. I am growing bigger, raising myself, feeling my worth. I don't know who I am yet, but I am starting to believe that I am more than a check mark.

Harley, Lydia, and I have been watching a television series called "24". I can totally relate to the theme of the show about twenty-four hours in the life of a person, about how much can happen in even a single hour. Just get through today. The program is about an American espionage agent searching for terrorists. I am not an agent, but maybe I could be. I am always searching for myself, looking for the terror, keeping it under control. Clearly, we are both having some success these days. There can still be some terror involved. The agent has a few key people upon whom he can rely when things derail badly, and I have Harley and Lydia. There is strength in numbers.

The interview is over. I didn't check the list until after I left, when I was sitting in my car in the airport parking lot. I forgot a lot of the good things about me, and I don't think I will get another opportunity. My state of mind leaves me feeling unfocussed. Another failure. When I walk through the door in the late afternoon, I throw my keys and purse on the counter, then head straight for the table. I pick up my list and check off the interview with a large mark. Done, done and done. I quickly flip through the pile of mail on the table, hoping to find a handwritten envelope with a postage stamp glued in the corner and a return address label in the opposite top corner that displays a little picture of a flower or a leaf printed beside the name to brighten it up. I'm not expecting a letter or a card from a friend, but when I do receive one, it connects me in a way that no other communication can. No such a letter for me today, and I feel my daily disappointment. There is, however, a letter from the University of Manitoba for Harley. I can only hope it is good news for her. I check the phone system for messages, hoping that someone, anyone, has left a friendly message. Let's go for coffee. Let's see a movie. There is a sale on moisturizing cream at the drugstore. The message indicator light is off, so I feel the same little disappointment inside. Nope. Why have I disappeared?

There should be a special place for people to go when they are lonely. A place that doesn't allow people who have lots of friends, or who aren't in need of them, or who can't, for whatever reason, be a friend. A place that would turn away at the door those people with lots of family in their lives, who don't have to try hard to fill their days and nights with the sounds of the living. Those people would stick out in such a place, and they would be resented for their success. There would be two learner's tables, one for the boys and one for the girls. Once friendships in the same gender had been established, they could then move on to an advanced table where they would learn to have friends of the opposite sex. The beautiful thing about such a special place is that only the truly lonely would be there, and there would be no shame in wearing your isolation like an armband. Everyone there would have such an armband. And there would be no tables where people might sit alone with an empty chair directly across from them that confirmed sequestration. There would be no dancing unless everyone dances. And on New Year's Eve, when the clock strikes the promise of new beginnings, there would be a group hug. Everyone's cheek would get kissed, and no one would be left out or behind. In that special place, the only reason anyone would talk to you is because they want to be a friend, or to have a friend. The not-allowed would include makeup salespeople, those only trying to make a deal, use the lonely, take the money, or leave behind enthusiastic promises of beauty or glamour or calm and empty promises of friendship. No users allowed. Pretty Ponzi posers. They would all be turned away at the door.

Harley has been out. I don't know where she went. She throws her backpack on the floor before flipping through the mail. I watch for her reaction when she sees the letter from the university, but there is none. She opens the envelope like a child, ripping the paper unevenly, the hand of one who is unpracticed at receiving mail. She reads the letter inside. I can see it is one sheet of thick paper. Still no reaction. She takes the letter and her backpack upstairs to her room without acknowledging me. No eye contact. I feel panicked for my friend, witnessing the horrendous crash of her dreams as they hit the floor, landing beside the scraps from the envelope. I want to follow her, asking questions, getting answers, filling in the blanks, but I resist. Harley's old soul needs privacy right now, and I must leave her alone to identify her feelings, to plan her Plan B. She doesn't know that I saw the envelope, buried in the detritus of junk mail.

I rise and go to the tiny kitchen and begin preparing a special meal. It will be my offering to Harley, my recognition that I know she has received word from the university. Lydia is working days right now, and she will be home for dinner. We will both be there, ready to receive Harley's disappointment, ready to offer options and false hope, but mainly to offer our friendship as a Band-Aid. The dogs are at my feet, unsafe around hot stoves and dropping knives, but I appreciate their stalwart presence and move carefully around them. I drop a bit of food, pretending my generosity is an accident, and they gobble up my carelessness. I drop another bit of food, and they are on to my game. Once is a trend; twice is a tradition; and they watch my hands carefully, waiting for me to offer them more. They can't be fooled by the likes of me. I set the table carefully, loving the preciseness and order of the process. Forks on the left, knives and spoons on the right. I have a friend who calls them tools. That term always bothers me. It makes me feel like eating is a job. I add some candles and dried flowers to the table, and three wine glasses. The table looks festive, like a place for a celebration. On second thought, I take the flowers away. There will be no rejoicing tonight.

Lydia comes in, not bothering with the mail. I guess she isn't waiting for word from anyone. Since my arrival at her house, she no longer leaves her purse and stethoscope on the stovetop, throwing them instead on the small table by the door. She wanders into the kitchen and pours herself a glass of wine. Decompression time. She offers me one, and I accept. It is no longer daytime, and I am not alone. A drink will be fine. I tell her about the letter and Harley's reaction to its contents. Her lack of reaction. Lydia's face drops, and in it I can read genuine sadness for her friend.

Harley comes into the kitchen to join us. Three women and two dogs in such a small space filled with the smell of good food should be an excellent place to be, but I am weighed down by the knowledge of Harley's letter. Lydia offers Harley a drink, and she nods her head. She rarely drinks, and Lydia and I exchange knowing glances. Perhaps a drink will take the edge off her bad news. Lydia and I wait for Harley to open up, but she remains silent. After taking a sip of the wine, she looks at us, raises her glass, and makes a toast to her best friends. I feel a lump in my throat as tears well in my eyes. The soft binking of our full glasses is the sound of friendship passing through crystal.

Harley then toasts her future at university. I am shocked, as is Lydia, and I am filled with such sudden and unexpected happiness and love for this young woman that for a moment I can hardly breathe. It takes another moment for her news to fully register and then we are leaping around the kitchen, hugging each other and spilling our wine on the floor and the dogs. We chatter excitedly. Such wonderful news. Why didn't you say. I was so worried. You didn't react. Fabulous. Cheers again. Double cheers. I put another bottle of wine on the table and put the flowers back. Of course, they were not really necessary. Harley's face made the small table clearly a place of celebration.

Chapter 17

Harley

Orval died in the summer. I had been visiting him in the hospice in Winnipeg where he was dying out his last days. He had no family to care for him, and I never saw anyone else in his room. He was shrinking, becoming small, and his energy seeped away with each pound he lost. He was yellow, and his green hospital gown loosely circled his thin neck, a few hairs whispering over the upper edge of the fabric, a reminder of the man of which there was little left. He was so thin that his head and neck protruded above the gown, as if there was no body below, like a turtle with no shell. I wanted to hug him, but there was barely anything to hold on to, and he was attached to tubes. I didn't know if I could bear to have him give me two pats, ending the hug, ending our friendship.

Before he died, I did manage to embrace his bony body and give him a small kiss, my lips touching his cold, rough cheek. He said something to me, his voice a whisper of a whisper.

"You got it in ya, kid."

Before I met Orval, no one had ever believed in me, and I took his words and filed them away for future moments of self-doubt.

Angels come in all shapes and sizes, and mine was an old, liver-spotted curler who managed a hardware store in the middle of the Canadian prairies, a strange and lonely young doctor, and a sad and neurotic unemployed hermit. It was only later, as I thought about that last hug, that I realized there had been no double-pat. There wasn't enough time for that nonsense at the end of his life.

In mid-August, Meaghan and I walked around the U of M campus. A university in the summer is a surreal place with no one around. It reminded me of the creepiness of a busy city street on a Sunday night when there are no people on the sidewalks and no cars on the road. Unnatural, but ready for business. We entered the buildings, some smelling of old varnish and paper and wax, warm brown and rich and full of history, and others smelling of new construction, the hard edges of steel, glass, and plastic reflecting an uncomplicated future. I took Orval's words with me and drew on them many times that day. I didn't feel like it was my world nor that I had it in me. Instead, I felt uncertain, and my thoughts kept returning to those nights at home in Brandon, pretending to study at the kitchen table. What made me think this would be different, that I was smart enough, that the people at the university wouldn't see me masquerading as a student, a charlatan with a bookbag? I was so sure I wouldn't understand their language, that I would be on the outside looking in, watching their lips move, not taking knowledge or meaning from them. I was so sure I would walk alone, that I would spend four years with no one in this new world seeing or speaking to me and that my isolation would crush me. I was so sure I should still be in Brandon, serving coffee, with my high school certificate the culmination of what I had in me.

How did my life change so much? There were eighteen more exactly like me, sisters and brothers, working sporadically, on welfare, their children wards of the province, a fun night defined as too much booze, drugs, sex, or violence. How was it that I found myself walking the pathways of a university, education and opportunity saturating the environment? It would be hard to avoid success in such a place. I thought of Orval, who had wanted his rather large bit to make a difference. I thought of his faith in me. I thought of Lydia and Meaghan who kept telling me to stop living in my biography, that the power was in me to change my future. I asked myself these questions, but my overwhelming emotion was that of fear. I would never be good enough, strong enough, smart enough, for university. I would always be fat Harley, in the jeans that didn't deliver, living on the outskirts of the world, across the street from the car and pet wash.

I knew I had to try to succeed, though. Orval had wanted his money to make a difference, and I at least had to try. His funeral was a quiet affair with Meaghan and Lydia standing beside me along with a few people from the hardware store and three old guys with bad knees who had curled with him for years. There was no one there from Tim Hortons. Orval's life had been a disappointment to him, and he had placed his hope in me.

I struggled through the mystifying process of registering for classes. Nothing came naturally to me. I hadn't been raised in the language of post-secondary education, and many times I felt so stupid I wanted to cry. But Orval's words rescued me. You got it in ya, kid. I wasn't so sure, but sometimes the best way to get to where you want to go is to put one foot in front of the other and then change feet. I simply kept moving through the things I needed to do, filled with self-doubt, uncertain about everything other than that I was making a terrible mistake. Who did I think I was? Well, perhaps a writer.

My first day of classes was on a beautiful and sunny fall day. The leaves had started changing colour, and although the days were getting short, the air was warm and full of promise. I told myself that September was a reset button month when I would get smarter, faster, and prettier. I expected that October was when reality would set in. That first day on campus, students were rushing from one building to another, knowing where they were going, knowing how to get to their future. I felt panic rising, and I wanted to turn and run, to go home, to give up on me.

I needed to talk to someone. Lydia was at work. I called Meaghan, needing a lifeline to get me through. She told me to look around. She said there were people around me from other countries who had no families in Canada, no friends, who couldn't even speak English. Were they running home? Was that an option for them? She again told me to look around. There were people with serious mental and physical disabilities, people who couldn't see or hear or walk. Or run home. A third time she told me to look around. There were people who believed in their dreams, were willing to face their fears, who were brave enough to go after what they wanted. Then she said to stop feeling sorry for myself, to be thankful for my opportunity, and to get on with what I had to do. And then she hung up on me. Click. And that was it. That was the start of the rest of my life.

Life can change in an instant and mine certainly did. Click. I was an adult. I began to believe my future was under my control, and that if I wanted a reason to lose, I would always be able to find one. What was trickier was to identify and hold on to my reason to succeed. Was it for Orval or for my squalid family or for the faith my friends have in me? Was it to be strong and certain of myself so that Barb/Bob wouldn't ever prey on me again? Was it so I could begin to make choices for myself? Was it because I had stories I wanted to tell? Or was it all of these? At the sound of the click, I moved from the losing team to the winning one. Thank you, Meaghan. Thank you. Thank you. I needed a moment of tough love, and you were brave enough to give me one.

Orval's money will pay for my education and much more, but I'm not used to having money available to me. I start looking for a job that will allow me to work some evenings and not conflict with my studies or my writing. I don't want to ever go back to Tim Hortons and decide instead to see what they might have at The Brick in The Wall, a bar down the road from the house. Our house. As I write up my resume, I convince myself it's close enough to walk to, the pay won't be too bad, the tips should be good, and I will meet lots of people, both good and bad. All excellent fodder for stories.

When I apply for work at The Brick in The Wall, I walk in through the main door as confidently as I can, intent on making a good first impression. I move slowly at first until my eyes adjust to the darkness, and then I carefully navigate my way around a taped-off area where electrical work was being done. I notice someone wearing a Humble Pie T-shirt, beckoning me to the bar.

I like my earrings, a gift from Lydia when I was accepted into school. Lydia said you had to celebrate every milestone in life. They are my lucky earrings, and I wear them all the time. Don't give luck a chance to get away. Meaghan had shown me how to wear makeup, but I rarely wear it because I like to be able to rub my eyes. Today, however, I had made the effort. Make-up, jewellery, and dress pants. Having a job close enough to walk to was important. I don't have a car or a driver's licence. Lydia is always pushing me to take driving lessons, but I don't see the point. Buses are handy to my house, and a bus pass was provided as a part of my tuition at the university.

"What'll it be, missy?" a man asks from behind the bar, putting down a paperback as he speaks "What can I get for you?" He watches and waits as I fumble in my backpack, pulling out a single sheet of paper.

"Are you hiring right now?" My voice is shy, reverting to that of a teenager in the unfamiliar surroundings. "Like, hiring people?" That didn't even make sense. "You know, for work?" What else would they be hiring for? "I've never worked in a bar before." That'll sell him on you, Harley. "But I am a fast learner." Am I? When I hand him my resume, he takes it without looking at it and places in on the bar-top on top of his book.

When the man holds out his hand, I place my small, uncertain hand in his. What a weird thing to do. I look down, never making eye contact. He moves my hand up and down twice, and then lets mine drop. I pull it away as if his hand had meant mine harm.

"I'm Jesus," he said. He pronounced it Jee-zuz.

My eyes flash up at him, only for a moment, and then I pull them down, looking at my knees. Was he kidding? Crazy man.

"What's your name?"

"Harley." What else do I say? I got it in me; I got it in me; I got it in me. "I'm a student at the university, and I am looking for work." My mouth turns slightly upward, uncontrollable, in a tiny, proud smile as I say that. Never thought I'd be saying that.

Jesus' eyes flash briefly at me when I say my name, then he looks away. Was she kidding? "Harley," he says. "That's quite a name. Were you named after a movie star?"

"No, a motorcycle," I answer. I need to work on a better answer for that. Or change my name.

"What kinda work you looking for?"

I don't know what kind of work I am looking for. Something that pays me. Something that is close to home. "What do you have here?" I ask.

He picks up my resume from the bar-top and starts to read it. He watches my gaze land on his book, trying to read the title upside down. "Do you like to read?"

I smile as I answer, nodding. "I want to be a writer. I'm going to university to learn how to do it. How to write a book, I mean."

"You old enough to work in a bar?" he asks.

I nod as I pull out my health card, my only identification, unless you count my high school student card. I have changed a lot since then.

He offers me a beer, and we sit across from each other. We talk about books, and he tells me about the book he is reading. He has read it a few times already, he says. Guaranteed happiness, rereading a book you like. It is that good. He picks it up from the bar and shows it to me. It is pretty worn and looks like it has been read more than once.

He finishes his beer first and then offers me a job behind the bar, pouring beer and polishing glasses and clearing tables if I have time. He is willing to make the hours flexible enough to work around my schedule. The pay is bad, but the tips would more than make up for it if I work hard.

He sticks his hand out again to shake mine, and this time, I put mine into his, only a little stronger and a little more confident. I look at Jesus and thank him.

As I leave, I note many things that need tending. I also notice a handsome woman, her eyes following me from her table in the opposite corner of the bar.

Chapter 18

Jesus

The owner of the bar is a man named Jesus Hernandez. His parents emigrated from Mexico to Winnipeg before he was born, and Jesus never learned to speak Spanish. He served in the Canadian military, joining as a young man in need of options and discipline. It was that or end up in jail. He spent time in Germany, and after a few tours in Afghanistan, he did a few years as a loadmaster with Search and Rescue. After seeing his share of rescues and recoveries, he was happy to leave the military life behind him. With few transferable skills and after a period of not working, he bought The Brick in The Wall for a song and ran it with Nancy, his girlfriend. Jesus wasn't much of a handyman, and Nancy didn't like him to pay for repairs to the bar. She was always trying to keep the profits in the form of readily accessible funds. As a result, there were half-finished or barely started projects everywhere, and orange cones and yellow tape warned patrons about hazards to avoid. Weekend nights were comedic with drunks staggering to the bathrooms, crashing into each other as they avoided construction projects, leaking ceilings, or each other.

Nancy was what people called a handsome woman, tall and big-boned, striking and imposing. She had moved to Winnipeg with her first husband, an agronomist whom she had met in her native Honduras. When he moved on to greener pastures, Nancy stayed behind, serving beer in various Winnipeg drinking establishments. It was at one such bar that

Jesus had found her, and over time, they moved in together. Nancy was teaching Jesus to speak Spanish, and he practiced his bad vocabulary and worse accent with his customers and staff. Nobody really understood Jesus, but he was used to that.

He had a big, loud personality, laughing hard and swearing harder. He was a storyteller, a collector of tales, and as time passed, the stories of his patrons became his own. There he was either the hero, the villain, or the buffoon. His favourite stories to tell were ones in which he was the butt of the joke, where he made mistakes or did dumb things. He loved to laugh at himself.

Jesus was Mexican by heritage, but most people thought he was of First Nations descent. His brown skin, dark eyes, and small, tough body made him almost indistinguishable from the indigenous population in Winnipeg. Since leaving the Armed Forces, he had grown his hair, and he let it hang down his back in a grey ponytail, bound with a thick blue rubber band from a broccoli package. He loved his collection of rock band T-shirts and wore a different one every day. He also wore baggy cargo shorts in summer, and baggy cargo pants in winter, and summer or winter, sandals with socks to keep his feet from getting cold and dirty. He particularly loved cargo shorts and pants because he could put all his stuff in them, and since no amount of ironing or folding made them look better, or worse, he left them on the floor at night, ready to put on again the next morning, the pockets perpetually full of his stuff, of things he needed for the day. He thought it was a brilliant system. Brillante sistema. Because his eyesight wasn't as good as it once was, he had to wear glasses, but he'd had the same pair with their aviator-style frames for the last fifteen years. His eyesight might have changed in all that time, but as the glasses were always covered in fingerprints and bits of dandruff, he didn't know for sure. He liked them because they adjusted to the light by themselves. He could go from the darkness of The Brick to the brightness of Portage Avenue without needing sunglasses. Brillante sistema. He shaved once a week. Sometimes. What little beard he had wasn't heavy, and it suited him fine because it saved time and effort. Besides, he thought that Nancy liked his scruffy look.

Jesus read voraciously, mainly science fiction, but anything he could get his hands on. He loved to reread books. It was a sure thing and a comfort, knowing he would like a book he had already read. He often read while he was at the bar when he should have been working on projects. He had accumulated a wealth of knowledge, both useful and useless, and could talk to anyone about anything. He had also accumulated a wealth of opinions, each supported by carefully selected facts. He loved to debate with people at his bar-top about politics, the state of the military, how to raise children, and the education system. Those were his favourites, but he could raise an argument about any subject. Being informed was often a by-product of those discussions. Nothing ever ended with raised voices, though. Gotta protect the clientele.

Jesus was liked and loved and tolerated. Sometimes, The Brick in The Wall ran out of beer, and Jesus would run out to the Palomino down on Portage to buy a few cases of off-sales. Nancy looked after the staffing, the money and the cleaning, and he looked after the maintenance and the ordering, although sometimes he was too busy to remember to do the ordering. His response to no beer in his bar was, "Hey, eso es la vida" and a shoulder shrug. That's life.

Behind him, Nancy would roll her eyes. Not her life. In fact, she had been trying to change him. To be something he wasn't. Anything he wasn't, it sometimes seemed to Jesus.

When Nancy first met Jesus, she was working at the Appaloosa. A Palomino wannabe, it was more a place where spray-tanned cougars and overweight Tom Selleck look-alikes found each other. The bartenders were scamming tips from the serving staff, and the cook was dealing dope out the back door of the kitchen. There were rooms for rent above the bar, but only the staff stayed there. The rooms were convenient, expensive, cold, and noisy, and the staff stole from one another. The bar was rife with drama, and fights among the workers were as common as fights among the patrons. Cooks slept with dishwashers, bartenders with servers. Jealousies were commonplace, and emotions ran high.

Nancy worked there for years as a professional server, and the customers loved her. She never threatened the turf of the cougars, only flirting enough to make good tips, but not enough to piss the old cats off. It was a living that demanded little of her other than a short skirt, cleavage, and a cowboy hat. She lived upstairs in the most coveted room with a window overlooking the street, down at the end of the hall. Over the years, she had accumulated keys to all the rooms, and when others were working downstairs she would dig through their tips, helping herself to their cash. Can't be traced, you know. Everyone knew she stole from them, but no one had ever caught her in the act. If they didn't like it, they found another place to live or another place to work. Nancy didn't care. She added to her coffers by accepting the occasional Tom to her room, ones with affinities for a strange accent, dark skin, and a handsome face. It all added up, and she had a nice little nest egg put away for her future. The girls were sagging a bit, and she was going to have to get some work done on them. That cost money. She was going to need her nest egg.

Back then, Jesus drank some and sat at the Appaloosa bar, talking with anyone around him, laughing and telling stories. He often arrived alone, always left alone, and he knew everyone. Sometimes he joined a group around a large table, ordering rounds of beer and plates of nachos, man-laughter bursting out often, filling the bar and making the lonely ones look around at them. There can be no better sound than that of a group of men laughing aloud. Nancy was already a fixture at the bar, and eventually, he got to know her. He chatted, and she listened. And she took notes. She knew he had never married, that he had some money saved, and had learned that he wanted to own a bar. He knew nothing about bars or women like Nancy, but he developed an affinity for her strange accent and dark skin and for the upstairs room at the end of the hall. When Jesus saw that a run-down neighbourhood bar called The Brick in The Wall was up for sale, Nancy encouraged him to buy it. She left her room above the Appaloosa and her job; and she moved in with Jesus. She didn't put any money into The Brick, nor did she get the girls lifted. Jesus liked her fine exactly the way she was. Instead, she banked her cash. And waited.

Over time, Nancy discovered that she hated his loud laugh, his swearing, his baggy shorts, his lazy ways, his stories, and his long, grey ponytail; but most of all, she hated his glasses that turned dark the minute he went outside. He loved everything about her.

I see her come in and wonder about a young woman drinking alone in the afternoon. I look hard at her. She doesn't look hard. She looks soft, too soft to already have a drinking problem. She is a solid girl, packed into a pair of black dress pants and a collared shirt, a small pair of earrings peek from behind her hair.

She hands me her resume, the usual young person list of few skills and little experience. A bit of babysitting, delivering newspapers, and the inevitable Tim Hortons stint. I will have to judge her for myself. She is respectful, smart enough to go to university, and neatly dressed. That was a strong start and better than many of the people who came through my door. Most were looking for a day's wages, enough to buy beers that night, a hit of something, or a bus ticket out of town. The Brick in The Wall was exactly that kind of place. This one is living close and going to school. The truth is, I need some help in the bar. Nancy isn't the same Nancy anymore, and there doesn't seem to be anything I can do to make her happy. She keeps at me about my hair, my clothes, and jobs that need finishing. She keeps at me about anything and everything. I avoid her, sitting in the corner behind the bar, reading and trying to stay out of her way. If I had someone behind the bar, I could get some jobs finished and make Nancy happy. She was supposed to do the hiring, but I figure it should be okay to hire a part-time kid to pour beer. Really. It should be. It is my bar. I like her. She has a quiet, calm manner that seems beyond the age on her health card.

She would stick around for a while, I think.

Chapter 19

Lydia

I have settled into a routine. Routine has never been a goal of mine, but it seems to work for me at the moment. Meaghan still hasn't found work, and Harley is still in school, although she works at a local bar whenever she can fit it in. When she's not at school or work, she is writing in her room, but she doesn't talk about what she is writing, and I don't ask. With three women in one house, it is hard to have privacy of any kind, but we do find our own ways to make it work.

Meaghan is great to have around. She cooks, cleans, does the laundry and the shopping, and looks after the dogs. The sidewalks are shovelled, my travel souvenirs artfully arranged, and she makes life easy for me and for Harley. She says she is looking for work in Winnipeg, and I know she has been for a few interviews, but I haven't sensed any urgency in her search. I wonder how close she had been to dying the day Harley and I went to visit, and how important this rest period is for her. She never speaks of her life in Brandon.

I must be feeling better too. I have started to date again. And I have changed my criteria for a partner. Height and weight are still important, but Meaghan is cooking our meals, and I don't feel so desperate for survival now. I seem to have moved up on the hierarchy of needs. I learned something from my time with Eugene, and I won't make that same mistake again. Despite my intuition telling me he was isolating me and stepping all over my self-esteem, I wanted him to be something other than what he was. What I have learned is to trust myself, to trust my judgement, and to honour my belief in myself and those I care about. That might not be the answer for everything, but I am confident this lesson will keep me safe. The truth is, I am lonely for a soulmate, even though I hate those two words. Everyone wants a soulmate, and it's the basis for an entire industry of dating. I am lonely for a man I can trust, who I respect, who loves me for who I am, and who I love for who he is. I am not looking for an identical twin, just enough sameness to find common ground, and differentness from which to learn about and grow with each other. I shake my head over Eugene. There were dealings with the police in the months after he broke into the house, but I never heard anything from him again. See ya lata, alligata.

I've been seeing someone for a few weeks now. Ian is forty, thirteen years my senior. Yikes, that seems old, but I think I need someone more mature. He has a son who lives with his mom, and I like that Ian sees his son regularly.

As my grandmother used to say, it is colder than a witch's tit outside. It has been a cold winter. The coldest in recorded history. Every morning it is creaky cold, and I feel like my shoulders are permanently hunched against the temperature. My old Volvo continues to run, and although the seats are as hard as bleacher seats and I can't lean against the seatback because of the cold, I am thankful the car starts every morning. I don't feel like I will ever be warm again. Even a hot bath is only a temporary solution. Winnipeg in winter. Winterpeg. The dogs don't even want to go outside. Everyone is tired of the cold and wants to stay home, under blankets, praying for spring and complaining constantly. It doesn't help, the complaining. A benefit of the weather is that because people don't want to go anywhere, we never need reservations. Restaurants are half empty, and theatres are like ghost towns. Every morning, I look longingly at my beautiful wool coats, high-heeled winter boots, thin leather gloves, and silky scarves. Then I put on my knee-length, down-filled, arctic parka, felt-lined snow boots, wool toque, and heavy mittens, and pull up my fur-lined hood to protect my face. I make a statement, for sure, just not a fashion one. The weather has been taking its toll on the old folks, and there are many in the hospital with pneumonia, the flu, and worse. Some of them can't afford to heat their homes in this cold, and there have been deaths in the city. People freeze to death when they can't get warm.

Ian picks me up to go to the movies. This is our fourth date. Our first time was for a coffee. He liked me enough to ask me out, and I liked him enough to accept. As we walk from the car to the theatre, he grabs my hand. Wait, that's a lie. His hand, heavy in its padded leather mitten, grabs my heavily mittened thumb, the only possible way to have outdoor contact in the brutal cold of the night. I turn to look at him, to smile, but my face is hidden by the fur of my hood, and I can't see his face through the fur around his hood. Because we are Canadians, we know that his effort to hold my hand and my effort to give him a look of appreciation are as worthy as a warm hand around mine and a meaningful gaze into his eyes. We have grabbed thumbs and exchanged furry glances, and that works for us. The snowy parking lot underfoot is squeaky, something that only happens when it is really, really cold. Squeak, squeak, squeak, squeak. We make our way to the building.

Once we are inside, we push our hoods down. My glasses frost up, and so do his. Neither of us can see anything as we fumble under heavy layers to pay for our tickets. It is almost comical. It is comical. A cold drink at this time seems the last thing on our minds, so we head to our seats. Off with the layers. With so few people at the theatre, there is plenty of room for our heavy coats on the seats around us. I tell myself that if anything drops to the floor, I will never find it in the dark, in the narrow space between the rows of seats, in the pile of hats, mitts, scarves, and parkas.

Free of the heaviness of its protection, my body feels almost obscenely naked. As I settle into my seat, Ian reaches over and takes my hand. I instantly change my mind. The outdoor thumb grab is not as worthy as his warm hand. I feel the rush of his strangeness, an unfamiliar man touching me, but I accept this gesture. His large, rough hand feels good around my small, dry hand. Many surgeries through the day means many hand washings, and my skin is always dry and red these days. I lean toward him and our shoulders touch. This is so intimate and a promise of things to come. I like this slow and easy way, the actions of a young and uncertain boy, executed with the sureness of a man.

After the movie is over, we go for a drink together. We sit and talk for hours, and I don't want to go home. The time comes, however, when I have to go, and I reluctantly tell Ian. Although tomorrow is Saturday and I don't have to work, I have a particularly busy day planned and need to get some sleep. We bundle up and head out into the midnight frost. He stops before we get to the car, and with his mittened hand, he pushes my hood down before doing the same to his. He kisses me, warm lips in the cold air, ice fog around our faces. When I get home, I climb into bed, but it takes a long time to fall asleep. I keep thinking about that kiss. Oh, Winterpeg, you do make things special.

The last week or so, I've been studying hard for a two-day exam and am exhausted. I know I don't really have time for a relationship with anyone and am burning the candle at both ends. Long days, call shifts, studying, and making time to see Ian. Harley and Meaghan joke about never seeing me, but it is no joke. Sometimes, they leave plates of food in the fridge for me. Sometimes, Meaghan leaves me notes as well. Harley is busy with school and her job. She seems to love working at a bar near the house. She often tells us stories about the cast of characters there. She is amused by them, and her stories about them are amusing. She has changed so much from when we first met. I don't know exactly what the changes are, but it is like when water is added to a wilting plant. She seems perkier, healthier, stronger, shinier.

I wake up early, not feeling exactly rested, but with some energy. Two dogs are on my bed, Captain snoring and Tennille curled under my armpit. I move carefully around them, trying not to wake them up but to no avail. We three then go downstairs to the kitchen together. Harley is already up, has coffee made, and is busy on her computer. I ask what she was typing, but she brushes me off.

"Something I am working on."

I'd love to know what she is working on, but I don't want to interfere. I pour myself a cup of coffee and head to the living room with my books. I need to spend the morning studying. I have a two-day exam in the spring, and it's an important one. If I don't pass, I can't rewrite for a whole year.

I try to knuckle down to work, but I can't seem to focus. Instead, I think about Ian and our evening together. Then my phone rings.

"I know you are studying, and I don't want to disturb you, but do you want to go for dinner tonight? Nothing fancy, just a quick meal?"

I am thankful for the invitation, partly because knowing I will see him later means I can put him out of my mind for now.

A few hours later, Meaghan comes downstairs, groggy and yawning. She starts breakfast. A real breakfast. Bacon and eggs and toast and juice. Meaghan treats us like humans, people who have to eat and sleep, and she tends to our necessities. I know she is unfulfilled, and I wonder who is looking after her necessities. After breakfast we all sit in the living room over yet another coffee, sharing stories like old friends who haven't seen each other in a very long time, rather than friends who happen to live in the same house.

I should probably stay home and study, but we make plans to go shopping later. It will be the perfect continuation of our morning of bonding. A girl's afternoon out, which will include a late lunch with wine, sounds like fun. I have a date later with Ian, so I can't be gone all afternoon.

There are rules for these shopping events. We can only look at items that are at least seventy percent off regular price, everything has to be modelled for the others, and each of us can only make one purchase. None of us has much spare money, so it makes for cheap entertainment. Back in the day, men were the hunters and women were the gatherers. This is our modern-day version of gathering.

We have to drag Harley away from her computer to go shopping. I don't know what she is writing, but she is so focused that she doesn't hear what is going on around her. When she tries to exclude herself from the girl's afternoon out, we gently insist. She doesn't take too much convincing though.

Outside, Meaghan calls shotgun, and we all laugh. Silly Meaghan, such a kid's game. We jump in the old Volvo, which thankfully, and predictably, starts. The back of the car is crowded with the remains of my life. The footwells are filled with old coffee cups, and the seats are covered with the usual array of medical books and journals and dog leashes. A light jacket and a sweater are in the same place I left them last fall. My usual. Harley climbs in the back, clearing the seat to make room. She was raised in a state of chaos, and this is her usual too. Same old, same old.

It is like the proverbial witch's tit again. There is clarity to the air when it is this cold. The whites are whiter; the blues are bluer; the shadows are blacker. The streets are surfaced with the shiny layer of snow that seems like it fell months ago, and intersections are dangerous, filled with white clouds of exhaust from vehicles. Look out, people on foot. We can't see you. Fortunately, it's only a short drive to Polo Park, Winterpeg's big shopping mall, and we park as close to the doors as we can. Squeak, squeak, squeak, squeak.

It is a wonderful afternoon, and we definitely make the most of every minute. When Harley decides to get her hair cut, Meaghan and I assume she is just getting a trim, but when she comes out, it is like she's a completely different person. She tosses her head, the shiny, short bob swinging around her chin. She is thrilled with her new look, and we are amazed at how much older and more polished it makes her look. It even seems like she has lost more weight, although that thought makes me immediately worry that she has been too busy to eat, what with all the running between classes at university, her job at The Brick, and her writing at home. Still, she looks beautiful, and she knows it. She grins at me, and I smile back. Such a fledged woman. I feel motherly. How did that happen?

Chapter 20

Meaghan

I still can't find work, but Steve and I have pried apart the financial aspects of our life together, and I have enough money to get by. Steve didn't argue much over small matters, and I chose to take my share of the joint property in cash. He took the house, the furniture, and the car, and I took freedom and the opportunity to reinvent myself. Both Harley and I agree to start paying Lydia our share of the house payments and food. Split three ways, the amount is small, but it's the right thing to do and speaks to our sense of fair play and independence.

Spring has finally arrived or at least a semblance of spring. The snow has melted, but the air is still unnaturally cold, and people are still miserable and complaining about the weather. I've cleaned out the gardens, and they are ready to nurture flowers, if only the sun would warm up the earth. The lawn is slowly turning green but still looks scabby from being covered all winter. I've become quite the expert at house repairs and am taking pride in my ability to learn how things work. I have fixed the fence, installed a new dishwasher, and changed an overhead fixture that had quit working long ago. Harley and Lydia don't seem to notice those things, probably because they don't know how to fix them, but I am enjoying both the adventure of learning and the end result. I am surprised by my own resilience, something I could have used a while back. Harley has finished her first year at university and seems happy with her results. She is so confident now. I suspect she has a boyfriend, but she isn't saying one way or the other.

I see more of her now that she is done school. She's still tending bar at The Brick and regularly brings home tales of the drama in the workplace. Nothing much of late, but the scandal of the winter was when Nancy left Jesus and took all the money with her. All of it. She had had access to the bank account for The Wall, and she cleaned it out before sliding out of Jesus' life in the middle of the night. He realized what had happened when he woke in the morning and found his aviator glasses, broken on the bedroom floor beside the empty jar in which they had poured the tips each night after closing the bar.

Other than shock and heartbreak, the biggest problem for Jesus was no money for paycheques or beer inventory. Most of the staff left, not content to risk working for nothing. Harley stood by him, however, tending bar in the evenings and helping him out as best she could. She had her money from Orval and told Jesus she could manage without a cheque for a while. When they had collected enough money from bar sales for a few more cases of beer, Jesus would head down the street to buy what he could and stock the fridge. It took a month or so, but finally there was enough money coming in to buy the beer and pay the staff. Jesus had lost weight during those months, and his cargo shorts, the overfilled pockets heavy with their burdens, dragged low on his hips. Rather than replace his aviators with similar ones, he had purchased a pair of dark horn-rimmed frames from the optical department at The Bay that apparently made him look wildly cerebral. He missed his brilliant system, though, the glasses that had effortlessly protected his eyes from the sun. Perhaps they had blinded him to the flaws in Nancy.

He leaned heavily on those around him as he recovered financially and emotionally, but he told Harley he felt no guilt about it. People either lean on, or are leaned on, he said. Eso es la vida. That's life.

More people are out and about now in the city. The Brick is getting busier, and according to Harley, Jesus needs more staff. When she told me that, I felt a rush. I could work in a bar, couldn't I? It's not what I have done, it's not what I expected to do, and it's not what I have been looking for at all. Reasons to say no all turned into maybes. Why wouldn't I work there? It's walking distance from the house. I have too much time on my hands. The hours are flexible if something else comes up. Still, I resisted when Harley first encouraged me to go and talk to Jesus. I have never been a feet-first-into-the-water kind of woman, but so much has changed. I have changed. Why wouldn't I work there?

Given my lack of employment and other prospects, I haven't been wearing much makeup or jewellery lately, but I decide that today is the day for a special effort. I slowly layer on my armour, step-by-step, until I am ready to face the world. Before leaving the house, I carefully place my resume into my portfolio case, making sure not to bend any corners. I don't feel resilient, afraid, or brave. I feel like I am stepping into the abyss, except it isn't me doing the stepping, it is someone else. Someone I barely knew. Someone who is stepping sideways, away from how things have always been. I feel a tiny, proud smile on the corner of my lips, but I don't know what it is that I am proud of.

Because of everything Harley has told me, I recognize Jesus the moment I see him. He is behind the bar, laughing with customers and talking loudly. He is wearing a Slade T-shirt, and his horn-rimmed glasses sit crooked on his nose. He doesn't look like someone who lost everything a few months ago. One of the waitresses yells an order at him, and he grabs a bottle from the fridge. I approach him, fumbling with my portfolio while trying to make eye contact. I want to get close enough so I can talk to him, but I am not quite sure how to get through the customers gathered around the bar-top. Then he leans down and almost disappears from my sight.

I move closer and, above the din, hear Jesus in deep conversation with two patrons directly in front of him. He is sharing his theory on how sink-holes develop. I grab the opportunity to slide sideways between the hairy man offering his own theory and another man intently listening to the whole thing.

Jesus looks up at me, and asks, "What'll it be, missy? What can I get for you?"

The group around the bar-top turns and looks at me, the talk dying down for a brief second. They want to see the missy.

"May I speak with you, please? I'm looking for work. My friend works here, and she said you were hiring."

Every head within earshot is paying attention now. This is their place, The Brick in The Wall, where they come to relax and be with friends. They are judging my suitability, and I feel their scrutiny. Will I be fun? Will I be fast? Will I stick around? Jesus is their friend. Will I be good to Jesus? The quiet is momentary, though, and everyone goes back to their conversations, the noise level rising once again.

Jesus yells across the bar to a server, asking her to take over for him for a minute. I wonder if he meant for her to just take over serving the customers or to also take over the conversation. He motions for me to step to the side, and I follow him to a small office in the back. It is filled with paperbacks, some closed, others open and pages down.

He offers his hand to me. "I'm Jesus."

I shake his hand and introduce myself. I tell him I am a friend of Harley's. He smiles at the mention of her name.

"She's a great kid and a godsend right now. I really appreciate everything she has done for me."

I give him my resume, but he puts it aside.

"Harley speaks of you and of Lydia. Highly, that is. She speaks highly of you. What are you looking for?"

We talk a bit, and I tell him about my time at the plant, the closure, and briefly, the hard times afterward. When I start to talk about my search for work in Winnipeg, he raises his hand.

"That's okay. I need someone, and if you are willing to learn to sling beer, I am willing to train you." He winks. "I assume you are old enough?"

I reach for my purse, but he laughs loudly.

"No worries. I believe you. When can you start?"

I walk home, that small smile still creeping around the corners of my lips. What have I done? What kind of adventure am I embarking on? Nothing ventured, nothing gained. None the worse for wear. All's well that ends well. Another day, another dollar. Any port in a storm. Not an original thought in my head.

For my first shift today at The Brick, I was both terrified and excited. I had hoped to be working the same shifts as Harley, but the more I thought about it, the more I realized it was probably better we weren't spending that much time together. I know nothing about working in a bar, other than what she has told me, but Jesus said he would teach me. And who am I to doubt the teachings of Jesus? I laugh to myself.

Fortunately, it was a quiet day and an excellent day for learning. Turns out that slinging beer, as Jesus calls it, seems pretty natural for me, and I have a good head for remembering orders. I was shy with the first few customers, but within a short time, I was talking with them and feeling more comfortable. Jesus is an okay teacher, but there isn't much to learn, and I'm not sure how much he actually knows. As I went around the bar, I noticed things that needed doing. Floor tiles that were lifting, windows that were dirty, toilets that didn't flush properly. Did no one else notice these things? Jesus was supposed to be looking after the maintenance, but he spent his time behind the bar, talking with customers or reading books.

My shifts at the bar have become pretty regular, and I enjoy the walk to and from home. At first, I didn't want to take on more responsibility than was my due, but slowly I have come to realize that Jesus isn't going to give me any direction. If something needs doing, I am going to have to do it myself.

I have taken it upon myself to assume a strange new role. In addition to being a server, I am now also the maintenance woman. I have started making lists again. I was almost afraid to start one, remembering the last months with Steve and how desperately I clung to them to get through my days. But now my lists are of unfinished projects at the bar and of the materials and tools needed to get them done. Each time I fix a leaky toilet or glue down some flooring or replace a light bulb, I feel such a sense of achievement. I have painted the bathrooms, washed the mirrors and windows, and cleaned the carpets. I asked Jesus to order new beer glasses, and they have arrived, with "The Brick in The Wall" etched on each one. Yellowed and dog-eared signs have been replaced by new ones engraved in plastic. Check. Check. Check. The neon sign outside the bar has been fixed, and now all the letters light up at night. I have been trying to get

Jesus to look into getting draught beer at the bar because I think it will bring in more customers. I also want him to start serving food. Nothing fancy, just chicken wings and nachos and mozzarella sticks. He never says no. Check. Check.

I am spending a lot of time at The Brick, definitely more than I get paid for, but the place is starting to look great. The only unchanged fixture is Jesus himself, sitting behind the bar, serving beer and talking with his customers. The place is busier that it has ever been, and people like the draught beer and the bar food. In addition to the regulars who hang around the bar, showing up each night to meet their friends, and who don't want change if they can avoid it, we are seeing more walk-in customers, people who are passing by and stop in for a drink and a bite to eat. Harley has noticed the changes, of course, and laughs about how much better her tips are.

I talk to Jesus about bringing in some entertainment on the weekends. He thinks he is the entertainment. Still, he doesn't say no, and I start to look for a folksinger who will play on Friday nights. A young singer/songwriter named Cliff stops in one day, making the rounds, asking if we need someone to play the bar. We try him once, and the clientele likes him. He agrees to play Friday nights for a month. He's going to school at Red River College and needs the money. We need the talent. It turns out to be the perfect arrangement for everyone.

Chapter 21

Harley

I have decided to go back to Brandon this weekend. Meaghan has the two days off and wants to check on some of her things in storage. Although Steve got all the furniture, she still has boxes of personal possessions. Clothes. Books. Pictures. Photo albums. The accumulation of the life she has lived so far. She is thinking about moving into her own place. Time to grow up, Meaghan. Again.

I am in my second year of university and have surprised myself with how well I am doing. It is much easier than when I was going to high school. I don't have to deal with the drunken debauchery of Mom and Dad, the low expectations of the teachers, and am no longer an outcast. I know what Jesus expects of me, and I know what the school expects of me, and I know that my expectations of myself are higher than theirs combined. I didn't expect to be given the opportunities I have been given, and I am not going to waste them. I am working hard to reach my goals.

Lydia is at the hospital most of the time. She wrote and passed her exams and qualified as a general surgeon at HSC, the big hospital in Winnipeg. Meaghan is at The Brick a lot, so I have the house to myself most of the time. Captain and Tennille are there, but other than when I walk them, they give me the time and space to drink my coffee, work on my courses, and write to my heart's content. I have been doing a lot of writing in the last year and think perhaps I have found my what next. As the teachers used to write in my report cards, there might still be room for improvement, but at least I have found my work ethic. No, Mom and Dad, no thanks to you at all.

I well up with anger when I think about home, about Mom and Dad, and about my brothers and sisters dumping their children there. I am consumed with rage when I think about my little nieces and nephews, mired in that muck of neglect. I shake my head when I think about those nights my parents drank and fought. I cry when I think about the number of times I was huddled in a bed with the little ones as we all waited for the noise to stop, for the danger to die. And when I think of all that, I want to reach out, to punch a wall, to pound my feet, to run down the street yelling about the unfairness of such a life. I want to scream at them all about how even a little bit of responsibility could have made such a difference to so many people. Yes, I am going to Brandon this weekend, but I am not at all sure that I am ready to visit them just yet.

I haven't spoken with Mom since the last time I was in Brandon, when I stopped at the house to say hello. When Mom answered the door and saw me on the doorstep, she moved forward to block my entry. Her eyes were hard; the set of her jaw was mean; and her posture told me I wasn't welcome. Dad stood behind her, his voice raised, talking about the runaway on the step who never gave a moment's thought to her Mom and Dad. Mom smelled of alcohol, and if she did, then for sure, Dad did. She asked me if I thought I was better than she was and then told me to go back to my high-class friend. I wasn't welcome. Not now. Not ever again. I looked at them for a moment, then turned abruptly, walked down the steps leaving the outside door ajar, and went back to the vehicle where Lydia was waiting.

I was embarrassed, but more than that, I felt such sadness for my parents. They had lived an unplanned life, short of money, short of self-control, short of birth control. They were long on addiction, long on anger, long on feeling like victims. They took their anger and their frustration out on everyone around them, and then, with no satisfaction to their anger, they took it out on each other. I had every reason to lose, but I was determined to win. I would not be a victim, and I would no longer blame them if things go wrong. They had not done the best with what they had, and they continued to make bad choices and to self-destruct. Fortunately, I had been yanked from their life by the mercy of a single phone call to a saviour lady. Lydia had allowed me to heal in her home. Orval and his bequest to me had elevated my opportunities. Meaghan and Jesus had shored up my self-confidence. The rest was up to me.

It is far easier to shut doors and leave them closed than it is to keep your foot in the crack of the door, just in case you want back in. When Mom told me to leave, I could have stuck my foot in that door. I could have done something different at that moment, something to make her remember me, her little Harley, and to take some interest in me. I'm sure there wasn't anything I could have done that would have erased a lifetime of being unimportant to my parents, but if I had just stuck my foot in that door, it might be easier now to build a bridge. All of which means that now I have a difficult decision to make. I don't know if I am strong enough emotionally to deal with them, but there is a part of the healing process that requires forgiveness. Not forgetting, just forgiving. I know it's going to be hard for me, but there are things I need to tell them.

Meaghan and I leave early to beat the Saturday morning traffic. Fall has come again, and the stubble in the fields is fresh and glowing against the blue of the sky. I love the morning light even more than I love the evening light. At both times, the shadows are long, but the morning light seems full of promise and possibility, and it makes me feel hopeful, alive. The evening light presents richer colours, but it also signals the end of the day, the last chance to achieve, and then it makes me feel unhappy, unfulfilled. As we travel the two hundred plus kilometres from start to finish, I distract myself by talking to Meaghan, listening to the music, and losing myself in the road ahead. The minutes click by much faster than they did when I was younger.

In what seems like no time at all, we can see Brandon a long way off, stubble buildings rising out of the stubble field. The small city is a hidden gem, tucked away from the highway, in the valley of the Assiniboine River, where flooding waters threaten the city year after year. Travellers often miss it altogether, assuming that Brandon is a few gas stations, a Tim Hortons, a couple of motels, and a McDonald's restaurant. What the they don't know is that they need to head south to really see it. There is only one escalator in the city. Only one way up. And one way down.

Meaghan drives up to the home of my parents. I put on some fresh lipstick. She asks me if I am okay, and I tell her I will phone when I am ready to leave. She studies my face for clues to my state of mind. I try to hide my fear from her.

"I am fine. Really."

She can see it, though, and reaches out and squeezes my shoulder. "Call me if you need me. Really."

I step out of the car and walk to the house. I can see that Meaghan has driven up the street a short way and stopped. She is waiting to see what happens next.

The house is smaller and more rundown than I remember. The grass has died from the heat of the sun. It needed water, but none was given, and so it died. The same empty flowerpots that were on the step last time are still there. The screen on the door is still ripped, and the latch is broken right off. There is an empty plastic water bottle on the front lawn and some old grocery bags stuck in the lilac hedge. Some red tinsel from a Christmas past winds its way up a post at the doorway, intertwined with a string of Christmas lights with broken bulbs. There is a stack of local flyers piled by the door, yellowed from rain, then sun, then more rain. Everything is weathered and worn and old. By comparison, I feel bold and cleanly garish and new, and wonder why I bothered with lipstick. I wonder if it was always like this, or if I am only now seeing it with new eyes. I do know that I don't belong here anymore.

I ring the doorbell, but I don't hear anything inside. When I try knocking on the door beneath the ripped screen, I see movement as the curtains of the living room, still closed, swing open for a moment. Mom has seen me, but I am not sure if she will answer the door. I look up the street to check that Meaghan's car is still there. I also check my pocket for my cellphone.

There is a shuffling sound on the other side of the door, and then the inside door swings in. Mom stands in the doorway, and I involuntarily suck in my breath. She is dressed in a pair of leggings and a camisole. Her fat rolls slide over each other like soft ice cream in a cone, each one larger than the one above. Her belly droops sadly, exposed. She has a fuzzy blue-green tattoo on her upper arm, a flower, its petals wilted and distorted by wrinkled skin, sagging down toward her elbow. Mom is old. Old, old, old. How did this happen?

"Hi, Mom. How are you? I'm in town with a friend and thought I would drop in to see you." Do daughters really ever talk to their mothers like this? "Do you have time for a coffee?" I am pretty sure that Mom has nothing but time. "I tried to call, but the line wasn't working." Didn't pay the bill again.

Mom looks at me suspiciously, not sure of my intent, but she remembers the last time I was at the house. She looks up and down the street.

"Is Dad home, too?" I hope not. Dad means trouble. Always.

She responds without any emotion, her voice gravelly from too many cigarettes. "I don't have any coffee, only tea. Dad's away right now."

She has gauged my mood and feels I am safe.

As she moves aside, I put my foot in the door. I glance down the street and see Meaghan's car drive away. I take off my jacket and shoes, and put them on the floor by the door, along with my purse. You never know when you are going to need them in a hurry, and it is best to keep them handy. I follow her into the living room and look around. I am in a time warp. Nothing has changed. Not one single thing. Even Mom's clothes are the same, only tighter and more faded. As far as I can see, the only thing different is that she is older.

"I'll go put the kettle on. Have a seat."

Instead of sitting down, I follow her into the kitchen. It is piled high with the usual dishes and garbage and empty bottles and cans. I watch as she clears room in the sink for the kettle and turns on the tap. She opens the cupboard for mugs, but there aren't any clean ones. She fishes two from the sink and rinses them out.

"Let's sit down while we wait for the water to boil."

She shuffles toward me and indicates that we should move to the living room. I am fine with that. She lights a cigarette, inhales deeply, and then exhales loudly with a sigh.

"How have you been?"

I don't know where to begin, how to even start to answer that question. Every step of progress, every single thing I have done to improve my life, has been in spite of her and Dad, not because of them. I see her eyebrow rise slightly, and know I have to be very careful. She can just as easily turn nasty. I want this meeting to end well. I don't want to make things worse. I am looking for the opportunity to forgive, not to build on the foundation of hate and resentment. So far, our reunion has yielded no moments of I Missed You hugs, no excitement or joy in the presence of each other. It is evident that we are simply going through the motions. If I want more from her, I will have to take the lead in this conversation, to steer it away from rocky waters. She watches me warily, waiting for my answer.

"I've been living in the city for a while now."

She nods. She already knows that. What she wants is some information into which she can sink her teeth, over which she can be indignant and angry. Something against which she can react, that says I am better than she is. Instead, I offer her something to which she can relate.

"I'm working in a bar, Mom."

Her wry smile says it all. She expected nothing better of me. Her expectation has been met.

"Where's Dad?" I change the topic, avoiding her gaze.

She watches me without answering for what seems like ages.

"Dad's away right now."

I look at her, expecting more, and getting it.

"He ran into a bit of trouble, and he's up at the pen right now."

Stony Mountain Institution. Wow. Not the local jail.

"He and Lionel were selling and got busted by the cops up at Small Town."

The Small-Town Bar is a rough watering hole in Brandon that welcomes customers who are not welcome anywhere else. Like my brother Lionel. He has been in and out of trouble for years, spending money earned from drug deals on cars and clothes. Usually he lives in someone's basement, and I muse that Stony might not be such a dramatic change for him.

"When are they getting out?"

Mom shrugs. Clearly, she doesn't want to talk about it.

I change the subject again and ask about the rest of my family. There ensues a litany of tales of woe. As she details each situation, I feel myself wishing that either I had not even mentioned my siblings or that there were far fewer of them. She is oddly animated as she goes down the list from eldest to youngest. How can one old woman be the original source of so much trouble? My tea is cold, but I drink it anyway, finally gulping down the dregs. When there isn't an offer of a second cup, I know it is time to leave.

I pause before I speak again. Don't bother. You won't get what you need from her. It isn't worth it. She will react badly. Don't.

"Did you ever love me when I was little, Mom?"

Oh, god. I don't think I am ready for the answer. Any answer will only lead to more questions. I'm not strong enough to hear her answer, whichever way it goes. I watch her face shut down. Please don't answer my question, Mom. I made a mistake. I want to take back my words, to continue the rest of my life without the answer. I know she is going to tell me, though. Her face has become a mask of protection, with nothing coming in and nothing going out.

"You want a beer, Harley?"

I shake my head no. It is the first time she has said my name, and the sound of it is strange on her lips, strange to my ear. I allow it to hang in the air without interruption.

I watch as she gets up and goes into the kitchen. I hear a beer can opening. Mom drinks from the can as she walks back into the living room.

"Yeah, I did. Still do."

I hold my breath and wait, but there is nothing more.

As I finally let out the air, I know it is the only satisfactory answer. There aren't any excuses attached to it. There is nothing but a simple statement. No, if only, no, wish I could have. Nothing. Just a yeah. I can't rail against a single word. I can't pick apart her justifications. There it is. She loved me. It isn't much, but it isn't a no.

"I love you too, Mom." I'm not sure I am telling the truth, but it seems the only thing to say in the silence.

She looks at me, her face still a blank. What level of pain does a woman have to go through to create such a mask of non-emotion? How much covering up has she done over the years? That she can completely conceal her feelings when necessary is a skill that has developed over a lifetime. Can this skill become so convenient that it remains on her face while her youngest daughter declares her love? Apparently so. She has watched her children fail in life, one by one. She has visited her husband and son in prison. I feel like I can offer her some hope, some pride, if I tell her of my success at university.

"I've been working at my writing, Mom. I've been going to the university in Winnipeg."

I want her to smile, to acknowledge my hard work. Instead, her face changes in an instant, from no emotion to complete disdain.

"Well, aren't you the hoity-toity? Ha, ha. You going to write about all the stuff we did?"

This isn't supposed to be about you, Mom. It is supposed to be for you.

"Keep our laundry in the family, Harley."

This time the sound of my name on her lips is like poison.

"Sure, Mom. Well, I have to go now."

As I stand on determined feet, I dial Meaghan and ask her to come and get me. Then I walk to the front door, pick up my purse and coat, and slide my feet into my shoes. Mom follows me, her posture guarded, her face black. She has found her way in, her reason to be angry. I reach forward to give her a hug, but she steps away.

As I open the door to leave, I issue a simple statement of my own. "Love ya, Mom."

The door closes behind me, the loose screen flapping. I walk to the road and wait for Meaghan to take me away.

Chapter 22

Lydia

The alarm on my cellphone goes off, a low, growly buzz. I grab it and put on my glasses. I wander to the bathroom and sit on the toilet. I check my phone for messages, scrolling through, deleting junk mail, checking to see what happened with my friends overnight. I go back to bed. Ian is still sleeping, but I curl up beside him anyway, knowing I will wake him. I only have a minute before I have to get ready for work. He spends a lot of nights at the house now, and I am getting used to having him around. Captain and Tennille are also getting used to sleeping on the floor. He rolls over and puts his arm around me. I love this man.

Meaghan moved out in the fall. She bought a small fixer-upper and has been using her newly found renovation skills to create her own safe space, a space that reflects the person she is today. The house isn't far from my place, and she drops in to visit sometimes. When she does, she brings bags of leftover food that I put in the freezer for desperate times. However, those desperate times are few and far between these days because Ian and I spend a lot of time in the kitchen with cutting boards, frying pans, and glasses of wine. We are learning together. If you can read, you can cook. There is an intimacy that comes when working in the kitchen with someone, a dance with sharp knives whirling and steam rising. Our movements aren't synchronized. We move around each other, sometimes colliding, sometimes embracing. It is an imperfect, physical dance, where all our senses are paying attention. The dogs are always underfoot, in danger, watching for opportunity, obstacles. Ian cuts bits of cheese and feeds it to them. There is no hope they will leave the kitchen now. We eat what we prepare. Most times, it is delicious, and we pair our accomplishments with good wine. The flowers are on the table. We light candles. Don't leave any occasion uncelebrated. Bink. Cheers. To us. To Us?

Unlike previous fence-post boyfriends, it seems Ian isn't threatened by my work. He says he is proud of me, for what I do, for how I do it, and he has given me every reason to trust him on this. I like the idea of trusting someone, of trusting Ian. It lets me believe in the possibility of us becoming Us. And if you believe something long and hard enough, sometimes it comes true.

He is a welder. He has a great job and enjoys his work. And that's about it. There is no drama. He shows up on time, does his work, and goes home on time. He goes out for lunch with his work buddies, and sometimes they all go for a beer on Thursdays. If he works overtime, he gets paid for it. His arrangement with his company is clear. He puts in a solid day of labour, and the company pays him for it. Fair is fair.

Because there is lots of Ian left after a day at work, he has the emotional energy to give to others. He is a great father and spends a lot of time with his son. He regularly calls him on the phone, and I love hearing the way he talks to his little boy, language habits of seven years. He still calls the little guy 'baby'. Cute, but I doubt his son will allow it for too many more years. He is so interested in the details of a seven-year-old's life. Yes, baby. Really, baby? I'm so proud of you, baby. He is a great friend and lover, and he spends a lot of time with me, too. Oh, baby.

We've been together for almost a year, but neither of us is talking about a permanent move yet. It is on my mind, but I don't mention it. We both have houses in the city, and moving in together would mean permanent changes. While I'm not sure I am ready for that, I do think of what living with Ian would be like, and I don't see a downside. I have dated men with children before, but I didn't feel any connection with their kids. I didn't feel the connection with their fathers either, so perhaps that was the underlying reason. Kids can be so fragile, and it isn't good to raise their expectations. But Ian's son Brayden is smart and funny and loving. I can see him as a part of my life, although I am not sure how to be a mother. He already has a mother. A stepmother? A friend-mother. That name settles over me and not in an uncomfortable way.

When Ian and I first met, there was an electricity that flowed between us, high-voltage jolts when we touched, pulsing current when we kissed. A motor is electric, an engine is fueled by gas. My heart is a motor, waiting for the next charge, searching for it. I am addicted to him. I can go hours without him near, but not days, and I don't have the confidence to handle long silences between us. A period with no communication and I start to wonder what is wrong, what I have done, whether he'll call me again. This is bad. I demand too much from him, expect too much, want too much. Settle the fuck down, Lydia. It will be okay. Accept him at his pace. I can't sit still though.

In the beginning, Ian was like all the others. Try-too-hard Ian. I expected his veneer to wear off quickly, his particle board to be exposed, to become soggy and stained, and then, I could gather him up and put him in a bag on the fence post out back. I waited, but it didn't happen. Surely it would, but it didn't. Oh yes, his try-too-hard veneer did eventually wear off, and he is no longer shiny and new and clean, but underneath the still wet and glistening topcoat is a rock-maple man, strong and heavy and able to weather the elements. Scarred from those elements, but able to hold his own. In a storm, I can lean on him, and he will lean into the wind, letting me know he is there and can support me. Where have you been all these years? Is this what I want? Is this what I have been waiting for?

He isn't like an old sweater yet, and I don't know for sure that he will exactly fit, that I can count on comfort when I go to him. But he hasn't disappointed me yet. He really likes Meaghan and Harley, and although he and Captain are still wary of each other, Ian loves Tennille. Why do large men love small dogs so much? Each time he comes to the house, she jumps up on him, wanting to be held. Captain sits by my feet, watching Ian, but his tail is wagging. After Eugene, he isn't sure who to trust, and he isn't taking any chances. Of course, the cheese offerings in the kitchen are helping Captain cross that bridge.

I have long wanted to finish my basement, and Ian has decided that he is exactly the man to do that job. Other than paying for the materials, fetching him beer and tools, and helping him as much as I can, I do all the cooking when he is working in the basement. One of the many things I learned from Meaghan when she was at the house is that we need to feed and water those we love. Ian needs feeding and watering, and while I know he appreciates my offerings, the best part is that I feel alive when he's around. And I'm not so exhausted any more. Harley and Meaghan have shared my load for the last while, and now Ian is carrying some too. I feel the benefit of this and can only hope I am doing the same for him. For them.

I take a box of nails and some drywall tape down to Ian. He is taping and plastering and there is mud and dust everywhere. His hair and face are white, a layer of dust heavy on the top of his eyebrows. When he removes his surgical mask, his face is completely white, except for his blue eyes blinking at me, the pink oval underneath where the mask had been, and the big ivory smile that is only for me. A strange creature, for sure, but one that I love. I hand him the box of nails and the tape, and lean forward to kiss him. I don't want to touch him, but he grabs me and I am immediately covered in white handprints. His son is coming over later, and we are going out for dinner. As I start to walk upstairs again, I hear clanging as something drops on the floor. He curses, and I smile, glad that he is not perfect after all.

Harley comes in from the library. She stops in the kitchen and tells me about her day. When she nods toward the basement and asks how the project is going, I show her the handprints on my bum.

"Ah, so he's drywalling now," she says, as she rolls her eyes in shared comic disgust over men and their ways.

She has a shift at The Brick that night. I ask if she has seen much of Meaghan lately, and she nods.

"Meaghan looks great, Lyd. And she seems happy. Jesus is so thankful for her and everything she has done for The Brick. It is incredibly busy at the bar, and he has been hiring a lot lately. The bar looks great, too. You should see all the changes."

I make a note to myself to go there for a drink soon and see what has been going on. Harley heads upstairs to write for a few hours.

If Meaghan looks great, so does Harley. She has lost a lot of weight, and her black hair is short and edgy and glossy. It is her skin that stands out, though. Pale and creamy, without a flaw, and her dark eyes are bright and observant. She is really beautiful. When I first met her, she was smoking too many cigarettes. Her skin was yellow and blemished, and she had dark circles under her eyes. She looked well fed in a junk food kind of way. Now she has completely given up smoking, has a healthy glow, and her clumping footsteps are light and full of optimism. Meaghan is right. It is important to feed and water those we love, but it is also important to love those we feed and water. Harley's mom had never understood the importance of that distinction.

Harley had come home from her trip to Brandon in the fall a different woman. During the time she has been living with me, she has grown from a girl to a woman, and now she has changed again. When she told me what happened out there, I felt crushed inside. Not for me, but for Harley. She told me she didn't feel that she could have any kind of relationship with her mom right now, that it would be just too hard to keep trying. She also said she wanted her mom to be someone other than who she was. Someone who was involved and loving and full of life, not distant and absent and worn out. Harley knew she couldn't change that, but she could change how she felt about her mom. As number nineteen, Harley was merely one in a crowd. She couldn't influence her mom, nor change her mom's existence or her past. And while she admitted she loved her Mom and knew her Mom loved her, Harley also knew that can mean different things to different people. As she talked, I felt Harley's old soul rise up and find a wise solution to an impossible situation. She gave me a hug and told me it was okay, that I shouldn't worry about her. Of course, I did, and probably always will, but I know now that Harley has found the power to understand and to forgive, and those two things combined have given her the strength to leave her past behind her in more ways than one.

Chapter 23

Meaghan

My little house in Wolseley is not far from The Brick or from Lydia's house. It is on the same kind of street that Lydia's house is on, lined with small, older houses on narrow lots and with huge trees shading the houses and their occupants from the hot Manitoba summer sun. There isn't any kind of a view, unless I count the alley between my street and the street behind me. On Sundays, a nearby street is closed to vehicle traffic, and people, dogs and bikes fill the street, enjoying the one-day-per-week park that the city by-laws have created for them. The house was a mess when I bought it for a steal. Other prospective buyers had been shown the home and walked away, daunted by the amount of work that needed to be done. I have done that work or sometimes paid to have it done. Knob and tube wiring has been replaced by an electrical contractor. Peeling linoleum replaced. Worn out and pockmarked hardwood sanded and refinished to a high sheen. Walls painted. Light fixtures updated. The list was endless and still is, but I try to make one improvement each week. Slow and steady wins the race. I usually walk to work, except in the winter when it's too damned cold in Winnipeg to walk anywhere, and then I catch a cab. I haven't bought a car yet.

Harley wants to move into my spare bedroom. Since Ian has been spending most of his time at Lydia's house, Harley feels in the way. I don't know how she can be in the way because she is never there, but I understand why she wants to give them privacy. We still work cross-shifts at The Brick in the Wall and rarely see each other, so I think it might work. She keeps asking, and I keep putting her off, only because I'm not all that sure about having someone else in the house with me. I need to talk to Lydia about it, to make sure there isn't some other reason for the move, something Harley isn't telling me.

From time to time, Lydia and Ian drop into The Brick for a drink or a bite to eat. The first time they came after the renovations were done, Lydia, in particular, was impressed by the changes we had made. She had been there a few times before and hadn't been impressed by the chaotic state. The bar is clean and repaired, and there's no more yellow tape or orange cones or leaking toilets. Jesus has hired a maintenance man, which means I don't have to do the repairs anymore. Although I miss that part of the work, my time is now spent managing the staff, ordering, and talking to the customers. We have added imported beers to the menu, which is bringing in many new customers. The place is always full, and Cliff the singer/songwriter attracts larger crowds on the weekend. Cliff is popular, and some people come just to hear him. Jesus still sits behind the bar, but he doesn't have time to read much. His customers love him, and he is also a reason people keep coming back. He remembers every name, but more than that, he remembers every story told to him. He makes people feel special, and even when the entertainment is playing, I can often hear his laugh over the music.

Jesus wants to buy the vacant lot behind The Brick. He has plans to fence it in and create a patio. There are large, leafy maple trees on the lot, and I love that he wants to leave them up, put tables around them, and string up fairy lights. They will shed their leaves in the fall, a messy business, but it will be beautiful in the summertime. Because he supported me in my ideas for draught beer and bar food, I am supporting him on this venture. It will be different from other bars in the area, even if is only for a few months a year. He is full of ideas now, and without the burden of having to physically carry out the ideas himself, he is hiring others to do the work. His creativity and business sense seem to be growing daily. Nancy, oh Nancy. You really blew it. Enjoy your grubby pot of coins and your saggy boobs.

When I arrive at work, Jesus is holding court at the bar. As soon as he sees me, he stands and walks toward me, leaving his patrons to continue their conversations without him. I am surprised to see he isn't wearing a T-shirt and cargo pants. Instead, he is wearing a navy suit, not fashionable, but certainly serviceable. I wonder if he has just one suit. He motions that I go to his office. As we walk, I comment on his clothing, teasing him about having a job interview or getting married. He sits down and asks me to do the same.

"Meaghan, as you know, I plan to buy the lot behind the bar. But I have found out from the tenant beside us that the unit is also for sale or lease. I also want to buy that space and put in a scotch bar. Because I don't have all the money to do this, I am suggesting it as an opportunity for you."

I look at him, not quite sure he has meant what I think he has said.

"What do you mean?" I try to think quickly, understanding that he is offering me the opportunity to buy into The Brick. Risk. My heart starts to pound. Fight or flight.

"What would you think about becoming business partners?"

This isn't a discussion I thought I would ever be having. Owning a bar in Winnipeg could not have been further from my mind.

We discuss in length how such a partnership might work and what the amounts involved would be. It is an exciting discussion, one that will be backed by the details that lawyers and accountants bring to the table, but to my ears at that point in time, it sounds like an excellent opportunity and a lot of fun. I like Jesus, and together we make a great team. As we part, shaking hands, I tell him I will seriously think about his offer.

And as I go about my work the rest of the night, I wear a small, strange smile on my face. I think about this new opportunity, one that is great enough to make Jesus change his clothes.

Harley has settled into my spare room and made it her own. I don't see her too much, but there is comfort in having someone else around. My earlier reservations about having Harley live with me were unfounded. She is tidy and quiet and pays her rent on time. She makes coffee in the morning. She is continuing her studies at the university and spends much of her time writing at the library, although she bought a small desk and a chair, and she has them wedged into her little bedroom. Sometimes I hear her working in there, to the background sound of folk music. Judging by the stories she tells me, she has a great imagination, so no surprise her book is fantasy fiction. Of course, I only know that because she says it is, not because she'll let me read any of it. When I ask her why not, she explains that her view of herself as a writer is so fragile, she can't allow any criticism, constructive or otherwise, to make her falter or to doubt herself. She is terrified she will not finish her book, that her university education will be for nothing. Harley is self-aware enough to protect the little author inside.

Lydia has purged her closet. This was a noteworthy event, as her closets and storage areas were full of clothes. Harley and I are using a lot of what she got rid of, and we are thoroughly enjoying her castoffs. Lydia has fabulous taste and is daring and creative with her wardrobe, something neither Harley nor I have ever been. Harley and I share a common closet filled with Lydia's old clothes. We have joint ownership.

Harley has her own style. She may not have a lot of confidence as a writer yet, but she has a lot of confidence when it comes to style. She has started wearing makeup more often, and again, I suspect she is seeing someone, although she isn't saying. I don't know where the chubby teenager has gone, but there is a beautiful and stylish woman in her place. And she continues to wear the lucky earrings Lydia gave her when she found out she had been accepted at university.

Harley is a nurturer, as am I. We live in harmony, each trying to make the other's life a little bit easier. On weekends, when we are not working, we go to garage sales together, looking for great deals and carting our finds home. It is fun and inexpensive and satisfying. Afterward we go for lunch, often stopping at The Brick for a drink and talking with our friends there. If the weather is nice, we sit outside on the patio. It is so welcoming and private, and it's hard to believe there is a busy street only metres away. The addition has increased traffic to the bar, and we are busy all the time. And there is often a waiting line to sit outside. When it cools off, people move inside, and through a set of inside double doors to The Scotch Room for a drink before they head home. It has been a great investment, and I am proud to call myself an owner. Jesus is a great business partner, and we each do our share of the work the best we can.

Harley's Bootstraps

Nancy was in The Brick last week. I didn't know who she was, but Harley pointed her out to me. She is a tough-looking lady, tall and brassy and mean. I am ashamed to admit that I took a look at her cleavage, to see whether work had been done. Sadly, none had, and Harley said they were worse than ever. Jesus saw her, but he didn't react. I suspect she was hoping for a reaction, so the worst he could have done was to ignore her. She finished her drink and left. She hadn't been enough to make Jesus change his clothes.

I have met someone. After so many years with Steve and the last few on my own, it feels strange to be with another man. I am not rushing into anything with him, but it is fun and I need to try my wings before I can fly. He is a financial advisor and works in the strip mall down the street from The Brick. I met him while having a sandwich at a nearby coffee shop. Mark is the same age as me, is outgoing, and loves to travel. I haven't done much travelling, other than my time in South America, and his stories intrigue me. For someone in such a conservative profession, he lives his life working toward his next adventure. I am nothing like him, but I love his stories and wonder if I could ever have the nerve to do some of the things he has done.

Mark is currently planning a trip to Panama. He has friends there with a sailboat, and he wants to spend some time on the ocean with them. As part of his preparation, he is studying Spanish and reading how-to books about operating a sailboat. I love his enthusiasm. He is a hard worker, and I know that when it comes time for him to go to Panama, he will be ready.

As he talks and plans and studies, I think about what it is that I would like to do next, where I would like to go, what my life will bring to me. So far, I have been taking my life as it comes, passively accepting opportunities as they are presented to me, but not pursuing anything on my own. What do I want from my life? I don't know. Yet. I am thinking about this more and more, though. Perhaps I want to drive the motorcycle and not ride on the back, goddammit.

Spring is the perfect time to learn to ride a motorcycle. Last week, I took a two-day course, and now I have my motorcycle licence. I also have chaps, jacket, helmet, boots, and gloves. Hmmmm. What is missing? I have been looking at motorcycles all week—used ones, new ones, bikes riding by, bikes in driveways, bikes in movies. I feel excited. This is my own adventure. I am making a decision about what I want and then taking action to get it. It is liberating for me, and I feel like a big door has swung wide open. A door big enough to drive a bike or a life through. I have the money, honey. It is time to make the move. Mark wants to help me buy the bike, but I want to do this on my own. If I make a mistake, it will be my mistake and not that of someone else. I have talked with Lydia and Harley about it, and they both think it's a great idea. They also want to know who I will ride with, but I don't have an answer for that question. Me, I guess. I am enough, aren't I?

I have been daydreaming about owning a bike, about riding down the highway, fringed leathers flapping, giving the low-hand wave to bikers passing in the other direction. I daydream about polishing the chrome, wearing racy leather vests and skimpy black T-shirts with tacky motorcycles printed on them, looking sexy in jeans and chaps. I daydream about pulling into parking lots on my bike, other bikers looking to see who I am. I daydream about a trip to the States, when I risk leaving my helmet off and riding with my hair covered by a do-rag. I daydream about pulling into a cheap motel and parking my bike out front, helmet hanging from the handlebar. I daydream about packing my bike with all the things I need for a trip, heading out on a Friday, going to where I still don't know, wherever the road will take me, I guess. Liberating.

I feel like I am changing, swaggering around like I just hopped off my Harley after a long ride in the hills. In my head, I am already the owner of a bike, part of a group that acknowledges fellow members as they pass each other on the highway. I am swaggering, but it is because I am taking control of my life. Be still, small smile. There is more to come.

Chapter 24

Harley

I have finished my book. Technically, it is a manuscript, but I feel like I am an author. I am not a published author, but still I have finished it. I haven't shared it with anyone, although Meaghan is pushing me to let her read it now that it is done. I couldn't let anyone read it while I was writing. I was terrified it would remain in a drawer, crushed and left unfinished because of a careless comment. I don't know what the process is to get it published. I don't know if it is good enough. I thought that I only had one book to write, but now that it is finished, I want to write again, to write another one. I didn't know how hard it would be to write, how exhausting it is to pour out my thoughts and my imaginations onto a piece of paper. I didn't know how to connect everything. But none of that matters now. It is done and ready for an audience.

Because I am no longer spending every spare minute tapping away, eking my story forward, word by word, I don't know what to do with my time. I keep rereading, changing a word here, a sentence there. It is like a tooth that I keep worrying. I can't leave it alone.

I sense Cliff in the doorway behind me. From living with Captain and Tennille, I know that whiskers deeply rooted in a dog's skin provide them with information about their surroundings. I have no such whiskers, but I know Cliff is behind me. His long legs are lost in his jeans, his T-shirt hanging like laundry from the clothesline of his shoulders. His feet are bare, and his long bony toes, cartoon toes, really, stick out below the hem. Crazy black hair curls up from the top of his feet. Strange man feet. His hands are similar, but there is a sensitivity to them that is missing in his feet. His hands are creative, building music, making songs from stories. Once done, his stories wander upwards, leaving his thin body in an incredible baritone voice, a growly sound that doesn't fit with his gentle character. My stories are silent, black characters on a white background. Cliff's stories fill a room, the details left unsaid but spelled out in the nuances of the music. He is tall, leaving the impression that he fills the doorway, but he doesn't. Two of him could fit in the narrow space. There is room for me in that doorway with him.

"I'm leaving now, Harley. I'll see you at the club later tonight."

I work nights, and he plays weekends at The Brick.

"See you, Cliff. Later." I smile at him as he leans over me for a quick kiss, then he slides on his sandals and disappears out the door and from my sight.

In his absence, my thoughts of him take over, a relief from the obsessive editing of my book. He has finished school now and is spending his days trying to get gigs. He has standing offers from cover bands, but they only want risk-free musicians on board, those who don't want to take the chance of playing something untested, original music, a new story, or even the same story told a new way. They want the richness of his voice to make their shop-worn music new, but they don't want his creativity. People don't hire cover bands for their creativity. They hire cover bands because there is guaranteed satisfaction. Like rereading a book. Cliff turns them down, even though he needs the money.

At first, I didn't think Cliff was my style. Where did I get that from? I don't have a style. I hadn't dated all that much in school, just the odd guy here and there. The odd guy with the odd girl. I got to know Cliff on his breaks, bringing him a beer and a shot between sets, commenting on his music, talking about the audience, asking about his lyrics. He was quiet, without a lot of words, but his eyes were soft and his voice deep and resonant. It rolled out of him when he was singing, but when he spoke, it settled gently, too heavy to float, a foundation on which to build conversation. Initially, we talked a bit during working hours, but after a while, when

The Brick closed for the night, we sat together while nursing a beer in the strange quiet of the bar. It wasn't only the two of us though. It was a ritual we all had, having a drink together after closing, talking about the regulars, the fights, the music. Each and every one of us were creatures of the night, sleeping in the morning and wasting our afternoons waiting to go to work. Most didn't eat properly, subsisting on bar offerings at work and canned food at home. I was the exception, with Meaghan insisting I eat properly, getting me out of bed at a normal time, and eventually enveloping me in structure. Thanks for the help, non-Mom.

Cliff lived in a rented house with a group of other graduated ex-students, some with big-boy jobs, others with hospitality jobs. Theirs was a squalid existence, with any housetraining left behind in their parent's nests. They were birds of a feather. Each bedroom was centred by a large television attached to the wall, speakers in every corner, and an unmade bed with sheets that had not been washed in a long time. Their new nests. Boy nests. These were not beds to which girlfriends were invited, and as relationships flourished, bedrooms were unused, the boy chickens spending nights in the beds of their girlfriends. Chicks with their chicks. Sometimes, a roommate would reappear, sometimes sharing the story of the breakup, other times not. Cliff was no exception, spending his nights in his rented room. With no girlfriend at the time, there was no other bed available to him.

At The Brick, there was no girl sitting at a table close to the stage, waiting for him to join her between sets. Sometimes groups of friends met there and were extra-enthusiastic in their appreciation of his music. He had developed a small, but loyal, following that arrived in groups and dragged their tables together into a raggedy mass of support. They asked for favourite songs by handing notes written on receipts or napkins or flaps from cigarette packages to their server, who then gave the requests to Cliff, pointing out the requesters. Cliff would sing their song, acknowledging the audience, and thanking them for coming down.

We were a group of friends, tired after a day at work. A night at work. We would cast our aprons to one side and feel the blood flow into our feet as we slid our shoes off under the table. I noticed that more often than not, Cliff would sit beside me, and slowly, over many nights and many decompression beers, we were a conversation of two at a table of many. At first, he was the singer, the guy that Meaghan had hired for weekend entertainment. Then, he was Cliff, the tall skinny guy with the deep voice. And now, he is the love of my life.

His manner is simple and his approach straightforward. He says what's on his mind, he is always respectful, and I never wonder where I stand with him. He grew up in north Winnipeg, was raised by his mother and never knew his dad. Burton Cummings grew up in the same neighbourhood, was raised by his mother, and never knew his father either, but the comparison stops there. Burton is Cliff's musical hero, known for his rock 'n' roll music, and usually performs with bands, while Cliff plays his stories out in ballads and accompanies himself on his acoustic guitar. He sits on the small stage at The Brick, his bony frame hunched over his guitar, and pours every emotion he has out to his audience. When the night is over, he looks thinner, paler, like he has physically given something of himself to the multitude. If Meaghan ever saw him then, she definitely would have tried to feed him. He would have liked that.

We have had the conversations about our upbringing, setting the stage for understanding each other's baggage. He knows I was raised by parents too busy avoiding responsibility to provide love or guidance. Nest failure. I know he was raised by a mother who, along with Cliff's two younger brothers, created a rich and nourishing home. He laughs about his early home life, acknowledging and cherishing the imperfections of that time, and when he speaks about his mother and his brothers, there is such warmth and love that I silently cry for this cavity in my own life. I want to have experienced this, but the lottery took place, and I wasn't one of the lucky ones. I never had that choice to make. Mom and Dad made it for me, and there is no going back to find a lost childhood, no joyous finding of it alive and thriving at the bottom of a well. Cliff shares the funny stories of his brothers and his mother, and while I genuinely enjoy them, I feel a simultaneous sense of loss. He knows this. I hate that the vacant place in my heart flavours everything I do. The vacant place that sometimes fills with envy for something I can never, ever have. What is most important for me is to keep that envy monster small, and I do this by appreciating the things in my life that are great. By making the most of the things I can make better. By not living in the past. As I appreciate the small details in other people's lives, I am working on living a vicarious childhood.

Cliff and I went on an amazing road trip last weekend to see the garter snakes at Narcisse. I had never been there before and didn't know what to expect. When we arrived, there looked to be tens of thousands of them, slithering effortlessly through the grass and huddling in moving green and yellow and red masses. When we picked them up, they wound themselves harmlessly around our hands and our wrists, looking for an opportunity to get away, to escape. Cliff told me the snakes leave their winter dens in the early spring to feed and search for a mate. They sleep in the sun above the ground, and return to their underground dens, via well-worn trails, only in the early fall.

I have been back to my den twice now. The first time Mom told me to leave; the second time I left on my own. There is a well-worn trail I could follow, but now I have a choice, and I choose not to follow that trail.

It feels wonderful to be doing normal things with a normal man. He holds my hand or puts his arm around me or places his hand on the small of my back. He tells me he loves me at random times, and I believe him. I wonder what his thought processes are that he will say he loves me in the middle of a silence, but when I ask him what he is thinking about, he only says, "This and that."

Tomorrow is Sunday, and we are going on another adventure, this time to Twin Lakes Beach. I have never been to a beach before, and I cannot wait. Both Cliff and Meaghan are stunned when I tell them I have never been to the beach, and they are determined to make this a wonderful experience for me. I don't have a bathing suit, and Meaghan lends me one of hers. It is a simple black bikini. I feel exposed in it, vulnerable, but Meaghan tells me I look fantastic. I choose to believe her. I trust her. I don't know to swim, but she tells me not to worry, but that when I go in the water, not to go past my waist. Thanks, non-Mom. Cliff is bringing his car and anything else we need, and Meaghan is packing us a special lunch. I have no responsibilities for the day, other than to enjoy myself.

Cliff picks me up early in the morning, coffees from Tim Hortons already in the cup-holders. Our lunch is safely packed in a small plastic cooler padded with frozen blue packs of ice. Cliff has prepared the perfect playlist of music for the road, and as we head out, he sings along to Joe Cocker's version of "The Letter", his voice blending with and complementing Joe's gravelly offerings. He grabs my hand and squeezes it while he is driving.

My excitement seems to get us there more quickly than it should, and by the time we park the car, I can already tell it is more than I ever expected. The beach is beautiful, and we immediately take off our shoes so we can feel the warm stony sand underneath our bare feet. The waters of Lake Manitoba are icy and still too cold for swimming, but that doesn't stop us from walking in the water. When my feet and legs ache from the chill of it, I simply step out to warm them in the sun. We watch as pelicans, powerful and ungainly, fly over the water in low formation. We see raucous gulls diving for fish. We examine bones of carp and jackfish and other bits of debris that litter the shore. Although the sun and the sand are warm, the wind off the lake is cool, and at times we sit covered in a blanket, talking, reading, sleeping, eating. It is an imperfectly perfect day.

"Harley, what do you think about moving in together?"

I have thought those same words many times, but wasn't sure of our what-next.

"I mean, it would save a lot of money, and a lot of travelling back and forth from your place to mine, and…."

I wait from him to finish, but he has stopped speaking, perhaps waiting for an indication from me before he … what? Commits himself? Embarrasses himself? Prematurely presumes something? The foundation laid by his deep voice, his words, suddenly seems less firm.

Something inside of me doesn't want to be too willing, too enthusiastic, but I love him and hate it when we are apart. What is that stubborn part of me that doesn't want to give in? Give in? This is what I want, more than anything. I feel my resistance wash away like the cold lake water, leaving me clean and fresh and honest. Trust fills the places where resistance has been.

"And?" I wait a moment for him to finish the sentence, but he says nothing, so I finish it for us both. "And I think this is such a good idea, Cliff. We would save money, and travelling, and…" Who was I kidding?

Who was he kidding? "I love you so much, Cliff, and this would be so fantastic. I absolutely want to be with you."

His face lights up, and in that moment, my life and his take a giant step forward, more defined, more purposeful, more us. Us, as Lydia says.

We are scouring the city for a place to start our life together. There are so many possibilities, but it seems we will know our home by the smell. Each time we walk into an apartment building lobby, there is a smell. A smell of old cabbage, old paper, old people, old cats, old mould. We haven't found one that smells like old Harley and Cliff, and although we both know whatever we decide on will not be our forever home, we need to find a place that seems right for us. I keep thinking about furniture and beds and linen and all the things we will need. I daydream about decorating our home together, about creating a special place for us. When we do find our place, it will be my first time in my own home, and I am so excited about it. Cliff will bring his television, speakers, and bed. I will bring my books and my clothes. I don't have much else right now.

Chapter 25

Lydia

When my alarm goes off at 4:55 a.m., my feet immediately hit the floor. There is no lounging in bed and no hitting the snooze button for me. If I did either of those, I would fall right back to sleep and be late for morning rounds. This is the disciplined part of my life, the part that gets no tolerance from me. I simply get up. It is not negotiable.

I shower quickly and head downstairs for a coffee before I leave. It is only a partial day for me at the hospital. I have Student Mentorship today, the program where I first met Harley. I had been an unenthusiastic participant back then, but now I look forward to it. I don't know when my slight influence, my smallest intervention, might make the difference to someone else. I can't take the chance that I won't be there for that as yet unmet person who needs me. Harley's reluctant tapping of my phone number into her cellphone has led to a remarkable transformation in her. She has gone from a hostile observer of the life around her to a flourishing participant, bringing joy to herself and those around her. It is the smallest of sacrifices, but I can't take the chance that some young woman who is at risk of never realizing her potential will not succeed because I didn't play my part. I will do my rounds at the hospital, and then head over to the College and meet my new girl.

Harley has changed the way I look at these young women. I no longer see them as victims of themselves, but instead as people who need someone to give them a leg up, to give them a time of peace and reflection, to remove them from the battleground long enough to see the horizon over the fight in front of them. They need to be able to imagine their future, and that can only happen if they can stop the daily battle for a short time. I remember how shortly after Harley moved in with me, she sat for hours and hours in the front porch, wrapped in a blanket, a cup of coffee by her side. She stared out the window, wanting nothing, needing something, unsure of everything, unaware of any horizon at all.

This experience has changed me, and I know I am a better person, not because I 'gave at the office' or was able to check off community participation on my resume or my work history, but because I am now incapable of climbing onto my high horse and looking down at people. In fact, I no longer even have the tolerance for such lofty heights, and as a healer, I am better if I can relate to the truth of the lives of my patients. This is the gift that Harley has given me. This is the gift that I have, in fact, given myself. Rarely do I think of Eugene and his pity for me in having to deal with such people. Well, Eugene, it is my calling to deal with such people, to understand and help them. Thank you for that lesson in life. I took so little away from my time with you, but I did take that, and it is extremely valuable.

Harley calls me often, a habit that developed after Eugene broke into my house, and it is a habit I appreciate. We are friends now, the saviour-saved relationship having been consumed by more alikes than differences. I value her opinions, her sage contributions to the impracticality of my doctor's life, and I value my joy in each development in her life.

She has finished her first book and sent it off to publishers. Meaghan was the first to read it, and although she added some editing, she said it was fantastic. She even suggested that Harley submit it for the Braxton First Novel Award Contest. Uncharacteristically, Harley agreed. She is clearly determined to be successful as an author, to be published, and she wants people to read her words, her stories. She wants to entertain them and give them respite from their harsh realities. Her book is a world of fantasy, of castles and monsters, where the good and the bad are clearly defined. Of course, in the end, the good win. That is the way of Harley.

Harley did hear back from a publisher. In fact, she heard back from a number of them. They were keen on the genre, on the style, and on the story. It had taken her some time to get her head around the steps involved, but two months ago, her book appeared online and in hardcopy at bookstores. There were mostly positive reviews, and some negative ones, but she is completely undisturbed by the criticism, choosing instead to take notes for future novels from disappointed readers. This is such a departure from how she was when she was writing her book. The published author is presumably less sensitive, less vulnerable, than the writer-in-progress. Harley was also shortlisted for the Braxton award, and we are waiting for the award announcements next week. She pretends the results don't matter to her, but I believe otherwise. Nothing matters more to Harley than her writing. She has already started a second book, a sequel to the first, and when I ask about the story, her eyes light up. I think she is having fun writing this one.

I arrive home from Student Mentorship, tired but satisfied. I spent the day with too-cool-for-school Rebecca, whose main goal was to sneak outside for a smoke. The doors were monitored for such efforts, and she finally accepted her nicotine-free day. She called herself Becca, and she was tall, pretty, and unhealthy. She was in high school, working part time, collecting social assistance, and living in a basement apartment on her own. She didn't talk about her family or about where Mom and Dad were in her life. We tolerated each other for the morning sessions, but over lunch and throughout the afternoon, we talked about her goals, what she wanted from life, how she could get what she wanted. My mantra was the same as it was for Harley. "Don't close any doors right now. Finish school. So much good can happen if you do." She had a lot of questions about how I became a surgeon, and I shared my nonlinear journey toward achieving what I wanted from my life. I probably won't hear from her again, but I feel that she was listening to me, and that I have left in her a small spark of hope. Tomorrow she will be on her own again, and either that spark will be doused or fanned into life. She tapped my number into her phone. I smiled as she did that, and said to her, "You just never know."

When I walk in, Ian is in the kitchen, chopping an onion. I open a bottle of red and pour two glasses, asking about his day, telling him about mine.

I can hear the television in the basement, and I know a seven-year-old boy is down there. I yell out, "Hello, Brayden!"

"Hi, Lyd." His words run up the stairs as he does. "Guess what's for dinner?" he quizzes, hugging me around my waist.

I know what Ian is making. The cans of tomatoes, sliced mushrooms, and chopped onions all point to spaghetti. Brayden's favourite meal. My favourite is anything anyone makes for me, and tonight, that is spaghetti. "I'm not sure," I tease.

"Spaghetti! My favourite! Yum!" he answers, squeezing me even harder in his enthusiasm.

"Mine too, bud." I bend over and kiss the top of his head. He is such a cute kid. I untie his arms from around me and pick up my glass of wine. "How was school today?" I hear about recess and what happened on the bus and what they did in gym. He runs back down the stairs with both dogs in tow.

With Harley and Meaghan both living in their own places and Ian staying most of his nights at my house, it was only a matter of time before we decided to move in together. He owns a house, as do I, so there wasn't an obvious right answer to where we would live. I am closer to the hospital, which was a major consideration for me. I am also closer to where Brayden's mom lives, which would make the custody arrangement easier for everyone. Finally, we agreed that he would rent out his house and move in with me.

I remember when Harley first came to my house and how the two of us had almost ignored each other. I didn't pay attention to much of anything other than what I was doing and what I wanted, and was unsure how to take care of another human being. So, I let her figure out what she needed and how to take care of herself and how she would fit into this new life. I didn't understand I had a role to play in all that.

Things are different this time. When Ian and Brayden moved in, I worried about the small details of their lives, about their creature comforts. With the addition of the finished basement, there is enough space for Brayden to have his own room. Mostly, he spends his time playing and watching television in the basement, but the three of us love spending time there, particularly given all the work Ian put into it. The new carpet, new furniture, the very big television, and all our personal knick-knacks make it feel more like a home than ever before. When Brayden is with us, four days at a time, our lives revolve around him and our work. When he is with his mother, our lives revolve around each other.

Ian is starting his own welding business. He wants the flexibility to spend more time with Brayden, and while he hasn't built up a large client base yet, he is making enough with his partial work schedule and his house rental to contribute his share of the financial costs of our home. More and more, as I leave work and walk toward my old Volvo, I am eager to get home and see him, to see Brayden, to share the events of my work at the hospital with them, to have them share their lives with me. Sometimes, when I arrive home and see Ian's truck parked in its usual place, on the road in front of the house, I literally run up the sidewalk to my house, but-terflies in my stomach, anticipating the joy of being part of an Us. I leave the hospital at the door, the hard cases behind me. There is something amazing happening right in my house. I can't believe it sometimes and laugh at myself. Ian has maintained his height and remains an acceptable weight. What was I thinking?!

The phone rings as we are finishing our spaghetti dinner. It's Harley, and she already has Meaghan on the line. A three-way call? I guess she has something important to tell us.

"I am going to Toronto for the Braxton Awards dinner."

We are all excited about what this might mean, but I can tell we are holding back just a little, wary of creating unfulfilled expectations, of building them up before they come crashing down. We agree that a shop-ping trip is in order to find a dress for the dinner. There will be no rules for this shopping trip. Harley, already a beautiful woman, will look gorgeous. We will find the perfect dress if it is the last thing we do. No prisoners. This is our mission in life right now. Fucking A. Damned straight. We end the call laughing at our language, looking forward to three friends out shop-ping together.

We meet at Earls, wine and appetizers priming the credit cards for the shopping that will follow. Harley has developed her own style, an edgy, arty style that is hers alone. She has some ideas about what she wants, and Meaghan and I listen intently. We laugh and we talk and we plan, but mostly, we are happy to all be together again.

After reluctantly paying our bills, we head over to Polo Park. Harley tries on what seemed like every dress in the mall until we finally find 'the one'. It is the colour of a boysenberry, a deep rich reddish purple that perfectly complements her dark hair and eyes. The dress is unembellished, the strapless sweetheart neckline accentuating her breasts, and the gauzy layers of the dress fluttering softly when she moves. It ends just above her knees, womanly, responsible, and a hint of sexy. With the dress found, it is on to jewellery and shoes.

"I'm wearing my lucky earrings. That's all the jewellery that I need."

We spend yet more time looking for shoes. A pair of black strappy heels add to her height, her legs appearing longer than they are. "I hope I can walk in these!" She laughs, "…and I don't fall in front of everyone!" Harley beams at me. She is ready. Full of optimism we declare that she will be the most beautiful, most talented author of all time. And she looks so happy. Because I am not sure if I will see her before she leaves for Toronto, I give her a hug and wish her luck. Meaghan does the same. I feel like a proud mother duck sending her duckling out into the world. I catch Meaghan's eye. She has the same look on her face.

After Harley leaves, I turn to my other best friend and ask, "Time for another one, Meaghan?"

We walk over to Earls for one last drink.

Chapter 26

Meaghan

Things with Mark didn't work out, but I am okay with that. We dated for longer than expected, each convenient for the other, but there wasn't any real chemistry between us. He was set in his ways, and I suppose I was, too, and our feelings for the other weren't strong enough for either of us to change. What he did for me, however, was instill in me the understanding that if I had a dream, I needed to work toward it. Dreams don't happen by themselves, he said. I still keep in touch with him. His trip to Panama had been exactly what he wanted it to be, and since then, he's had a few adventure trips to exotic locations. I like hearing his stories, but I am busy living my own dream. He is a nice guy and a friend, but nothing more.

The Brick is doing incredibly well, and I know I made a great decision. The Scotch Room is filled with groups of people learning about single malt and other fine whiskies, sampling new ones, and enjoying old favourites. We hold tasting sessions from time to time; a growing number of customers are eager to exercise and develop their new passion. The ambiance is warm and comfortable, and it is a wonderful place for friends to gather. Harley is still getting a few shifts at The Brick from time to time, and she is always ready to help if we need it, but her main focus now is writing.

After receiving the Braxton First Novel Award and with her book continuing to sell well online and in print, she has gained a large following of readers who are anxiously awaiting the release of the sequel. Eager to meet their expectations of another excellent story, she writes every day, developing engaging characters and fascinating stories to inhabit the world she has created.

She is still with Cliff, and they are as much in love as they ever were. They are made for each other, and I feel the energy of their love when I am close to them. Cliff's music has become especially popular in the southern Manitoba market, and we can't count on him playing for us anymore. He comes in from time to time, though, and when he does, Lydia and Ian and Harley and I get a table at the front and send him relentless requests for our favourites. He has made a few CDs and is getting some commercial success from them. He has a small band that plays with him now, and is still writing his own music. His face lights up whenever he sees Harley. He has even filled out a bit since they started living together. I suppose there wasn't a lot of food in the house of boys he lived in before he met her. He is handsome and wears his hair long, and his beard is short and scruffy. It is a look that girls like and young men copy. His clothes are casual in the way of a singer-songwriter, and his manner is easy and friendly. He is making money at what he does, and the confidence that brings him shows in his face. He is so proud of Harley and mentions her at every show he does. He also mentions his mom.

I finally bought myself a bike. After much discussion with Mark and experts at the dealership, I listened to advice and bought a Harley Davidson Softail Low Rider. I took more lessons. I rode it around the city. I took it on shorter trips. Even after the lessons, riding it around the city, and taking it on shorter trips, it still feels heavy and unmanageable. I don't feel comfortable on it. It is like a big dog on the other side of a fence, barking and growling, but I am not in any danger unless the dog gets out. I know I bit off more than I can chew, but I am keeping it and hoping for more control. Stay the course, Meaghan. Sometimes I sit on it, ready for a ride, and go over checklists, the same kind of lists I made during my worst depressive days. I have started obsessing over my hands, that I will drop the bike and my hands will be broken and scarred. I am wearing heavy gloves, but they don't help me control the bike at all. I am not having fun with it. When I approach intersections, I am terrified I will be hit by a car because the driver doesn't see me. I wear my heavy leather jacket all the time in case I fall, but that makes my rides hot and sweaty and uncomfortable. I am not sharing any of this with anyone; I am keeping it to myself. I should take my bike the short distance to The Brick, but I walk, saying I need the exercise. I am afraid of the bike, and I am too proud to say that I made a mistake. Riding just doesn't feel the way I thought it would.

Finally, I talk with Jesus about the bike. He has been asking me a lot of questions about my new hobby…I think he senses my fear. Why don't I take the bike to work? Who am I riding with? Do I love my new ride? I avoid his questions, but he knows me well and is relentless in his efforts to get more information from me. I tell him about my fears, about how I don't feel I can control the bike. He looks at me oddly, raising his eyebrows, and spreads his hands out, palms up, like the solution to all of this is so simple. "Trade the bike, Meaghan. Get rid of it. Find something that suits you, that fits you, that you can have some fun with. This isn't a wrestling match, a zero-sum game, a winner takes all battle. You are supposed to be enjoying this new venture in your life, not dreading every time you get on your bike."

I stare at Jesus, wondering why I didn't arrive at that decision myself. It was so obvious. In my efforts to prove something to myself, I was stripping my own confidence, sinking the bravado and thrill of riding into a quagmire of quivering fear, leaving only a shell of why I wanted to ride. While my pride doesn't want to admit it, I acknowledge to Jesus that he is right, and I should take his advice.

I tell both Harley and Lydia that I am trading in my bike for something more manageable. I sense that they are relieved, and they encourage me to make the change. I will lose some money on the deal, but not that much, as the mileage I put on the bike is minimal. I find an 800 cc Kawasaki that is a dog that I can tame. I have been riding it around town, and it feels like fun…like it should feel.

I have a trip planned to South Dakota. I am going on my own, solo time, and I am taking my cue from Mark. I have planned everything down to the last detail, and I am ready to go. I have reviewed the details of the trip with Harley and Lydia, and although they know little of riding or of

South Dakota, they try to help. I am still a novice, but at least I am not afraid of my new bike. I spend time riding the highways around Winnipeg, trying to make sure I am comfortable.

The day comes for me to head out. I am nervous, but not terrified. The bike still feels strange to me, but not alien. I don't feel ready, but I don't know if I ever will be until I take my first big trip. Lydia and Harley wave me off, telling me to have fun, to keep my eyes on the road, to be safe, safe journeys.

Finally out on the open road, I'm not making the time on the highway that I thought I would. Riding a long distance is hard work. I am physically exhausted, and my arms feel weak. My shoulders are so tight from the stress of riding that I feel totally inflexible. I pull into a gas station along the way to have a coffee and gather my nerve for the next stretch of highway. I am nervous about this journey, and I'm sure the other bikers can smell my fear, like dogs smell fear. They avoid my eyes. When I leave, I see it has started to rain. Back on the bike, I don't feel confident or sexy. My hands are glued to the handlebars of the bike. I ride slowly and am so afraid of losing control that I don't give the low wave to passing bikers. I am a bad and unfriendly motorcycler.

The rain is coming down really hard now, and I stop to put on my rain gear over my jacket and chaps, then I get back on the road. The nylon rain suit is doing its best, but it's still not quite up to the task. The water is getting into every crevice and driving itself into my clothes. I can't see well through the windshield, which is covered in beads of rain. I am soaked, cold, and tired. I want to stop, but I have a reservation at the Blue Sky Motel, so I steel myself to push against the dusk to get there before dark. I am wearing gloves, but they aren't waterproof. My hands are stiff from the cold and rain, and my butt is numb from too many miles in one position. Although my windshield is high, and thankfully deflects the rain from my face, sometimes the rain comes down so hard that I have to pull over to the side of the road and wait for it to let up.

I thought this trip would make me feel stronger and more in control of my life, but I don't feel that way at all. Maybe I will feel that way when I get back to Winnipeg, but for now I am longing for the routine of my work at

The Brick, the comfort of my home and my friends in the city, and for the opportunity to make another decision, a different decision, to not buy a bike at all, to do anything but this. I can't just leave the bike at a gas station and go home. I have to continue on, to get to my hotel, to calm down, to relax and appreciate my bravery, and to reflect on pushing my own boundaries. I keep having visions of sliding on the highway, the bike hurtling forward, me flying through the air, my head bouncing on the pavement, fading to black, then death. I try to shut them out, but they are there and will not leave. It occurs to me these visions could be self-fulfilling.

I am close to the Motel. It is almost dark, and the rain is abating. The terrain here is hilly, and there are twists and turns in the road. Even though I slow down to manoeuvre the bike around corners, I am still afraid it will slide sideways. As the rain lets up a bit, the traffic increases. More people are willing to brave the weather.

I go around a bend in the road, watching the pavement in front of me intently. I look up, and in the darkening light I see the green reflective eyes of a deer in the roadside ditch. Please don't cross the road, please. The deer begins to move across the road in front of me, and I swerve to miss it, into the oncoming lane. I am off the bike, sliding along the pavement toward the cars. I put my hands out to change my direction, but the gloves simply wear away on the uneven pavement.

My world becomes silent, my vision a reality.

Chapter 27

Harley

Early morning is the best time to write, and I am working at the kitchen table as usual. I used to like being alone and curled up on my bed when I wrote, but that has changed. Now I need a quiet space, but also something more structured. Complete isolation is too lonely now. I don't need to escape; I need to focus, and the kitchen has reminders of Us that comfort me while I write. Cliff has a studio and spends much of his day there, working, recording, rewriting, and rehearsing. He needs more space because he has musicians who work with him now. I miss him when he is at work, but I know we both need space, that each of us is a distraction to the other.

When my phone rings, it is Lydia. She is calling from the hospital. Her voice is choking, thick with tears, and at first, I can't comprehend her words. She tells me that Meaghan has been in an accident, killed while riding her bike in South Dakota. I hear the words but they don't register. Then my blood stops. My breathing stops. The world is silent. The lights buzz. The words register. Meaghan is dead.

When Orval died, it seemed like a natural part of life. We are born; we live; we die. I was sad but okay with that. It is the way of all things. But Meaghan? It seems not like a natural part of life, but a part of untimely and unnecessary death, something yanked before its time. And it means that another piece of me is gone forever.

In the permanence of that moment of understanding, there is no going back. My life will pitch forward without Meaghan. She will be a memory, one that always ends with this dreadful news. I ask the hows, the whys, the wheres, but none of that really matters now. Meaghan is dead. She is gone. Her life is over. I press the button to end the call. There is the softest of clicks. Over.

I call Cliff, but he doesn't pick up. I leave a message for him to call me back, but instead of waiting for him, I call Lydia back. She is still at work, struggling to finish her shift. I tell her I can't get in touch with Cliff, but I can't be alone right now. She reassures me she will get away as quickly as she can. I sit, motionless, on the sofa, thinking about the loss. Meaghan has a family, a brother and a sister, a mom and a dad. My limbs feel heavy, and I can't move. I just sit.

When the lobby buzzer for the apartment interrupts my sorrow, I stand up to answer it. In moments, Lydia is at my door, her face blotchy and swollen, and we collapse in tears in each other's arms.

"Does Jesus know yet?"

Lydia shakes her head. "No, I tried to call, but his phone is shut off. He must be sleeping. We need to go over, to let him know…" She pauses. There are no words for the immensity of what we will be letting him know.

"Has anyone been in touch with Steve? With Mark?" My mind is trying to cover all the bases.

Lydia says that Meaghan's mom is trying to get in touch with as many people as possible. I thought about that mother's job, letting those people important in her daughter's life know that Meaghan is dead. That should not be a mother's job. Who else, though? Who else would know who to call, who was important, who needed to know? I rage inside at the unfairness of such a task, wanting to make the necessity for those phone calls go away.

As I make coffee, tears fill my eyes until they overflow their brims and run down my cheeks. Those tears are sometimes replaced by an anger I can barely control, but then they revert to tears again. I can see similar changes in Lydia's face. We share such a feeling of helplessness.

There are things I could do, of course, but those thoughts came later.

Then, for some reason, I decide to call Steve. He is completely consumed with anger that she had been riding alone.

"What was she thinking? I would never have let her ride alone. She didn't have enough experience."

No, Steve, but you did let her get away. You failed to look after her in her time of need.

After I hang up, I feel the need to blame someone, to vent my anger at such a senseless death, but there isn't really anyone. Perhaps my anger should be directed at Meaghan, like Steve's, but I'm not sure I can do that. My sense of loss is greater than my anger. I miss her too much.

I meet Lydia at the funeral home. It is filled with a sea of dark dresses and suit jackets, the air scented with flowers and shoe polish, and heavy with loss and sadness. When we are old, many of our friends and relatives have died, or moved away, or lost touch with us or with reality. But when we are young, the ties that bind are still strong, and there is a greater need to say goodbye. People are here to shed their grief, to support her family, to show that Meaghan had been valued in their lives. There were so few people at Orval's funeral, but Meaghan was young, and the funeral home is full.

Jesus is wearing his navy suit and his hair is neatly combed and pulled back. He is alone in the pew, so Cliff and I slide in beside him. I reach over and touch his shoulder. We don't talk. There is nothing to say.

Asked by Meaghan's family to speak at the funeral, Lydia's tears roll down her cheeks as she shares stories and memories about her friend. Her voice is strong, and her love for Meaghan almost too much for our broken hearts to bear.

There is a group of young people, both staff and patrons, from The Brick, uncertain of how to attend a funeral. Ironically, I think that if only Meaghan was here, she would help them through this. She would tell them what to say to the family. She would walk with them to the tearoom for sandwiches, coffee, butter tarts, and the opportunity to share their feelings. Meaghan is here, of course, but she is not helping them at all.

There are also people I have never seen, and I wonder how they were a part of her life. There is an old couple—he in clean, wrinkle-free pants and a dark sweater, she in a lavender overcoat, both dabbing their eyes. Neighbours? Aunt and uncle? Teachers? Meaghan's ripple effect was bigger than we ever knew.

They say that time heals all wounds, but our pain is still fairly raw. The four of us are a little stronger; Meaghan's death no longer consumes our every conversation, and we are starting to move on, sort of. We still talk of her and miss her, but it is a different type of missing, a different type of talk, one that allows us to occasionally smile and laugh and remember more of the good times we shared. Of course, that does not mean we don't sometimes end the sharing with tears or anger, which often leads us to The Brick. Jesus sometimes joins us at our table in The Scotch Room, in Meaghan's place, in her creation. It seems like she is right there with us. I can almost see her moving around the room, looking for details undone, and then fixing, moving, straightening. Check, check, check.

Jesus is not doing well. He misses her, his business partner, his friend. His hair is untidy, his whiskers long, his shorts dirtier and more wrinkled than ever. He is going through the motions at work. He feels her absence in every minute. Que es la muerte. That is death. He is drinking too much, ignoring his business, and taking his anger out on the staff in the bar. Meaghan had become quite the businesswoman and took care of every-thing. She even made sure that if anything happened to her, there was enough insurance in place for Jesus to buy back her share of the bar. I think he will thank her for that down the road, but right now, it is the last thing on his mind.

I have started writing again, but my words have taken a dark turn. One day, I killed off the heroine of my story, killed by a dragon she sought to conquer. I had to start again the next day, deleting the previous day's work. My book characters are not happy right now. They are all struggling with their own particular demons, some real, some imagined. They are filled with anger toward each other, their friends, their families, their enemies. I will need to find a way to resolve their conflicts, to bring them back to a peaceful, loving place. The good must win in the end. That is the fantasy of my book, but it is not the reality of my life. Meaghan was good, but she didn't win.

Cliff has written and recorded a song about her. It is soothing for me, and I play it often. It brings back strong memories of her. Lydia remains sometimes angry, unaccepting, and has thrown herself into her work, spending more and more time at the hospital, railing against patients damaged in boats, in cars, and on bikes. We must each find our own way through our grief. It will take time, but we all need to help each other.

I think about Meaghan's mantra, that we must feed and water those we love. Then I pick up the phone, and invite Jesus, Lydia and Ian over for dinner on Friday night. I will put out candles, and wineglasses, and of course, flowers. This will be a celebration. We need to start celebrating her life, and I know that is something of which she would approve.

Everyone arrives on time. Jesus has someone with him. A friend? A date? She is short and round, and her hair is prematurely white and without any particular style. She looks like nobody, but also like everybody. Perhaps I have seen her somewhere, but there is nothing spectacular in her appearance to make me stop and notice her, and I am sure that if I saw her in the grocery store, my gaze would go over her head. Her name is Margaret. Of course, it is. Nothing spectacular about that name either. She wears no makeup, and her skin is clear and pink. She wears gold-rimmed glasses, and her eyes are a bright blue. They try unsuccessfully to draw me in. Her clothing is simple, neutral. Not stylish, but definitely serviceable, clean, and comfortable. She is attractive in a plain kind of way, and I guess that Margaret is tidy. What's to like? What's not to like?

I am slightly put off that Jesus has brought someone new to our celebration dinner, but I keep that to myself. He has been struggling so much lately and needs all the support he can get. Besides, every word she says that night is kind, understanding, and helpful, and she works hard to both celebrate the life of our friend and to help us get past our sorrow.

I shelve my first impression and decide I like unspectacular Margaret.

Chapter 28

~~Margaret~~ *Maggie*

Nothing beats being out on the roads of the Canadian prairies. All the places I have been with ~~Johmuch jacketn~~ over the years tried, but never succeeded, in coming close to the beauty of these perpetual skies and the never-reachable horizon. I appreciate having a job that allows me to criss-cross this province while doing something I love.

I returned to Winnipeg for school, and then after that, work, almost six years ago. I am a Herd Reproduction Specialist at the Canadian Association of Animal Breeders. There, I work closely with students to instill a healthy attitude toward the program and to raise purebred cattle profitably. I teach proper insemination technique, semen handling, and reproductive management, three elements crucial to herd reproduction. I teach these techniques at the agricultural centre outside the city, but I also have a private practice that takes me out to the farms in the province. Raising beef is big business in Manitoba, making use of grasslands and a natural abundance of clean, accessible water. As most cow-calves are marketed at about eight months, it is crucial to profitability to ensure that the reproduction cycle is perpetuated. This is something that cannot be left to chance, to a bull in a loving mood.

Raised on a large beef cattle farm in the province, I was the only daughter in a large family of sons. The boys stayed to work the farm, but I wanted to get away to the city, to get an education. I moved to Winnipeg right after high school and went to Red River College to study business administration. A serviceable education. While out with friends one night, I met a soft-spoken young military pilot named John, and we married soon afterward. Two years later, he was transferred to North Bay, Ontario, and after that, we moved every few years from air force base to air force base across the country, and I followed, first with one, then two, and finally, our three children. It was a happy life, and we were comfortable, but never wealthy.

I loved him completely. At first, I was infatuated with the quiet, handsome, young man in uniform. Over time, my feelings for him transformed into something less consuming, but more powerful, his very being impacting every moment of my world, sometimes in big ways, sometimes small. I felt his love, his support, and his goodness permeate my life.

John died of cancer six years ago. He had complained of constant lower back pain and had begun to lose weight. From the time of his diagnosis to his death was a shockingly short seven weeks. We were stationed in Edmonton at that time, far from our families in Manitoba. It was an awful time in my life, with a series of doctor's appointments, which were followed by medical tests, then surgery, then…watching my first and only love fade away, his death fast and cruel. I still miss him terribly. At the time, the kids were grown, but I needed to work. He had left me with a military pension, but it wasn't a lot, just enough to get by on. I found my days long and so lonely. I made the decision to go back to school, but I wasn't sure what to take. My brothers suggested that artificial insemination was reliable and important work. It fit with my childhood background on a cattle farm, and so I returned to Winnipeg to go back to school and to begin to build a new life. I have been teaching and consulting for almost four years now and have a steady income. My practice has grown moderately over time. Life is good, but not great. Through my work, I see people; but in the evenings, I am alone, but not miserable, much of the time.

John had fancied himself a connoisseur of scotch whisky and had dragged me along for company. At first, I found it horrible, its taste smoky and it burned the back of my throat. Over time though, I developed a taste for it. Recently, I discovered that a bar in my Winnipeg neighbourhood has a scotch bar, and I dropped into The Brick for a drink. I went alone but found that the warm quiet of the bar suited me, and I returned on an infrequent but regular basis. Used to being on my own for the last six years, I enjoyed my own company. Over a period of time, I began to recognize the regulars, and they recognized me. Sometimes I chatted with them, sometimes I read my book or a newspaper, and sometimes I watched the television over the bar. I could have stayed home and had a glass of whisky, but I needed to get out of the house, to have the hum of people, of life, around me.

I had met the owner of the bar, Jesus, and he was outgoing, always laughing and telling stories. Recently, his business partner, a lady named Meaghan, was killed in a motorcycle accident. After the accident, I could see that Jesus had changed. He was angry. He would sit behind the bar, reading books and talking to no one. One time when I went into the bar, there were no quiet tables, nowhere for me to sit alone and sip my whisky, so I sat at a stool at the bar and started talking with Jesus. He told me about his military background, and we shared stories of the air force. I told him about John, his fast death, and how unprepared I had been. He talked about Meaghan and what a friend she had been to him. He also told me about Nancy, and we both shared a laugh, although his tale of Nancy's theft was only funny in hindsight. It was wonderful for me to be able to talk to someone who was not involved with the impregnation of cows, and more often than not, I sat at the bar when I dropped in for a drink.

I had been sitting at the bar when Jesus' phone rang. He talked for a few minutes, and then hung up, a look of resignation on his face. I gave him a questioning look, inviting him to share his feelings. He said that Harley, a young woman who had worked at the bar, had called and invited him to dinner. He said he felt overwhelmed by the thought of going anywhere alone. Even if it was with good friends. He looked at me, sipping my drink across the bar-top, and asked, "Do you want to go with me? You know, as a friend?" I sensed the second question was polite, that he didn't want me to turn him down because I wasn't interested in him. That way. I laughed about the manner of the invitation, but told him that I thought I would like to go. I liked Jesus. Maybe not in that way, but I liked him. Although maybe in that way.

Jesus picked me up at my apartment, which was not far from The Brick. He wore a clean Billy Nicholls T-shirt, had changed his shorts for a pair of jeans, and wore sandals. When we arrived at Harley and Cliff's apartment, I was surprised by how young everyone was. Jesus was about my age, or older, and from my conversations with him, I had expected that his friends would be older, too. Harley was dressed fashionably, seemed genuine, and appeared to be sad. She was withdrawn, observing the group chat, but not really participating in the conversation. She is an author and had recently won an award for her first novel. Cliff is tall, stretched out, and hovered around Harley like she was his prized possession. He had an easy manner, his rich voice soothing, making small talk easily with his friends. He is a singer/songwriter, and I had seen him perform at The Brick a few times. Ian is a welder and the father of a young boy. He is handsome and out-going. Lydia is smart and witty, and drank single malt whisky, like me. She is a surgeon and has a piercing in her nose that matched her piercing way of asking questions. She cuddled into Ian on the sofa, and their love was obvious. She was clearly fond of Harley and very protective of her. I already knew some of their backgrounds but was content to have them play out as time dictated. I sat and listened as this group of friends talked about Meaghan and each other and celebrated their friendship.

Before dinner, we sat around the tiny living room, drinking wine and beer. When Harley announced it was time to eat, we all crowded around the table. I sat beside Jesus. The food was delicious, and the wine poured easily and often. We finished the meal and continued sitting around the table, laughing, and telling stores, mainly about Meaghan. Sometimes, one would grow silent, sometimes, another. I knew they were thinking about their dear friend, the one who wasn't at the table. They talked until the candles grew too short and went out, first one, then the other. It was time to go home.

On the short drive home, Jesus and I talked about the evening. I told him that I really liked his friends, that they were all great—fun and wel-coming. Jesus looked relieved. He had shared a part of his personal life with me, a life that had, until the last few years, been one lived alone, and he didn't want to have to defend these people who were important to him. He had been very much a part of the celebration of Meaghan that night, sharing his stories of her in a way that only he could. He missed her, and he wanted, needed, perhaps, me to tell him how special his friends were.

When he dropped me off at my apartment, he thanked me for going to Harley's house with him.

"No, thank you," I answered. "Goodnight, Jesus. I'll see you sometime next week."

My apartment was on the second floor of a 1960s red brick, three-storey walk-up building, located on a quiet side street. There was no view, other than that of the cars parked on the street. It had cheap carpeting, and eggshell-coloured walls. As I entered my apartment, I dropped my purse and keys on the floor and slid out of my shoes. I sat in the darkened living room without putting on any of the lights. I wanted to enjoy the quiet moment.

This was the first time I had been out with a man since John died, and I had had fun. Even though it was only as friends, it felt like a milestone in my life. I knew it was time to start making some changes. My kids told me so. I told myself so. I turned on the lamp and poured myself a shot of scotch, neat. I sipped it, wondering how things would work out. If it wasn't to be Jesus, and it might well not be, practical me told myself, it would be someone else. I had too much to offer the world to live it out alone. I turned on the television, which often kept me company, but continued to mull over the events of the evening. I had enjoyed my night, and wanted to stretch out the enjoyment, to make it last a little bit longer.

I looked around my apartment. It had the colour scheme of the constantly moving. Beige couch, beige curtains, and beige rugs. Everything went with everything. No matter where I go, it will still work. Even the lamps were beige. And the throw cushions. And the blankets. This didn't seem like my home, it seemed like a stopping-off place. Who was I in this sea of no real colour?

The next morning, I woke early and had my cup of coffee in a beige mug—I had two, in fact. As I sipped my coffee, I looked over the ads that came with the weekly community newspaper. I got dressed in the same clothes as the night before and headed out the door in my sensible shoes and with a determined look on my face. I was on a mission.

When I got home later that afternoon, it took me almost an hour just to unload my car. I had decided to brighten up my home with colour-ful new cushions and blankets and candles, pictures for my walls, towels and bathmats and shower curtains, dishes and placemats and napkins and fresh flowers for my table, a silk rug, picture frames, floral curtains, and baskets, and vases of dried flowers, pillows and a bedspread and shams for the bedroom. Everything was bright and colourful and in my favourite colours of cherry red and lime green.

I was exhausted, but I was not done yet. I spent the rest of the weekend putting everything in place and moving out the no longer wanted. By Sunday night, I had a home that was all about me and what I loved. Before collapsing into my newly bright bed, I made a note to call the Goodwill people first thing in the morning. I'd ask, no, beg them to come and pick up my load of beige that day. I couldn't wait to be rid of it. I did have an appointment to inseminate a cow at some point in the afternoon, but I could work around that.

When I woke up the next morning, I looked around my room, at the bright colours, my colours, and hopped out of bed, refreshed and energized. I raced into the living room like a child on Easter morning and viewed my handiwork of the past two days. Oh Margaret, life is for the living! I had my coffee in a bright red cup with a green happy face. The face was winking at me.

Chapter 29

Lydia

To my surprise, I receive a call from Becca, the young girl I mentored at Girls of the Future. When my phone buzzes, I see who it is and hesitate before answering. I remember her, of course, but instantly think of Harley and her call years ago. How much my life has changed since then! How much Harley's life has changed!

Becca wants nothing except to thank me for taking the time with her and helping her. She is graduating this spring and going to university in Thunder Bay in the fall. She wants to be a teacher. We chat briefly and say goodbye. I know she will do well. She knows enough to take a hand when it is offered to her.

I still miss Meaghan, but I know I always will. She was such a big part of my life, and I seem incomplete without her. Ian and I have settled into our life together, and it is an easy, harmonious home, but occasionally, it does feel like something, like someone, is not where they should be. My friend.

Harley called me last month to share her news that she and Cliff are expecting a baby. She is now seven weeks pregnant and taking weekly pictures of her belly. Of course, there is little to see right now, but that will change quickly. What I can see, however, is that her skin and eyes, always clear and shining, seem to be extra bright, and her usual smile is beaming. In fact, she and Cliff are so delighted with themselves that sometimes when I see them, they say, "What have we done?!" with giddy grins on their faces. They act like they are the first parents in the world. They are the first parents of their child, and I am delighted for them too!

She has assured me she is taking the proper vitamins, eating well, and getting a lot of rest. She says she gets tired more easily, but makes sure she goes to bed early each night. All that tells me she is taking care of herself and their precious package. I smile to myself. So many women who come to the hospital have not taken care of themselves or their precious packages. They are exhausted and not ready for motherhood. Their babies are born small and weak.

I am proud of Harley. She is reading books and following the growth of their baby and exercising. She calls almost daily, and I welcome and appreciate her including me in this wonderful part of her life. She has an ultrasound scheduled in the next week and is agonizing over whether to know if it is a boy or a girl. Cliff wants to know, but she isn't so sure. They are going through books of baby names, short-listing some, discarding others, and laughing out loud at many of them. She tells me that Cliff's car won't be big enough, and they'll also have to get a new place. She already knows there is a never-ending long list of changes that a baby will make to their lives. For now, she is still writing her second book, although she admits it may take longer for her to finish this one, given that she is so distracted by her pregnancy. She feels bad about that, but mostly for her fans who have been waiting so patiently. I tell her not to worry about it, that now is the time to focus on herself, to do what she can while she can, that things will happen how and when they are supposed to, and in the end, there's only so much she can do about any of it anyway. I tell her to enjoy the moment for as long as it lasts. Turns out I was talking to both of us.

After a bit of a slow start, Ian's business is picking up, and he has hired two men to work with him. He has a small storefront in a strip mall near the house, and can walk to work from home if he wants. He never does, though. He needs his truck for work. He has been bidding on some large jobs and hopes to hear soon about whether he will be awarded any of the contracts. He started his own business partly so he could spend more time with his son, but it hasn't worked out that way. Still, he does whatever he can to be an involved father, which is great for Brayden. In fact, Ian coached his soccer team this spring. My job was to bring the post-game snacks. Popsicles and orange slices. Of course, the popsicles were the hit, and I took home the orange slices at the end of each game and ate them myself. As a doctor, I felt obliged to regularly provide a healthy snack, but did I honestly think any of them would choose an orange over a popsicle?

The day before Harley's ultrasound, I take a home pregnancy test. I have been feeling sick and tired, and my period is late, but I am on the pill and don't really think it even possible. Just to be sure, I tell myself as I wait for the results. Then I look down. I am wrong. I am pregnant. Two lines. I rush to the store to get another test, just to confirm. Yup. Two lines. Positive. How pregnant? I count back the days to my last period, and figure I am about five weeks along.

I'm not sure how this happened. Well, actually, I am absolutely sure how this happened, but I wasn't sure I wanted it to happen. Not now, anyway. When I tell Ian after he gets home from work, his reaction is similar to mine. His face clouds over slightly, and I can tell he is controlling his words and thoughts. We talk about the news. He is clearly not delighted, but it is a surprise and the prospect of a baby will take some time for both of us to get used to. Still, I tell myself that he loves Brayden, and he loves me, and he will love our baby.

I have been to see my family doctor, and she confirms what the drug-store tests indicated. I am going to have a baby. When Harley calls me with her latest update, I wait until she is done before telling her my news. She squeals with delight and says something about birds of a feather flocking together. I am going to have to get happy in a big hurry if I am to be a part of her flock. We chat about the books she is reading and which vita-mins she is taking, and I make a mental note to pick all these things up for myself. In for a penny, in for a pound.

My big challenge right now, however, is getting my head around the very idea of it. Maybe now is the right time. Is there ever really a right time? I think back to when I wasn't sharing my life with anyone who interfered with what I wanted. And then I wonder how is it that a few short years later, I find myself living with Ian, his son, and being pregnant with our own child? I wish I could talk with Meaghan about this, and it makes me so sad to think she will not be a part of Harley's or my child's lives. And then I think about how all our lives will change in some way. I don't know what I will do about work, but doctors have babies, so both the hospital and I will have to be flexible. Even my practice babies, Captain and Tennille, will take on a different role, but they have done so ever since Brayden and Ian moved in, and it doesn't change the fact that they will always be part of the family. My family. Our family.

I have told family and close friends. Margaret has become a part of our group and a friend, and I shared our news with her. She has been calling and giving me all sorts of information and advice. She is wise and calm and has three grandchildren of her own. I am so thankful for her. She drops in from time to time on her way home from work and brings me fruit, fresh-baked cinnamon buns, or some other delight from the Hutterite farms she passes. I keep trying to send her back out on the road to buy more cinnamon buns, but she laughs at me and warns of too much of a good thing. She and Jesus have something going on, but I don't know for sure what the extent of it is. I know they spend time together. He has been lonely, and I sense that she has been as well. She has dyed her hair and her clothing is bright and happy. Jesus is combing his ponytail more often. Something is definitely going on.

Ian's company was awarded a contract for rig welding and pump jack repairs in the Bakken oilfields. This is a stretch job for his little company, and he has hired two welders and is ordering materials. While I know he is excited about this new venture and spending a lot of time travelling or at his shop at the strip mall, he seems quiet. I am so proud of him for taking this risk, and I feel certain it will pay off for us. I worry that he has concerns about our growing family. He leaves early in the morning for the shop, his client's office in Virden, or the Sinclair oilfield site, and sometimes I don't see him for a whole day. Sometimes, he overnights. In my first trimester, I am tired and going to bed early, but I can hear him come in, feel him slide into bed beside me, quietly so as not to wake me. I can feel the warmth of his body in the space between us. I reach over to touch him, but he doesn't respond. Asleep so quickly.

I am on call tonight and arrive at work for 6:00 a.m. It will be a long day and night, and I am weary before I even get to the hospital. My stomach is still queasy from the pregnancy, and it doesn't help that I won't get much sleep in the call room overnight.

When I arrive home the next morning, the house is dark. The dogs greet me, tails wagging and wanting their breakfast. I feed them before making myself a cup of chamomile tea. Ian is already gone, but that isn't a surprise. What is a surprise is that he has left his computer running on his desk. He doesn't usually leave it on. I don't have the energy to get up and turn it off, but I am not sure when he will be home. Lunch? Dinner? Late tonight? I finish my tea, rubbing Tennille's little head while I allow relaxation to settle into me. I am now ready for sleep.

"Let's go, kids," I finally say to the dogs as I start toward the bedroom upstairs. I decide at the last minute to stop and turn off his computer. As I reach for his mouse, the screen lights up. Outlook is open and there are new e-mails. I glance briefly at the names of the senders, not interested in the details, or the titles, or even who is emailing him. Work, mainly, although some junk mail, too. I notice that Eliza has sent him something. The subject is "Later". Eliza is not his ex-wife, or anyone else I know.

This doesn't sound like junk mail, nor does it sound like something from work. I click on the e-mail and see, "Last night was fun, Ian. I am at work until 3:00 but call me after that. LE." LE? Love Eliza? My heart stops. I use his mouse to search for other e-mails from "Eliza". I find many of them, all referring to their relationship, their times together, a relationship and times of which until this moment I have been completely unaware. She loves him. He loves her. I am pregnant. He doesn't know how it happened. He doesn't know how to leave me. He still cares for me, but it isn't love. Honestly, Eliza, it isn't. I start to read the e-mails, but there are many, going back several months. This is not a one-night stand or even a brief affair. Ian is involved with Eliza and has declared his love for her. Does he mean it? Can she trust him? Can I trust him?

I am tired and want to get some sleep, but instead I head into our bedroom with other things on my mind. Sorting through his jacket pockets, I find an open box of condoms. Really? I am pregnant. It is unlikely these were intended for Us. us. I write a note on the box. "Hi, Ian. I think we need to talk. LL." Love Lydia. Then I go back downstairs and sit at his computer. I call up Later, and respond to LE. Send. Click. Eliza will let him know I have e-mailed her. No take backs. Life will change now.

An hour later, Ian walks in the door. He had been at the shop. His face is pale, his blue eyes avoiding mine.

"You are home early, Ian. Forget something? Home to eat?" Sarcasm drips. Floods.

He looks surprised. Where is the anger he expected? Then we make eye contact.

"Home to pack?" I ask him.

His shoulders, so broad before, slope downward. He has seen the anger in my eyes. Busted. You. Are. So. Busted. LL.

We talk for a few hours. He tries to act normally, but the pitch of his voice is higher than normal, strained. His words sound false. As they have been for the last few months. He tries to explain. At first, he says it didn't mean anything, that she is barely a friend, that they haven't done anything wrong. I quietly look at him, waiting for some truth. He says they crossed some emotional boundaries, boundaries they both knew were wrong, but he hasn't been unfaithful to me nor she to her husband. Mr. Eliza. I continue to wait for the truth. He says they did sleep together, but only once, and it was a terrible mistake. And I continue waiting. No truth yet. He says they'd had a brief affair, but it is over now. More waiting. He says he is in love with her, that he wants to leave me, that he didn't know how to tell me. And there is the baby. Wow. That wasn't planned. I tell him if he'd used the condoms in his upstairs pocket when we were having sex, I wouldn't be pregnant. His eyes flash. Yes, I know about those too. He talks about my job, about how it makes him feel that his work is so much smaller, that he is less of a man around me. He talks about wanting to be the hero in someone's eyes. He talks about nights alone when I am at the hospital. He talks about everything I have done that makes him feel small. The truth.

I take a deep breath and look directly at him. "I think it would be best if you leave for a while. I haven't had sleep in twenty-eight hours and my emotions are a little out of control." My tone is even, my words slow. I don't sound out of control. I just need him away from me.

He shakes his head in disbelief, as if he can't believe I would look through his private emails. My house, mister. My rules. Then he goes upstairs to get his jacket, and I watch him read the note on the condom box as he walks back down. He doesn't even acknowledge me as he grabs his computer and walks out the door, leaving me alone to try and figure out what has just happened to my life.

I go upstairs and take a sleeping pill. Is that bad for the baby? Maybe, but I need some rest and to free myself from his betrayal. I sleep most of the day, sleep providing a respite from my reality. As soon as my feet hit the floor, I remember the events of that morning. I so want to talk to someone, but I am ashamed and embarrassed and know that I can't erase what happened. What will my friends think of Ian? What will they think of me? I spend the evening sitting quietly on the sofa. Captain and Tennille lie at my feet, as if waiting for an invitation to comfort me. Soft, emotional, depressing country music is playing on the stereo, as if in concert with my life. I am sad and angry and without a future. I have no what-next right now. The only thing I know is that I have to be at work early in the morning, so eventually I go back to bed. There is no warm curtain of air beside me. Ian hasn't come home, nor had I expected him to.

He leaves a message on my phone, asking me to meet him for a walk after work. I am hesitant at first but tell myself that only one of two things is going to happen, and I may as well find out which one it is, so I can get on with my life.

We meet at Assiniboine Park and follow the cedar chip path along the river. Big trees spread their pale green, new leaves over us, as if protecting us, but the damage is below them, already done. The Assiniboine River is full from the spring melt, the edges high on the banks. This is a walk we have taken many times, sometimes with Brayden, an energetic, child-focused walk that ended in ice cream or French fries. Other times it was only the two of us, a slow and romantic hand-holder, ending with a beer at a pub or a movie on television. This evening is still warm, and I think about our first kiss in the dead of winter. A distinct contrast to where we are now.

At first, we have little to say to each other. I walk far from him, keeping plenty of space between us. No touching allowed. Touch fucking Eliza if you need to touch someone. I look at his face and his hands. I imagine him touching someone else. What would that look like? Just thinking about it makes me ill.

"Lydia, we need to talk."

Duh. No kidding. Why did all the childish answers always come to my mind?

"Lydia, I don't know what is wrong with our relationship. It's me. I know the problem is me. I need to leave."

Does pretending the problem is with him get him off the hook for sleeping with Love Eliza? There is no pretending, however. The problem is real. He did sleep with Love Eliza.

"I simply can't be with you. I can't commit to you. I need out."

You may not have a choice, Ian.

"I'm under a lot of stress right now, what with the new business, the contract, employees, you know…." His voice trails off, begging for my understanding, begging for me to let him leave, pride intact.

Sure, Ian. You are a great guy. You slept with Love Eliza for months, impregnating me while you were having sex with her, lying to me, lying to her. I understand your life is hard, and having an affair was the only option you had. Who could blame you?

Me. I blame him for giving what is rightfully mine to Love Eliza. He has given her everything that belongs to me—the affection, the conversation, the hugs, the sex, the time. And now I am left with nothing to fight with in the battle for his love. He stole that from me as well and gave it to her. She stole it from me, too. Hate Eliza.

We continue to walk as he continues to justify his affair. I listen but have little to offer him. His self-effacing list of things that are wrong with him, reasons for his affair, morph into things that are wrong with me, reasons for his affair. And then it is all my fault. He has slid himself completely off the hook.

When the focus of his words shifts, I realize he is trying to sell me on something.

"…about the baby…"

Co-custody? Child-support? Full custody? Access rights? Where was this going? Wherever it's going, I'm not buying.

"Do you really want the baby, Lyd?"

Not Lyd. Lydia to you. We aren't on informal terms anymore.

I know what he wants. He wants me to have an abortion, to end the life of the child that is in me, our child. I knew he wasn't excited about the baby, but I hadn't known why. Now I know why. He tells me he is okay with an abortion, that he already has his hands full with Brayden. Even the mention of Brayden makes me angry. Brayden and Lydia. We were a part of each other's lives. Will I be surgically removed from him, something that later he might remember he'd had, but really didn't need after all? Lydia the appendix? I won't forget him; I know I won't, and the thought of missing him makes me feel worse than ever.

We walk to the end of the trail, and I say I will let him know what I want. Across Portage Avenue, I see the Star Grill, the restaurant we had loved so much. The neon sign in the window says it is closed.

Fuck Eliza.

Chapter 30

Harley

I am in love with the beach at Lake Manitoba, and Cliff and I are staying in a cabin for a week. The Lake is huge, like a big, shallow, inland ocean. On calm, quiet evenings, the water provides a sheer and reflective platform for sunsets that are like no other—eye-blisteringly bright as if trying extra hard to make the short summer special. When the winds blow out here, however, they blow hard. The waves are stirred up easily, and each time they slam the shore, they take away sand, add sand, a little here, a little there. It all breaks even in the end, though. Nothing really lost, nothing really gained.

There are only two drawbacks to being at the beach at this time of year. Mosquitoes are our constant companions. When they bite, the welts are small, but there are so many of them that we don't even know where to begin to scratch. Fish flies are also out right now. In fact, the air is thick and grey with them, and they hang like dirty snot from the side of the cabin, the windows, the car, and even the leaves of the trees. I'm trying hard not to be squeamish, but a walk outside is not pleasant, and if we breathe through our mouths, we won't need to eat dinner tonight. We cover our noses lightly with our hands to keep from breathing them in. They cover the screens, wanting inside. I stand inside, watching them, and don't want to go out. We can't turn on the lights because that attracts them. A happy fish fly is no friend of mine. It is no consolation to me that their presence indicates a healthy ecosystem, or that they only live for a few hours, or that they don't eat. They have sex and then die. Sex to die for. Any bug around me is creepy, especially when they number in the millions. We have a fire pit and I want to sit outside at night, poking the fire with a long stick, listening to the frogs, melting the tips of my runners in the heat from the flames. But we can't do that. Too many mosquitoes. Too many fish flies.

This morning, I wake up early. I leave Cliff sleeping and walk down the hall, from the bedroom in the back of the cabin into the living room. I open the windows to let in air, the screens keeping the insects out. There are so many flies that the air hums, a soft, low buzz from the sound of their beating wings. Above the noise from the flies, I can hear the raucous call of the yellow-headed blackbird and the screech of gulls fishing in the lake. I look around the cabin to see the floor and tables littered with buggy carcasses. There were a few that snuck inside when the door was opened, and there is a price to be paid for last night's fun.

My belly is growing, a little at a time, the change hardly noticeable, but I can tell that our baby is growing inside me. It is a mystery to me how life can start from a little of me and a little of Cliff, and then grow in a nice warm place for nine months until finally making his or her entrance into the world. It feels magical, like someone has been created out of nothing. It is such a massive responsibility to grow a human being, and it is a responsibility I do not take lightly. That we do not take lightly. And as I cherish this little baby, so does Cliff cherish me.

We have nicknamed the baby Cletus the Fetus, or Cletus for short. That won't be his or her name when he or she arrives, but for now, it makes us laugh every time we say it. Ha ha. What also makes me laugh is when Cliff makes up songs about the baby. Cletus the fetus is going to meet us in the winter. It's silly stuff, but in his deep growly voice, the songs sound loving, as long as I don't listen to the ridiculous lyrics. My love for Harley the genius, my Venus, is the deepest. Ya, Ya, Ya. I love Cletus the fetus to pieces. Ya, Ya, Ya. I am now going to go eat fajitas. Ya, Ya, Ya. Thanks, Cliff. You are clearly the genius in the family. Our family.

I know that strength lives here with us, but sometimes I feel like I am in a soap bubble. A world that is fragile, perfect, beautiful. And as I float through life, Cliff is with me, making sure the walls of the bubble keep us safe from harm. It means everything to me that strength lives here in our perfectly round world.

This past winter was warm and so there was more snow than usual. Manitoba is either really cold in winter, and little snow falls when it is frigid, or slightly warmer with lots of snow. It was late to melt and combined with heavy spring rains, there have been huge threats of flooding. Everyone is nervous. The government made the decision to divert excess rainwater and spring runoff into Lake Manitoba, and the lake water here is high. Much higher than normal. Expensive real estate in the cities were kept from the danger of flooding, but it has put this little strip of cottages at risk. We were simply told by the authorities that if all goes well, there shouldn't be a problem. Bad risk management words. Ed the Water Guy for the government has retired, and there is a new Water Guy in the golden throne. Under the Golden Boy. Making a mistake, but hey, everyone makes them, right? Give him time, he will get it right.

Cliff emerges from the bedroom and joins me on the sofa. We look out through the drippy snot fish flies on the window screens and comment on the high level of the lake. It is completely flat, but off in the distance there are roils of clouds, and here and there we can see the fluttery ripples on the surface of the lake that come with a change in wind direction. The birds are strident, screeching, flying fast. After breakfast, we watch the storm clouds come closer. The waves pick up, small white caps appearing more frequently. The wind is blowing harder, and the fish flies have all disappeared. Where are they? Where does a fish fly go in a storm? Where do a hundred million of them go? How much time does it take for them to fly to safety? They only live long enough to have sex. Perhaps they are at the back of the cabin, having a quickie in case there isn't time later. We can't see them anywhere, though, and can only guess what is going on. The mental image of a million flies going at it behind our backs makes me laugh.

The wind is starting to blow much harder than before, and some of the trees around the cabin are creaking. It is a scary sound, like a low tree growl. Get out of my way or pay the price. Too late for us to go anywhere, so we stay put and listen as the howl of the wind cancels out all other sounds, except for the ominous creaking of the trees. The temperature has dropped, and inside the cabin is cool. As Cliff gets up to close the windows,

I grab a sweater from a chair in the kitchen and put it on. A few drops of rain hit the front window. Looks like we are in for it.

The storm clouds are above us now, and there is lightning every few seconds. The thunder is deafening and a little frightening, and I move back to the couch and curl up against Cliff. I was worried about Cletus until Cliff put his arm around me and said everything will be okay. Genius and protector. We try to watch the impact of the storm, but the wind is driving the rain so hard against the window that it's hard to see clearly. We can tell, however, that the waves are higher now and are hitting the shore hard. It doesn't look like break-even at all. It looks to me like the lake is winning, taking more than its share, leaving less behind, encroaching on the beach, reclaiming some land. The lake is bigger and stronger, and it needs more space. It has a right to more land, and it is taking it by force.

We can't believe it, but the wind has picked up even more, blowing harder and bringing more rain with it. Branches and flowerpots and plastic pails are flying through the air. The sign from Mike and Betty Piros' Heavenly Haven blows past, its beachfront post apparently undermined by the waves. Before long, the beach is lost. The canoes, rowboats, and kayaks are no longer piled neatly on the shoreline. They have been freed from their sandy moorings and are frantically roaming the lake. Unused to being alone in the water, paddles and oars crash around with nothing and no one to guide them.

The wind and the water continue their work. Creaking trees are flung to the ground, foundations are stripped from buildings, and broken cottages and boat houses are carried away. Cliff and I are terrified, but there is nowhere to go. The lake is all around us. No longer snotty with flies, our car is slowly drowning. So far, the cottage is dry, although all the trees around it are gone. We have moved as far as possible from any window, fearing that something will crash through, shattering the window and showering us with broken glass. There is no power, no heat, and there are no options.

And then as quickly as it came, the storm is over. The sun is out, beaming its silly, sheepish smile, almost apologetic, as if it was caught sleeping on the job. There are no winds, no birds chirping, and no flies or mosquitoes. The beach is silent, as if waiting for something, but nothing comes. The fat lady has sung. Cliff and I cautiously step outside to survey the damage.

The devastation is complete. Our cabin is one of the few that have no damage. Many others have been completely washed away or have slid into the lake, while those still standing are missing roofs, have broken windows, or have been crushed by trees. Shore buildings have all gone, as has the shore. Sloping sand beaches have been reshaped into sheer sand cliffs, small but steep. Fish are flopping on the land. The lake is full of debris, as well as possessions that represent the summer lives of the people of Twin Beaches. A few other people are wandering around and assessing damage, but mainly wanting the comfort of their own species. It is unbelievable that no one seems to have been injured. Not so unbelievable is that the only way out has been washed away and blocked by fallen trees. We are only renters, but no one is leaving for a while.

The community of Twin Beaches came together, unified by their history of shared cottage life and their anger at the government's failure to take full responsibility for their decision. Town hall meetings developed group strategies for dealing with the arbitrary decisions of the Water Guy, who sacrificed the people of Twin Beaches for the sake of those in the cities. The cottage owners railed against offers of compensation that were deemed inadequate, and they spat at the idea of only compensating year round residents, leaving the owners of summer homes and boat houses to fend for themselves. Television stations showed footage of the beach devastation, followed by clips of cottagers, angry at the poor efforts to reclaim the beach, but it was all for naught. In the end, the Water Guy won, and the cottagers were defeated. They had no power. They took whatever money they could get and started rebuilding.

It is a few days before we finally get home. It wasn't just another day at the beach, and we are so thankful we are unharmed. All three of us. Chalk that vacation up as one for the memory books. Cletus the fetus, that vacation was grievous, ruined by the Water Guy cheatahs. Ya, Ya, Ya.

Chapter 31

Maggie

I don't know yet if I like it a little, or a lot, that I have been spending time with Jesus. We share our military background, an understanding of moving around, of having our friends move on to different locations, and of starting over again. That ability to start over, to begin again, is underrated, but it is an ability that most military folks share. That feeling of not being from around here, of being the new one, of being the third wheel, of not having a best friend. We leave a piece of ourselves, of our story, in each new location, but these are pieces that we can never reclaim. Houses, schools, and friends are all left behind. Left behind as a fond memory. An occasional phone call. A line on a Christmas card list. Then one year, the card is returned. Address unknown. The last physical reminder of a piece of our life is gone. That feeling of not quite fitting in eventually becomes a way of life, and I believe it has hardened me. I don't and I can't, therefore I won't. Instead, I will form myself into a square peg, always trying out a new round hole for a better fit, and if it doesn't work, I will simply move on to the next one.

Jesus and I have talked about this at length, he with his beer and me with my scotch. We understand the longing for a shared history, the envy of those people with deep roots to a city or a town. I think this is why I like The Brick so much. It is a place I can go where I am known, where Jesus pours me a drink when I walk in, where people say hello to me as if they have known me all their lives. They have nicknamed me Maggie. I have never had a nickname before, and I like it. It makes me feel special, that there is a familiarity and an appreciation of me. Margaret is somewhat limited by her self-expectations, but Maggie can do anything she wants, be anyone she wants. I feel like my nickname has given me permission to change.

For me, September is the start of fall, my favourite season. I hate late August, though, when the days shorten, the sun loses some of its power, and the flowers stop blooming. That is also when people usually give up on summer. Grass doesn't grow as quickly, and people don't mow their yards as often. The weeds in their gardens are permitted to grow. Once I have accepted both the death of summer and the inevitability of winter, I make the most of the relatively short season in between. I love the cool nights and the sense of new beginnings as people go back to school, buckle down at work, start a yoga class, or take lessons in Mandarin.

Thanksgiving is my favourite holiday. Family, friends, good times, and walking off the pumpkin pie after a most delicious dinner. It isn't like Christmas though. Christmas is hard, burdened by expectations and traditions, the peer pressure of the past, disappointments and jealousies, ending with the big rip. Months of preparation conclude spectacularly in only a few hours. Everyone is packed inside in cold winter weather, grating on each other's nerves. Feathers are ruffled. Everyone knows which buttons to push, and there is nowhere to hide your buttons. Tempers flare. Thanksgiving is not at all like Christmas. It is a dinner and a time to give thanks for all that we already have in our lives.

None of my kids are coming for Thanksgiving. Unfortunately for me, they are all in different cities, the by-product of their transient military childhood. To fill the void, I have invited Lydia, and Harley and Cliff, and Jesus. Jesus.

We will be a small but merry crowd. Lydia and Ian didn't find a way to get past what Lydia calls the Love Eliza affair. I hoped they would. Lydia said he felt small in their relationship. Eliza was his plan B. Plan to be Bigger? Lydia was sad, of course, but mainly angry. I'm glad she has decided to keep the baby. I think it has helped her to get past Ian and to focus instead on her future and that of the little one.

The baby is a girl. Lydia had to know as soon as she could, and she wanted a girl so badly. Of course, before she knew exactly, she said the usual. I don't care if it is a boy or a girl, as long as it is healthy, but now that she knows, she says she wanted a girl all along. I can picture Lydia mothering a small version of herself, but in my imagination, the little girl has a nose ring and an attitude.

I love the look of pregnant women. People say that pregnant women glow, but I think that if everyone ate as well, got as much rest, and generally took care of themselves the way pregnant women do, everyone would glow.

Harley looks so beautiful pregnant. Her baby bump is neat and tidy, barely sticking out in front of her at all. Her skin, always creamy, is flawless. She and Cliff talk of little else. I suppose it could be boring to some, but I love to hear them talk of their plans for Cletus. I don't like that name at all, but they giggle every time they say it, so it must be a joke. Harley has also finished her second book, and it will be published about the same time as their little baby is due. I was surprised when she said she had finished it, as I remember how hard it was for me to concentrate when I was pregnant. Both she and Lydia ask me questions about my pregnancies, but I don't remember too many of the details, and so much has changed. And not changed. We have sex, get pregnant, and have babies. That hasn't changed. I didn't have a book about the development of the babies. My maternity clothes were designed to cover my bump, not to show it off. I tell the girls what I know and what I remember, but mainly I try to ask them questions. I know that is what they actually want. To talk about this exciting time of change in their lives. I am truly thankful to be a part of it, especially with my own grandchildren so far away.

So, five for dinner unless Lydia finds someone to bring along. I am cooking the turkey and making the stuffing and the pumpkin pie, and everyone else is bringing dishes of food. My apartment is small, but we will make it work. I am nervous. I haven't had people over to my place for dinner for a long time, and I keep telling myself it will be fun. I used to love to entertain, but John was around then, and I didn't have to do everything myself.

I set the table carefully, and it looks beautiful. The girls won't be drinking wine, but I know that Jesus and Cliff will have a glass or two, and I certainly will. What is a celebration without a glass of wine? I bought new dishes for this dinner. They are brightly coloured Mexican dishes. I wonder if I chose them because of Jesus and his heritage. Some people do that, I know. Maybe I didn't, but maybe I did. I also bought some candles, and some expensive paper napkins with Happy Thanksgiving printed over a picture of a worried-looking turkey. I thought they were funny when I bought them, but now I am not so sure. Oh well. Too late to worry about things like that. The main thing is my apartment smells like turkey, and it looks expectant, ready for company. I am excited about this dinner. I love Thanksgiving. I am thankful.

The buzzer in the lobby jolts me from my thoughts, and I press the button that opens the door to the building. They have all arrived at the same time, and my tidy apartment, resplendent in its bright colours, becomes chaotic, with people coming in and slipping out of their shoes, handing me coats, tucking their purses out of the way. Three bottles of wine arrive with the group, and I quickly take them to the kitchen. Two are white and one is red, and I can't remember which goes in the fridge, so I put them all in. There are dishes of food arriving as well, and everyone has ended up in my small kitchen. The men are looking for the wine and glasses, and laughing about me putting the red in the fridge. Harley and Lydia are giving me instructions on last minute preparations for the food they brought. Jesus lifts the tinfoil on the top of pie.

"It looks great. Ice cream or whipping cream?"

"Both, of course!" I laugh, pleased that I will make him happy either way.

Cliff has gone into the living room and put some music on. It is too loud, and everyone is shouting over the top of it to turn it down. Eventually, we all end up in the living room with our drinks, waiting for the turkey to finish cooking. It is a warm and comfortable night, fueled by conversation and the company of friends. When dinner is served, we eagerly take our places and share looks and words of gratitude. We are not gourmet cooks, but the food on our table is good, simple fare, and the meal declared a success by all. Lydia and Harley are tired, and so it seems that almost as quickly as they arrived, they are gone, home to rest themselves and their precious bundles.

Jesus remains behind, and I pour him a beer. I have a shot of scotch, and we sit in the living room, talking about the food, our friends, our hopes and dreams, and our disappointments. We talk for hours over more beers and more glasses of whisky, and the music plays on.

It is getting late, and Jesus says it is time to go. He is a bit wobbly from the drink, but fortunately he doesn't have far to walk.

"Night, Maggie. I'll see you later."

I see him out and close the door to my apartment. I am not sure if I am happy or sad that nothing further happened with Jesus, but I am grateful for this man, this friend with whom I can share my stories. Jesus has so many stories, some of which I suspect are not entirely true, but he is a skilled storyteller, and I can listen to him for hours. Even though I know I will regret it, I pour myself another drink and sit alone, happy, thinking about the night. I think about my life with John, my children having their own dinners in other cities, and I shed a drunken tear or two. Still, I have made a life for myself, and I am both happy and extremely thankful.

Chapter 32

Lydia

Time passes slowly as I watch my belly grow bigger. A watched pot never boils, and a closely monitored baby will never be born. Both are nonsense, of course, but I am fascinated by the development of my baby. She is strong, and I am healthy. Together, we will conquer the world.

I don't expect to hear from Ian ever again. We made a firm agreement that he would leave and never come back. There will be no visiting on Sundays or Wednesday after school. He will just get on with his life, and l will get on with my life and that of our little baby girl. I do worry he will change his mind, but I try to keep myself calm, to provide a peaceful bubble for my baby to grow in. My little girl. Sometimes I cry and rage and question how my life changed so quickly, but I am resilient, and I am determined to be the strongest, best mother I can be.

I daydream about my future. About pretty bedrooms full of ruffles, tiny lace dresses, and pink, popcorn-stitch knitted booties. I also had a dream about being a mother. In it, I am playing house, and when my mother calls me to dinner, I leave my doll on the basement floor. I play outside after dinner, and then go to bed. In the morning I go get my doll, who is waiting patiently on her back on the floor. Not hungry, not in need of a diaper change, or a cuddle, or being fussy at all. None of this makes any sense, of course. Dreams don't.

There are some women at the hospital who share with me their tales of maternal hardships, no detail forgotten. In my head, I hear their unspoken pleas, and I guess at the reality of the lives behind the stories. Their voices echo in my head.

"Please, tell me I am special. Let me tell you about me and my pregnancy many years ago." "Let me tell you about me." "I have not had enough attention in my life." "I have done the caring, but have never been cared for." "Those births are about me." "I won't tell you about the disappointments I've had as a parent, about how my children didn't live up to their own dreams, never mind my dreams for them." "Who can I tell that even though I love my children, they do not love me?" "I had failed in my responsibility to raise solid citizens."

I have listened to these stories of childbirth and parenting and guessed at the stories of motherhood behind them. Women can forget that I am a doctor, and that I have seen many births, and the mothers in awe of their creation, moments after expelling the child from their bodies, after setting these new beings free. And they forget that I see people who were once these awe-inspiring babies, wheeled into the hospital with flank wounds or stomachs full of pills, or bodies worn down by years of excesses. When does the imperfection start? When does the mother realize that her baby is not a perfect creation, that it is real and has needs, some of which can never be met? When does a mother realize that no matter how hard she tries, or if she even tries at all, she will never be able to control the outcome, that her little baby has a say of its own? Is control over at the moment of birth? Perhaps that is what that moment of pure love is about, a tug-of-war as the mother stares into the eyes of her newborn child.

I will not control you. I will not be controlled. You are on your own. I will lead my own life. I will help you if I can. I will accept your help if I can.

Harley calls me every day. I think she is checking up on me. She isn't writing right now, probably because all her creativity is focused on her little Cletus, imagining the world that she and Cliff will live in once the baby is born. Cliff has been travelling a lot and has been named in *The Globe and Mail* as one of Canada's best new voices. He is making serious money now and has had to hire a manager. He and his band are touring, and their next gig will be at the Interstellar Rodeo in Edmonton, a festival that appeals to the fans of artistic outlaws and musical mavericks. Harley is earning royalties on her books. The goodness of two of my favourite people is clearly paying off for them. They are making a life for themselves, pushing away all that is bad and living in their bubble of happiness.

If anyone deserves such a life, it is Harley. I often think about the day I met her, how angry and resentful she was, pushing back against everything, failing in all areas of her life, so alone, and so very troubled. Harley had told me about that day, about counting backwards to see who her saviour lady would be. I sometimes wonder what would have happened if instead of me, she had been influenced by the lady in the polyester suit. I am not patting myself on the back because I know that all of the heavy lifting has been done by Harley herself. I am, however, thankful that I was able to offer her whatever it was she needed that day.

Harley is shorter than me and a few weeks further along in her pregnancy. Her tummy, full of hope, is huge, and she waddles when she walks. When she sits, she falls back into her chair with a loud sigh, her short legs sticking out in front of her. Cletus is wildly active, kicking her almost constantly, pushing her ribs out, standing on her bladder. She can see little feet travel across her skin or an elbow push out against her side. There is a life inside her, waiting to get started. She is due in only a few weeks and has been busy gathering what she needs for their baby.

Cliff hovers around her, getting what she needs, what he thinks she needs, and what he needs. He cannot do enough for this woman, for Harley, who will soon bear their child. He is determined that his baby, their baby, will be raised in a loving home, a home with both a mother and a father. Harley is determined that her baby, their baby, will be raised in a loving home, a home that will be nurturing and supportive. Harley will ensure there are two signatures on all report cards. Cliff's and hers. She will ensure that if skating is what the little one wants, then skating there will be. Not just skating, but Mom and Dad standing and cheering with the other parents. There will be no late-night partying, no raging-bull father, no sobbing, button-pushing mother.

I am sad that my little girl will not have a father in her life. Ian was, is, and would have been a great dad, and it would have been so much fun for us to share in the parenting of our little girl. I have many regrets about him, but not that he is the father of our baby. She is kicking and turning, a busy baby indeed, and like Cletus, she is getting ready to start her life outside of me. I am getting ready to give up control, to let her grow into the best person she can be, and I will be there to help her in every way I can. I wish things had gone differently with Ian. I totally loved him and saw us spending our lives together. I wish he had been more honest about his feelings, or talked to me about his insecurities, or turned to a counsellor for help, instead of to Eliza. I am still angry, but not so much about the affair. I've accepted that Eliza was a symptom of a problem between Ian and me, and that I was blind to it. Jesus has seen Ian at The Brick and has relayed to me that he isn't with Eliza anymore. I actually feel sorry for her, but only a little bit. Two broken hearts, and maybe Ian's will make three. Poor Eliza.

When my phone rang this morning and I saw it was Ian, my world went silent, so silent that all I could hear was my heart beating in my chest. When he spoke, my breathing stopped, a lump formed in my throat, and each second of time seemed to last forever as my head caught up with my heart.

He wants to go for a drink, somewhere quiet.

"What about, Ian?" I eventually asked, my voice quiet, but registering all my emotions that had suddenly risen to the surface. Anger, love, hope, disappointment, betrayal. Hope.

"What about The Star Grill?" he suggested.

The Star Grill is a small restaurant across from Assiniboine Park, on the other side of Portage Avenue. In the past, we often went there for a glass of wine and something to eat after a walk in the park. It was, is, a place of warm memories, so his choice of meeting place spoke volumes. It told me what he might want from me. My head was racing, trying to figure out what I wanted from him.

"I'll have to call you back later, Ian. There is a patient coming into emerg." Liar, liar, pants on fire. God forgive me. I need some time to think.

If there is anything I have learned from Harley over the last few years, it is the need for resilience. This is, by far, the greatest gift that she has given me, and it is something I value very much. Harley came from a background bereft of love, and yet she has achieved everything in life that she wants. She knows what she wants and has found a way to reach her goals. She doesn't stand on ceremony, doesn't let other people form her opinion, and believes that what others think of her is none of her business. She watches, learns what is good and what is bad, and takes the good and builds on it. She doesn't wallow in her past, there is no 'poor Harley' in her vocabulary, and she appreciates everything and everyone that has helped her along her way. I imagine her walking barefoot along the beach, her footprints slowly filling with water until they completely disappear. She, of course, is unaware of this because she has her eye on the open beach in front of her, on the sun in the sky, on the waves on the shore, on the limitless possibilities of the horizon in front of her. I have so much respect for her, and often wonder what she might have done if she'd had the same opportunities that I have had in my life.

I dial Harley's number, and she answers right away.

"I was going to call you, Lyd." Not surprising, given that she calls me every day now. "What's up?"

I tell her about the call from Ian and what I think is coming.

"I don't know what to do, Harley. I think I know what he wants, but I am not sure. I think I know what I want, but I am not sure of that either."

We talk about my past dreams of life with Ian, Brayden, and the baby. We talk about how it is okay without Ian, that there are many single-parent families. We talk about my feelings of betrayal. Harley keeps pushing, pushing, pushing me to identify what it was that I want. Not what Ian wants, or Brayden, or the baby, or what the people who care about me want. Not how I feel about what happened in the past. She keeps at me, pushing my yeah-buts out of the way until I finally say to her, "I love Ian, and I really want a life with him. I want it so much that I am willing to do the work it takes to make it happen."

There is a pause, then Harley says, quietly and a little bit smugly, "Lydia, I think you do know what to do."

I call Ian back later in the day, and we agree to meet. He is in the oil-fields right now, but he will be home the next day.

"So, I'll see you at The Star Grill at 7:00 tomorrow night."

As I hang up, I feel like I am heading out to sea and can't see the horizon, but I also feel prepared for the journey. My thoughts are consumed by what could be in front of me, just out of my range of vision. As I walk the dogs that night, I look hard at my life as it is. I have a great job, a great home, two practice babies, a real baby coming soon, and a group of friends who support me. My life is good. I could settle for good; really, I could, but I think I want to shoot for great.

When I walk into The Star Grill, I see Ian in the back corner, facing the door, in a small booth for two. He smiles when he sees me, and I smile back, a tentative, unsure smile, but it is definitely lip corners up. Why is it that a person's physical appearance is so overwhelming in times of stress? I am aware of every hair on his head, the colour of his eyes, what he is wearing, his aftershave, the drink in front of him. My senses are on high alert, and I take everything in.

"What are you drinking, Ian?" I order the same-only-virgin, and we verbally stagger our way around some opening conversation.

His business is going well, and he has done quite a bit of hiring for the new contract. Brayden is in gymnastics and shows some real talent. I have been feeling okay, after the first trimester, which was a bit rough, and Harley's baby is due pretty soon. He comments on my belly and asks for news of the baby.

After some more chitchat, my inside naughty person speaks up. "How is Eliza?" I actually want to ask how Fuck Eliza is, but my inside adult person checks the Fuck word on the way out of my mouth.

Ian groans and opens his hands toward me, palms up. Welcome, Lydia. Come to me.

"Eliza isn't a part of my life anymore, Lydia. We had something together, but it wasn't permanent, couldn't ever have been permanent." He looks at me, his blue eyes fill with tears, salty tears from our sea horizon. "Lydia, I am so, so sorry. I know you can never forget what I did, but I only ask that you can, at some time, find a way to forgive me. What can I do, what can I say, to show you how bad I feel about what happened, for the whole Eliza thing, but mainly for not being the man you thought I was?"

It sounds like a prepared speech, the kind of blah blah blah that so many men deliver in such times, but it isn't disingenuous, at least not to my ears. In fact, I get the distinct impression that he has thought hard about what he wants to say to me. As he continues, taking his time and talking about how he was feeling before and during his affair with Eliza, I listen closely, my spider senses on full alert for any blame he puts on me for his betrayal. To my surprise and delight, there isn't any. He blames himself for his weaknesses and tells me that he owes our relationship the bravery to address his insecurities head on with me. He is a coward, he says, an ashamed coward, a sorry, ashamed coward.

"I get it, Ian. You are a sorry, ashamed coward." I almost laugh, not because of his words, but because he is trying so hard to get his words out, to find a way to make me understand that he was wrong. And then, no longer blocked by guilt and apologies, the words I expect to hear are set free.

"I want to try again, Lyd."

I don't correct the nickname.

"I can be everything you thought I was, and I promise you I will be. Please let me back into your life, Lyd."

Now it is my turn to talk, and I don't hold back. I tell him how much he hurt me, how difficult it was to understand, how betrayed I felt, and how much I had loved him.

"Can you forgive me, Lyd?"

"I don't know."

"Do you think you could ever love me again? Or even like me?"

I successfully suppress an imperceptible grin trying to reveal itself. "I don't know."

"Would you be willing to try?"

I pause, grateful for my conversation with Harley. "Maybe.

Time and words pass between us, and in the end, we agree to meet again for drinks and to talk some more. Before we go our separate ways, I tell him I will work on forgiveness and that I am willing to take our relationship to that of friends, at least for now. I know, however, the energy between us belies that relationship. We can never be friends because we are already connected as lovers, at a higher level, but we can pretend, at least for now.

As we leave the restaurant, he steps sideways, around my pregnant tummy, to kiss my cheek. Friends. Pretend friends. I get in my car and drive home, feeling lighter than I have in months. I feel resilient. Thanks, Harley.

Chapter 33

Harley

It is almost baby time. Not quite, but soon. Cliff is away at the Interstellar Rodeo in Edmonton with his band. It is the last stop in a longer-than-usual tour that has taken in folk festivals right across the prairies. I really miss him, and maybe it's the hormones, but I am a little bit angry he is away right now. Of course, I understand that he needs to make a living, that he can't simply drop his career for his personal needs, but still, this is the biggest event of our lives, and I definitely want him with me when our baby is born. When he promises that he will be with me, I tell him I am going to hold him to that.

The doctor wants to do another ultrasound tomorrow. He says I am bigger than normal and wants to check my blood sugar levels. When he asks if there are multiple births in my family medical history, I almost laugh.

"I'm the youngest of nineteen, Doctor. Of course, there are multiple births."

I know what he means though. Twins, or triplets? No, Doctor. Mom had nineteen babies, one at a time.

Inside, my heart takes a leap of excitement. Twins? Is that even a possibility? I call Cliff from the parking lot of the doctor's office and tell him about tomorrow's ultrasound. He is over-the-moon excited about even the thought of twins, and I am immediately worried that if there is only one baby in my tummy, he is going to be extremely disappointed. When he says he will fly home for the ultrasound, I tell him not to, even though I hope he does. Of course, I can handle it alone. All I have to do is lie on my back and let the technician oil my tummy and roll a sensor around my stomach. I am a passive participant in the ultrasound process, but I want him to be here with me. It would be exciting for us to hear the news together, whether it's one or two Cletuses.

When I tell Lydia, I can tell she is really happy for us. Her voice sounds chokey, like she is crying. Tears of joy. She says that if for some reason Cliff doesn't get back in time, she is happy to stand in for him. She doesn't want me to be alone, but she also doesn't want to interfere. I tell her I will let her know, one way or the other.

When Cliff calls back, he says he has booked a flight and will absolutely be there. He's not playing at the festival until the night after tomorrow, so it will only be a quick trip, but I am beyond thrilled. After I hang up, I feel like I can no longer control the outcome of anything. Then, of course, I realize that I never could.

I wake up early and fuss around the apartment. It will be great to get into a bigger place, but right now we need to concentrate on getting ready for the baby. For Cletus. es. The weather is terrible outside, windy and raining, but this is Manitoba where the normal state of the provincial weather is guaranteed to be crappy whenever something important is happening.

I turn on the light over the kitchen table and start writing in my journal. I have been writing daily about my pregnancy. Ever since my second novel was sent to the publishers, I've missed working on a book, and my little journal is a way to keep writing and chronicle the development of the baby, my feelings and my thoughts, and what Cliff says or does. It has assuaged my creative soul.

Some women tell me they hate being pregnant, but I have loved every moment of it. I know I am going to miss my bump and how contained it has been. The skin over it, my skin, is threaded with silver and red streaks where it has expanded to accommodate the baby. I can see blue veins running near the surface. My belly button pushes outward, like a tongue sticking out. It's an odd sensation when I sit down naked and my pregnant stomach rests on my thighs. I have never felt that part of me resting on that part of me before, and it is almost like a heavy stranger sitting on my lap. Hey you, naked ball, get off my lap! Ha ha.

The phone rings. Cliff is still in Edmonton, but he is on his way to the airport and will meet me at the clinic. He says again how sorry he is that he can't pick me up, but it was the only flight that will get him here on time. I am so happy he is coming home, even if it is only for one night. I call Lydia to let her know, but she doesn't answer. Working, most likely, so I leave a message thanking her for her offer anyway.

I shower, but am unable to clean my feet. I suppose they are disgustingly dirty, but there is no way I can reach them to scrub them off. I soap my belly several times. I like the feel of it. It is round and hard and alive, and I like to rub my soapy hands all over it. Oh, Bump, how much bigger will you get? I step out of the shower and dry off as best as I can. I swipe the towel at my ankles and feet, but end up walking around leaving wet footprints. I pick clothing from the closet, but nothing fits anymore. I will not miss one single item of maternity clothing when the baby is born. I make a cup of tea and wait for the time to leave. Fidgety.

I grab an umbrella. It is pouring outside, and in my excitement about seeing Cliff and knowing the results of the ultrasound, I waddle-race to our car, parked on the street. Cletus seems to be lower, and I suspect the baby has dropped. The home stretch is here for sure. I park the car in the lot and walk toward the clinic entrance. As I arrive at the front doors, a taxi pulls up, and Cliff climbs out of the back seat. He looks nervous and proud. He smiles when he sees me and rushes to me, hugging me. He kisses me and then holds me gently away from him, looking into my face, my eyes, at my bump, checking me to make sure I am okay. He feels so good, and I feel stronger with him here. The clinic isn't crowded, but that doesn't mean I'll get in right away. I still have to sit and drink cup after cup of water, creating a water bubble inside that will push Cletus (es?) into full view for the ultrasound. So much water. I am terrified I will pee on the examining table.

The nurse calls my name and we follow her into a dim little room. After I put on the nightgown, she helps me onto the table. As Cliff holds my hand, he stares at the monitor on the wall. The nurse adjusts the nightgown so she can prepare me for the ultrasound.

The oil is warm, but the sensor is cold, even though she tried to warm it in her hand. As she moves it over my bump, I see Cletus in the monitor, and am impressed by the size. I see arms and legs and feet and hands. Everything is jumbled in the image, and I can't clearly see what is what. Then the technician says she is going to bring in the doctor to look at the images. I immediately worry. Is something wrong? What is wrong? Why does she need the doctor? Cliff talks to me quietly, calming me, telling me not to jump to any conclusions. After a while, however, I can hear in his voice that he is concerned as well. It doesn't help that the nurse is gone for what seems like a long time, but finally she and the doctor walk into the room. The technician picks up the sensor again, tries unsuccessfully to warm it again, and rubs it over my belly again, apologizing again for the cold metal. The doctor takes the sensor and guides it over areas of my abdomen.

"Twins for sure, my dear. One boy, it looks like. Can't tell the sex of the other baby. Both are a normal size. Definitely two heartbeats." He continues scanning my bump. "Placenta looks fine, nothing out of the ordinary, other than twins." He smiles and winks at me, sharing this small joke.

Well, no surprises for us now, except whether the other baby is a boy, or a girl. Cliff's hand is locked tightly onto mine, and I move my hand to loosen it. He loosens his grip but keeps my hand in his. He asks the doctor to explain the image on the screen, and the doctor points out the back of one head, the front of the other, and the genitals of the boy. It is absolutely fascinating, and I want to lie there forever, with Cliff holding my hand, and the two of us watching as the little lives we created move around inside me. The doctor advises us that he will send the results to my family doctor right away.

"Twins are often born early," he cautions with an authoritative tone of voice. Then he smiles and says, "Congratulations you two, or should I say you four."

The nurse groans and rolls her eyes, but she is smiling as well.

When we are finally alone in the room, Cliff and I take a moment to hug, to share our joy, to express our disbelief. I am so thankful he is with me and that we could share this happy news together.

I dress quickly and race to the bathroom.

We go for lunch together, and then spend the afternoon shopping for additional baby things. Another car seat, more diapers, more bottles, more clothes, two of everything. I call Lydia and Maggie to tell them our joyous news. They are happy to hear it, and Maggie says she will tell Jesus.

It's probably my imagination, but as we eat and shop and make phone calls, it seems to me that the two babies are more active. Maybe because it has been confirmed that they are twins, I am more aware of their constant movement, as if they are busy packing and getting ready to be born. It is amazing to me how much they can wiggle in such a confined space.

Cliff flew back to Edmonton this morning, but not until I made him promise to answer his phone the next time I call. He didn't really want to go, but it can't be helped, and I plan to keep myself busy making sure everything is ready for the big day.

I spend the morning checking my bag for the hospital, washing the new baby clothes, putting the diapers and clothes in the cupboard and the drawers, and making notes of anything else we need. I eventually take a break and sit down with my journal, but before I write a single word, I am surprised by an overwhelming desire to call my mom. Instead, I call Lydia and ask her what she thinks I should do. She encourages me, but advises me not to get my hopes up or to upset myself if I can avoid it.

I call Mom's house and let the phone ring and ring. She doesn't have an answering machine, so I can't leave a message. I tell myself she might be outside. When she finally picks up, her voice is rough and gravelly. Too many cigarettes and too much yelling. I chat for a minute, and then let her know I am having twins. The line is silent, in the way that only a landline can be. Mom says nothing. I wait and wait. Finally, I hear her voice, soft, something I haven't heard for a very long time.

"I always wanted twins, Harley. Congratulations."

At that moment, something hard inside of me melts.

"How's you been feeling? Were you sick? When's yer due date again?"

My world rocks slightly as she peppers me with a myriad of questions in a soft, quiet, unfamiliar voice.

"Do you need any help? Can I do anything for yous?"

We chat for a few more minutes, and then I tell her I will call her later. I check to make sure she has my phone number. As we hang up, I hear unexpected words. So quick, I almost miss them.

"Love ya."

Well, Grandma, you just made my day.

I sit staring at the phone for what seems like ages. I remember the last time I saw her, when I put my foot in the door to keep it open. Wonders will never cease. I look through the living room window, watching the rain come down, and think about my mom. They are understanding thoughts.

A few hours later, Mom calls me back to say that she would like to come to Winnipeg for a visit. She is going to Stony Mountain to visit Dad and will stop in to see me, if it is okay. I'm not sure it is okay, but my life is changing, and maybe this is one of the changes that will come to me, not from me. Mom didn't change for my sisters or brothers when they had babies, but she is older, and alone, and alienated from much of her family. She also doesn't have Dad's influence in her life right now, and she sounds lonely. And different.

With many mixed feelings, I suggest we get together for lunch, since she will be in the city anyway. I sense she is hoping for something more, a sleepover perhaps, but in no way am I ready for that. Baby steps. I can't bring myself to forgive her, and my foot must remain firmly in the door. Ready to enter or ready to make a quick getaway. With every part of my common sense, I resist trusting my mother, resist believing that she has my best interests at heart. My preferred option is for Cletus and his brother or sister to grow up without knowing my family, but I'm not sure that should be my decision. Then I remember many nights with my nieces and nephews, huddled under blankets, waiting for the storm to pass.

Chapter 34

Viola

I like watching TV in the afternoon. I like all them ladies that have problems and need them fixed. I like what Dr. Phil says, we do the best we can with the information we have at the time. Not true for me. I know a lot of stuff that I don't pay attention to. And I don't usually make decisions anyways. There is always someone else to make them, and I just go along for the ride.

Harley is expecting her first baby, although she called yesterday to say she was having twins, so I guess that would be babies. Lucky her. I always wanted twins. It ain't like I needed them coming two at a time, but still, two at once would have been pretty neat. I might have been famous, if all mine had been twins. That would have been thirty-eight kids or thereabouts. There sure wouldn't have been room for that many. Not sure what Aaron would have said about so many, but he wouldn't have stopped what caused them either.

Aaron is away and has been for a long time. He got into a pinch of trouble while selling drugs with Lionel. I didn't like it much, but I did like the extra money it brought in. And as I told myself, people is going to buy them somewhere, so might as well be from us, making sure the stuff is good and all. No bad drugs from us, is what Aaron said. Well, he's away for awhile yet, so someone else is selling in his place. No shortage of people wanting to make a quick dollar. Mainly, it was Lionel though. He got Aaron involved, and well, once there was the cash around, it was just hard to stop. It felt good to have the money and not to have to fight with him for it. There was lots to go around for everyone. He hardly thought about it being against the law, just helping out friends in need.

It's quiet with Aaron away, and I guess I miss him, but I do like the quiet, although sometimes it's a bit too quiet, even for me. I never did make many friends, what with all the kids and their troubles, and Aaron didn't like no other women around anyways. He just liked me all to hisself, and he'd get mean if others came around. He didn't get mean once he was dealing though. At least not too much, but his habit was hard to break, and besides, he still feels bad about never getting work.

None of the kids come here too much. They is all busy living their own lives, like grown-up kids is supposed to. I'd like to see my grandbabies though. I used to, but not so much now. Everyone is so busy. A few is away, but mainly they just stay clear. Busy, busy, busy, they say. I know how it is, for sure. I was always busy too. Too busy to go home, that's for sure, so I understand why they stay away. Not away like Aaron and Lionel, just away from me.

I wish I had kept up relations with my brothers and sisters, but we all moved on when we was young, too young, really, to fend for ourselves. We wanted out, with Dad pounding on Mom all the time and sneaking into our rooms late or when Mom was out, and he didn't care if we was boys or girls, he loved us all. I couldn't wait to get away, anywhere, the same as the rest of us.

I had twin sisters, Emma and Alva. They was younger than me and cute as bugs. Shiny little faces with big, wide grins, spaces between their two front teeth. They was always dirty, digging in the mud, climbing trees, chasing each other, bare feet dusty and calloused. They didn't need to talk either. They had a way of getting their point across to the other one without even saying one word. It was a bit spooky, but that was just the way they was. Emma was bigger and smarter too, and Alva just loved her sister to bits. They was always together, curled up watching the television or in the tub, playing with margarine tubs and dish-soap bubbles. Once they was clean, outside they went again, the neighbour dogs following them for fun or scraps if the twins could get them. In the summer, they got all tanned, and it was hard to tell if they was tanned or dirty, so on Saturday Mom would wash them anyways. Just to be sure. They had some dolls that the Goodwill had given to us, and Emma would try to dress them the same, the way twins was supposed to, she said. We didn't have the financial resources to buy the girls matching clothes, and I think they resented Mom and Dad for that. Mom especially. Dad, they was just afraid of. There was just no use in resenting Dad, in case he got wind of it. Mom would just say to them, "Yous guys will know how hard it is once you have kids of your own."

Neither of those shiny little stars of girls gotta have kids of their own. When Emma was fourteen, she got pregnant by Dad, then she killed herself by hanging herself up on the pipes in the laundry room. We was all really sad, and then Alva couldn't live without her sister, and she did the same thing just a bit later. I still think about those big smiles they had, and how much I loved them. But I had other brothers and sisters, and they didn't hang themselves; they just moved away, and I don't know where they is. Sometimes if I get a chance, I look in phone books for our last name to see if I can find them, but I don't get a chance to do that very often, and so far, I haven't found any of them. I still get broke up when I think about my little sisters and how they was just too young to even have a chance.

There was one bar in our town, and about as soon as us kids could reach the counter, if we had money in our hands, we got served. I never had much money, but when I did, I hung out there, and anyways, there was usually someone who would buy me a drink. After it closed, me an' my friends would get up to the highway to the Husky for a bite to eat if we had money left over. It was open late, all hours, for the truckers passing through. The best was the roast beef on white bread with canned gravy and canned peas, mashed potatoes, and a cute little cup of cabbage salad. Coffee, too. Come with it, and we didn't have to pay more for refills.

Aaron was from the same town and a few years older than me. If he saw me in the bar, he would come over and buy me a drink, and we got pretty friendly. He had a bike, a big motorcycle that he loved. I was done with school, and in the daytime, I would sit around with him, drinking coffee and watching him polish his bike or fidget with motor bits. He would take me for rides. He only had one helmet, and we was supposed to wear them because of the law, but he would put it on my head and swear he would keep me safe. It wobbled a bit because it was way too big, but it smelled like his sweat, and I found it sexy to wear it. Dad didn't like Aaron much, but Dad didn't want anyone coming around his kids. For Aaron, the feeling was mutual. He knew about Dad and didn't want him coming around me.

We two got pretty comfortable together, and the next thing I knew, I was expecting a baby. I knew it was Aaron's baby, and I was pretty happy about it. I think that eventually Aaron got there too. We moved in together at his place, but it was just a single room he rented from his cousin. There wasn't much in the way of work in our town, but Aaron got pogey each month. Dad wasn't happy about what was going on, so Aaron and me left on the bike in the dark, early in the morning and headed to Brandon. He needed work, and I needed to get away, away from Dad. I didn't trust Mom not to tell Dad where we was going.

I'm no Dr. Phil, but sometimes I think that I took up with Aaron just so I could get away from home, from Dad. I wonder what I woulda been if my family had been normal like. I like babies, and maybe I coulda had one of them daycares where you take care of other lady's babies or been a teacher, but I never liked school much. Our family had a secret, and it's only a short step from keeping a secret to telling a lie, and once that starts there is nowheres for it to stop. Everyone tells you not to lie, but nobody teaches you how to stop if you do. Besides, if you lie, you can be anyone you want. That can be better than who you really is, even if it ain't real.

Brandon is a pretty rough town, and it's hard to make friends there. At least it was for me. I wasn't drinking too much because of the baby, but Aaron said this was his time to have some fun, that when the baby came, he would have to be responsible for the rest of his life. He tried to get some work, and I cashed at the convenience store nights. There wasn't much money, but there was always enough for a drink or two. Aaron kept trying to get some work, I know he did, but everyone kept saying he needed to go back to school. He quit after grade eight, and I thought he was ashamed of that. It made sense at the time. His Mom and Dad didn't care too much either way, and he just gave it up. He thought about going back and finishing his high school, but he said it was too long since, and he would have to start over. How far back should he go to get started over, he would ask me, laughing, "Kinnergarden?" He had a point, I guess, but I didn't argue with him. He was sad and angry and frustrated, and a few drinks would turn him in on himself. After a while, he started blaming me, saying that I got pregnant and that was keeping him from his dreams. He took a swipe or two at me, but I think he was scared of hurting the little one.

He was a stud in those days. He was tall and strong, his skin was pale and clear, his hair was shiny and dark. He smoked rollies mainly, although sometimes when he was flush from his pogey or my payday, he would buy pre-mades in a bag down at the reserve and share them with me. He was always at me, even when the baby was in me, and I think that is why we ended up with so many kids. He was bored too because of no work, so he used me to fill the time. When the first baby was born, he was up at the bar with some friends he had made there, and I couldn't get in touch with him. Off I went in a cab. I was a natural, the doctor said, the baby sliding out, not real big but pretty healthy. The doctor said baby would have been bigger except for the smoking, which I already knew. Gal's gotta have some fun, right?

I remember looking down at that little girl and thinking how she was the most beautiful thing in the world. Imagine, Aaron and I made that little thing. My life changed after that, getting pregnant, having a baby, and then it would start over again. I wasn't too pretty no more neither. I ate too much, and anyways, I was always pregnant and ugly, but Aaron didn't care if I was. Then he turned mean, and I think it was because he couldn't never get a job. We was always out of money for food and diapers, and I would have to ask him for it. He would get all pissy because he wanted the money for going out with his buddies, then we would get into it. He was mean alright, and our battles became our way of life. The kids, whichever was around, would go to the bedrooms in the back of the house. Out of sight, out of mind, they hoped, and for the most part that was true.

I felt worn down by life. I had too many kids, not enough food, no one around to care for me, and a history that couldn't be shared. It wasn't like now, when everyone gets on television and talks about their stories. Back then, it was a secret to be kept in the family, no sharing that dirty laundry. I had a bad-ass biker for my baby-daddy, although Aaron sold his bike one time. He said he was gonna buy a bigger one, but course he dinnent. If Aaron was mean, well so was I. I wasn't taking shit from anyone, especially them little kids, and, just like me in the old days, they couldn't wait to get away. They would come back now and then, leaving kids or sleeping on sofas, needing a place to stay for a bit. Sometimes, if they was in a bad way or up at the pen, the kids stayed around for longer. And now, I hardly see them.

So, Harley has been back a few times since she left right after high school. She was touch and go, that one, whether she would get her leaving, but in the end she did. Not all of them did, but mostly they did. The first time she came, she was so full of herself that I sent her packing. Aaron was in the hall behind me, and he was mean and spoiling for a fight, and I didn't want Harley to see him in that way again. The second time she came, I was alone, and Aaron was away, and I was surprised to see her. I thought she was doing pretty good, but then she got all self-important about going to the university, and it just made me mad. I never had a chance to do that, and maybe I couldn't have, but maybe I could have, too. Anyways, she left, and it wasn't the worst visit ever. She called me few months back to let me know she was expecting. She ain't working neither, just writing away at books, like she always did when she was little. Back then, I used to snoop in her folder she kept under her blankets and read her stories. She was pretty good, that one. A real gift for making up stuff and writing it down. I never told her that, so she wouldn't get all uppity. She ain't married, and she's with some guy named Cliff, a travelling musician or something. Heh heh. The apple don't fall far from the tree, do it?

Anyways, she called me last night to let me know she is having twins. I kinda liked that she called to share her news. Things is pretty quiet around here, and it was good to hear her voice. It is days between times the phone rings, and when it does, it always gives me a start. I never expect it to ring. Harley sounds happy, and that ain't a sound I hear too much. I'm going up to Stony Mountain to visit with Aaron, and thought maybe I would go to see her in Winnipeg afterward. I was pretty scared to ask her, in case she said no. I'm feeling lonely like and don't know how I would feel if she just turned me away. I was hoping for an invitation to stay over, but she said lunch, and I'll have to be content with that. I usually just go along with the plan. She's a good kid, and really, she's the only one that ain't in big trouble of some sort. Except that she got herself knocked up. With twins. Heh heh.

Chapter 35

Maggie

This summer has been pretty busy with visitors coming and going. The kids were here for a week with the grandchildren, and I got my fix of their bright little faces. I missed them as soon as they left. Spring was busy as well but mostly because of work. I was doing a lot of travelling around Manitoba, teaching courses to farm boys and girls.

Speaking of girls, Lydia and Harley are both due soon, and what a surprise that Harley and Cliff are having twins. If reading about child-rearing makes good parents, then those two will be at the top of the heap. They are so informed. Harley calls me with updates and questions, although from her reading she knows so much about the babies that I don't have much to offer her. Perhaps because I am a herd reproduction specialist, she thinks I have advice for her. That's my own little joke, and I laugh at it every time.

I am now Maggie to a wide circle of people. Sometimes, in my quietest moments, I think of Margaret, living in her beige world, not fearful, but always so careful. Did that come from being the only girl in a family of boys, the sole sister to carry the mantle of all that is proper and feminine? I won't ever know, but I have broken the ties that bind. Maggie doesn't exactly rock boats, of course. That isn't my way, but like my new décor at home, not everything has to be a perfect match. I am cautious by nature, and I test any new waters carefully.

Perfect matches. I don't think Jesus and I are like that. He has become a dear friend, but I doubt it will go any further. There isn't that spark, that contrast, that attraction, those things that make for something other than friends. We spend a lot of time together though, and it helps to have a friend my own age. I am quiet, a listener, and Jesus is loud, a raconteur, and it amuses me to hear our mundane, normal activities embellished with his imagination. Sometimes he steps over the line, adding things that didn't happen. When I asked him about that once, he answered in a way that made perfect sense. He said that everything he says did happen, but when he is telling a story, if he remembers something that happened some other time, he adds it in. The dishonesty is in the timing, not in the happening. It is a small thing though, and they are his stories, not mine, to tell as he sees fit.

Last year, after Thanksgiving, I realized that I had a life with which I am content. I have my children and my grandchildren, and although I don't see them too much, we talk a lot. I have fun shopping for them, and I send them notes in the mail. I am Grammy, and that name feels warm and comfortable. My daughters send me drawings and stories made by the children, and these I proudly display on the fridge. There is no better place for the creations of kids. My mom used to do the same.

Mom. She is failing now. Her physical health is still okay, but she has succumbed to the ravages of Alzheimer's disease, which has created a tremendous sadness in me. I am unable to connect the small, bent, papery lady I visit at the personal care home to the lively powerhouse who ran the farm, the family, and the finances. There was more common sense in her little finger than there is in most people I have known in my life, and she provided her very best advice to everyone about whom she cared. She didn't ask you to take it, though. She always prefaced her thoughts with, "You might consider…," and over time, we knew the words that followed were likely to be the best advice we were ever going to get. Mom was so smart and so busy that she didn't have time to follow up on whether we took her advice. If we didn't and things went badly, she would look at us and raise one eyebrow. She never said, "I told you so," and she never raised a hand or her voice to any of us. That eyebrow said it all for her. When we were little kids and our play became too rowdy or we were too noisy when guests were over, that eyebrow was enough to quiet us down. So much power in that little muscle over her left eye.

When John first got sick, she cared for me, and while I was still hopeful he would recover, Mom was hopeful alongside me, never letting me waver in my faith that he would beat the cancer. I felt her strength; I leaned on it; I learned from it; but in the end, it wasn't enough. When there was no hope, when the disease had taken hold and I had to accept his inevitable death, Mom was with me the whole time, absorbing my sorrow like a sponge so there was never so much that I couldn't bear it. Then he died, and my sadness overflowed, filling every room, every relationship, every thought. At that time, Mom let me collapse completely, helping me as I immersed myself in my loss. She cooked and cleaned and shopped and listened. She really, really listened, and she didn't offer advice. I don't know how I could have made it through that terrible time without her. Knowing that she was near was like a big hug, tightly wrapped around me, holding me together.

I remember the first time I noticed something odd with her. It wasn't long after John had passed away. We had gone to the mall to pick up a few things and then have lunch. Mom wanted to go to Walmart and I had to go to the drugstore, so we agreed to meet in fifteen minutes at the food court. I arrived there before her, bought a coffee, and sat and waited. When I saw her coming, I thought her step seemed slower than usual, a bit uncertain. She stopped at the entrance to the table area, and the look on her face was complete bewilderment. She didn't seem to know where she was or why she was there. I went over to her, and called her name. "Hey, Mom. Did you get what you needed?" She looked at me, suspiciously at first, and then her face brightened, and she looked at the parcel in her hand. "Yes, dear." Shock ran through my body, that awful moment when I recognized that Mom wasn't infallible, that something could be wrong with her too. I said nothing to her, and I wasn't sure if she was even aware that she had been disoriented.

After that day, there were increasing moments when she forgot details or thought she was living in a past time of her life or was out of touch with the passage of time. Over time, our roles slowly reversed. Long, supportive conversations, the sharing that women do, became a thing of the past. I don't know if she was aware that her conversation or her memories were no longer appropriate, out of touch with what was going on around her, or if she simply couldn't remember enough details, events, or people to contribute much at all. Mom shut down, and rarely did our talks touch on anything deeper than the weather or things immediate to her life. She stopped asking about my life, and I stopped burdening her with my grief.

When my brothers went to Winnipeg for business or shopping, they would bring Mom with them and drop her off at my apartment for a visit. During those visits, I could tell she was getting worse, more forgetful, but I had no idea how bad her illness had become. There came that terrible time when it was clear she was no longer able to care for herself. My brothers had been talking about her being dangerous to herself and those around her, but I thought they were exaggerating. They told me to go to the farmhouse, to see for myself. I hadn't been to the farm for awhile, and as I drove toward it, I thought about how insistent she was that she stay in the family home alone after Dad passed away all those years ago.

"This is our home," she told us. "And it will stay that way for as long as I live."

Although I'm sure she was lonely from time to time, Mom was also proud and independent. And she was steadfast in her determination to not only keep the house as clean and tidy as it had always been, but also to keep alive the memory of all who had lived there. I have to admit that I was a little bit afraid to go there that day, afraid of what I might find.

When I entered the front door of the house, I was struck by the smell of old people, old furniture, old carpets, and old clothing. Mom was sitting on the living room sofa, the lights off, staring out the window. When she turned toward me, I could see that her hair, normally a ball of grey fluff, was stuck down on her head, the front combed but the back forgotten. Normally, she was well groomed, but that day, her clothing was dirty and unmatched, and nothing about her looked fresh and clean. She had lost weight, and she looked small and frail, her skin the white translucent skin of the very elderly. Or the very sick. Looking around the living room, it felt like the bloom was off the rose. Nothing looked cared for, cleaned, or loved. Not the house, not Mom. I went into the kitchen to make coffee. The dishes had been washed by hand and placed on a plastic rack to dry, but most of them were still dirty. Mom was also clearly forgetting things on the stove, and her pots were burned thickly black on the bottom. The scariest thing, however, was the smoke detector lying on the counter, the battery removed. I felt a sick, twisting feeling in my stomach as I realized that it was only a matter of time until Mom set fire to her house. I understood what my brothers were saying, and that it was time for a permanent change.

In some ways, what was even worse was that she was still driving. On my way into the house, I saw her car in the driveway. The fenders were covered in scrapes, the front bumper hanging down on one side. When I asked her what had happened, she didn't know. Maybe she did, maybe she didn't. Maybe she didn't want to lose her licence, her independence. Maybe she would lie to me to keep her independence. Anybody would, I thought. Whether she was telling the truth or not was irrelevant. She shouldn't be driving any more.

I never wanted to make my mother cry, to break her heart, and I never thought I would. I never thought I could. But when I talked with her about a move to a nursing home, she cried out like a small child. Just one word, "No." Her tears, tears I had never seen in my life, emptied down her face. I wanted to do the right thing for her. I wanted her to be with me, so I could care for her in her final years as she had cared for me in my initial years and, most recently, when I had needed her more than ever. But I knew I couldn't leave her alone in my home while I worked any more than I could have left a small child alone, any more than I could leave that day without doing something. I called my brothers, and together we tried to come up with a different solution, but there was no other solution. Mom needed fulltime care, a home with resources that would keep her safe.

She is so frequently disoriented now that she often doesn't remember me at all, but her face lights up in delight when I walk into her room. Although she doesn't know who I am, I tell myself she knows I am someone she loves. We talk quietly for a few minutes, and I stroke her hand or brush her hair, then she falls asleep in her chair, my tiny and white Mom. She doesn't remember my visits from day to day, and she tells me that no one ever visits her. She isn't happy where she is. She wants her old life back.

Through all of this, Lydia and Harley and Jesus have been with me. They all helped move Mom to the personal care home and get her settled, and they sometimes stop in to visit her if they are in the west end of the city. It doesn't require a lot of time to visit with the elderly, but it makes Mom so happy, and I am grateful that they care enough for me to do this. Each of my friends, in their own way, have helped me through this grieving process of slowly losing my mother, providing support and counsel, and accepting her for all her graces in her dotage.

Chapter 36

Harley

Mom is coming into town today, and I don't know how it is going to work out. When she called me back and asked if she could visit me in Winnipeg, I meant to say no, but yes came out. I meant to say some other time, but let's go for lunch came out. Perhaps it is because I am pregnant that I am more forgiving to my mother, worried that I too will make mistakes, that I also won't be the mother my babies need me to be.

Cliff is home and doesn't plan to be away again until after the babies are born. Once they are born, I don't think I will let him leave. I have gone from being super excited to nervous to terrified about being a mother, but it's too late to stop the show now. Help, let me off this train. It keeps speeding up, and there are no stops scheduled between now and motherhood. I've changed my mind. How about next year? Nope. You are on this train until it reaches the station. I don't think I am ready for this. No one is. I can't do it. You will do it. Cliff senses my nervousness and is doing whatever he can to calm me. He sings songs that I love, brings me drinks, rubs my back and my feet, and makes me my favourite dinners. Makes me annoyed.

What is wrong with me? All I want to do is lash out, make this birth go away, or make the birth happen now. I am tired of waiting. I am big and awkward and overtired, hormonal, and bored and terrified, and hot and sweaty. I can't concentrate on anything. My clothes are too small, tops riding up, bottoms riding down, and everything is faded and ugly, washed too many times. I remember the first time I bought something maternity, a loose, flowy long blouse, boho and cool, that I couldn't wait to wear. Now I hate it. I actually hate it. It doesn't fit, and when it did, it made me look like a grandma. I dream sometimes of wearing the clothing in my closet, my neat, dark clothing with clean, sharp lines, silver trim, silhouette slim. I don't even wear jewellery anymore. I can't be bothered. I had a pair of maternity jeans, but my belly is so big that they roll down, resting uncomfortably on top of my underwear, which has done the same thing. Two rolls of fabric nestled at the bottom of my belly. If I pull them up over my tummy, they are tight and make me itchy. My boobs are bigger too, but not beautiful big. Big and pale with blue veins. I hate them. They rest like total strangers on the top of my belly. Not huge, but not mine. I could set a whole dinner placement on top of all that extra mess. People I don't know touch my stomach. I want to scream at them. I am not public property, and I am not happy right now. Keep your hands to yourself. What? One's a boy, not sure about the other one. Next week, if the dates are right. My first. And second. Ha ha. Some names picked out, but we aren't saying yet. First few months were rough, mainly sick in the mornings, and I am pretty tired now. No, no help, only Cliff and me. Pretty ready, as ready as a person can be. Just found out it was twins. A shock. On and on, same questions from well meaning, caring people. Always the same answers from me. Why, why, why am I so bitchy?

I stand in front of my closet, trying to decide what to wear to lunch. I feel tense, my emotions close to the surface, and I realize I would rather go to bed and sleep or watch television. I don't know if I can handle lunch with Mom. I'm not actually all that hungry, and I don't know if I even want to eat. I finally choose a pink cotton top and some leggings and sandals. I put on lipstick and a pair of earrings. I feel the waistband of the leggings roll down. My boobs are bulging out over the neckline of my top, and I put on a scarf to tone things down, to hide those big girls.

I check my purse to make sure I have my wallet. Mom isn't likely to offer to buy lunch, I think resentfully.

"Where are you meeting her," Cliff asks as he comes into the room.

"The Olive Branch. Mom wants to do some shopping at Polo Park after lunch, so I picked a restaurant close to the mall."

Cliff bursts out laughing, and it takes me a second to understand why. The irony of the name of the restaurant. I laugh right along with him, and the act of laughing cheers me up, giving me the will to make this lunch a success.

I park in a Moms-2-B stall and am grateful for the fewer steps. The weight of the babies on my bladder makes me feel heavy and stiff and awkward. My swollen feet are thankful for the sandal weather. I enter the restaurant. Compared to the brightness of the summer sky of Winnipeg, it is dim, and it takes a few moments for my eyes to adjust. Slowly, silhouettes come into focus. A hostess offers to seat me, and I say I am meeting someone there for lunch, a single lady.

"Viola?" she asks.

I nod, and follow her through the restaurant.

I see Mom sitting in a booth by the window, a coffee in front of her. She has been there for a while, waiting. I can tell she has made an effort to be on time. I suddenly have a thought that Cliff should have come, that it would have been a good thing for him to meet her, but the thought leaves almost as soon as it enters my head. It would not have been a good idea. Mom and I have some trust to build before I can dare share her with anyone else. I put my purse on the seat of the booth and try to sit, but my pregnant tummy is too big. I won't fit unless I sit sideways, which means that either I will have to eat my lunch twisted around, or we will have to move. I want to say something to Mom, but hesitate, expecting the worst. You shouldn't be a baby. Why are you making such a fuss? You're not the first person to have a baby, you know. But she surprises me, peeks over to see how tight the squeeze is and speaks first.

"Why don't we move to a table?"

As I sit more comfortably at the table, she goes outside for a cigarette. While she is gone, I look at the menu while the babies twist and turn, fighting inside of me for space. When she returns, I can smell the tobacco on her, old and stale and dirty, but strangely comforting, a smell from my childhood, the smell of my mom. She reapplies her lipstick, a bright coral colour that is too bright. Her face seems washed out, overpowered by the orangey slash on her lips. The smell of the lipstick is as familiar as the tobacco. My sense of smell is heightened by my pregnancy.

We catch up on old news while we wait for our food. We are both on our best behaviour. I know that if this lunch ends badly, there won't be an opportunity to make amends for a long time, perhaps ever.

I ask her how Dad was when she saw him in Stony.

"He looks good, but he's lost some weight, and he's smoking too much. He's been good in the pen, and he hopes to get out early. Not Lionel. He's had some trouble there, in with the worst of the bad. Dad's trying to stay out of it all, but it's hard, you know. Lionel's his son after all."

I nod, amazed that this is the reality of my mother's life, the reality of mine as well.

Mom is cheerful and starts asking lots of questions. The same questions strangers ask, but it doesn't feel like she is invading my privacy. I answer her without any hesitation, wanting to open myself up to my mother, this stranger who isn't one. The smart person, the one in my head, tells me not to trust her, that she will let me down again, but my heart wants and needs my mom at this time in my life. We have a lot of catching up to do, and as we eat and afterward, over coffee, I share the details of my life during the last few years. Mom is interested and doesn't make the conversation about her. I can tell she is very lonely, and I sense her surprise that she is so alone. I know her life didn't work out the way she wanted it to, the way she dreamed it would. I am filled with sadness for her, but my smart person is telling me that Mom is not my project, that I don't have enough of anything to make her life what she wants it to be, that there isn't enough of anything anywhere in the world to make her life what she dreamed it would be.

As I talk, as Mom asks me questions, questions about me, it occurs to me that I know nothing at all about her, about the person she is, about her likes, her dislikes, about how she feels about politics, or whether she likes to read books, or what her favourite colour might be. I only know her as my mother, the failed nurturer, the hard-drinking sparring partner for my father, the selfish attention-seeking mother who did not deliver. I only see her as the result of how I have reflected off her, and I think back to my brothers and sisters and my dad as we were growing up. I don't recall any conversations that any of us had with Mom. I suck in my breath to keep this realization inside me, to hold back my recognition of how completely and fantastically isolated she must have been all those years. My attention is drawn briefly to the squirming little lives inside me. What if, what if, what if, they ignored me, left me alone, like Mom had been left alone? Of course, back then we were children, and we didn't have the responsibility to make her happy. That was up to Dad, and he did a piss-poor job of it. Slowly, the tables are turning, and as we talk, I begin to ask her questions.

"Did you have pets growing up?" I ask her, not knowing how to begin. It seemed like the wrong question, but also a safe one.

"When I was little, I had a beagle named Bugle, and one day Bugle was hit by a car in front of our house. The driver of the car was a man. Bugle wasn't hurt or killed, but forever after he hated men, and would bark and bay in circles around them if they came too near the house. I wanted a dog for you kids, but Dad wouldn't hear of yet another mouth to feed. So, I made do with little budgies instead. I love their bright colours and friendly ways and how they try to talk to me."

They did try to talk to her. We didn't.

"What kind of music do you like?" Another safe question. How do I not already know this?

"I don't like country and western music."

That's a surprise. All we ever heard on the radio at home, day in and day out, was country and western music, except when the Wheat Kings had a home game.

"My favourite band is Metallica."

Say what? I laugh out loud when she says that. She looks a bit hurt when I laugh, but then she smiles over the top of the hurt, and I think she is just so glad to be talking that she ends up laughing with me. I ask her to tell me about her brothers and sisters.

"I had twin sisters once, but they killed themselves when they were in their teens."

A lump forms in my throat, but I swallow it.

"I would like to have had twins."

I feel a mixture of guilt and joy.

"Dad was so handsome when he was young. I always liked tall men."

On and on and on we talk, me asking her questions, Mom answering. Sometimes, I think her conversational ducks don't line up properly, that she is leaving out bits or adding in things, making her life sound bigger or better that it ever could have been, larger and more successful than I know it has been. I don't call her on it though. I don't want to take anything away from the here and the now.

As we talk, she seems to grow bigger and brighter and prettier and younger, to sit up taller, her defensive posture and facial expressions completely dissipating. Her lipstick, overpowering an hour ago, now compliments her skin and makes her look alive and engaged. I imagine how pretty she must have been as a young girl, how Dad could have fallen in love with her. With barely one hour of me caring about her, asking about her, letting her know she matters through the gift of my complete attention, she has come to life, like wilted flowers finally placed in a jar of water. Sandblasted by the reality of the neglect she has endured all her life. I feel raw and ashamed.

When it is time to go, I happily pay the bill. Mom is out for a smoke when the server comes for the last time, and Mom is not even given the opportunity to offer to pay. But that is more than okay with me, and I smile deep inside. I walk her to her car, a grey-pink-brown Impala she's had for ages, never classy in its time, never owned at its best. She drives away, a cigarette between the fingers of her left hand as it hangs out the open window, rock music blasting on her radio.

Lunch has been a success. A truly huge, incredibly massive, unbelievably gargantuan success. Write that down, Harley, I say to myself as I stand in the parking lot watching her taillights brighten at the distant intersection. Then I feel warm fluid gush down my legs as my water breaks.

"I like the Liberal Party. My favourite colour is violet. That's a kind of purple, you know."

Yes, Mom, I know.

Chapter 37

Lydia

It came as no surprise to me that Ian and I went from pretend friends to lovers to living together again in a heartbeat. I made promises to myself to take it slow, to give myself a chance to say no, but instead we went fast, and I said yes. I like to think that is the way of true love. If I am honest with myself, I knew the moment I saw him sitting in the booth at The Star Grill that we would find a way to be back together.

Ian and I dated before we became lovers again. Two whole dates. One drink at The Star Grill, then lunch the next day. That was it. So much for resolve and taking it slow. I put Ian back on like an old pair of yoga pants, a perfect fit, worn a bit thin, but easy-peasy. As we left the restaurant after lunch, he grabbed my hand and pulled me toward him. Then he leaned over the baby bump to kiss me on my lips, not on my cheek. It reminded me of the first time we kissed, the cold and frosty one, and the excitement and strangeness of his foreign man-lips on mine. I compared that kiss, special in its own right, to the one on the sidewalk outside the restaurant, and decided to take the second one every time. It was the kiss of two people in love, accepting that our lives were changing yet again.

The biggest hurdle we have to overcome is the previous discussion about the baby, about abortion, about taking the easy way out. I've never been the kind of person to take the easy way out in life. I want to do all the hard work, take all the chances, grab the brass ring. That is why I told him right before he left me that I wanted our baby, our child, and whether he was around or not, I wanted to be a mother. He says now that he is ready to be a dad again, that he's had a long time to think about it, and he knows what he wants. He says all that talk of abortion was a reaction against his situation at the time, and he is so very thankful that I didn't end the life of our little girl. I want to believe him, and I think I'm starting to. Yes, he has taken the easy way out twice—his affair with Eliza to fill his needs and insecurities instead of working them all out with me, and his suggestion that I have an abortion—but that is all in the past. I think he is fully committed to this relationship as both a partner and a father.

Whenever I talk with Harley about all this, she always says to look forward, not backward, to work for what I want and not to wallow in the past.

"Don't look at those footprints in the sand behind you, filling with water, disappearing. If you do, you will spend a long time looking for them, and as you look, you will continue making footprints, going backwards or in circles. You might as well walk in the direction you want to go."

Clever girl, that one.

Sometimes I sense I am being judged for resuming our relationship, not by Harley or Maggie, but by others, people who only see the outside. They see what happened and then assess us, judge us, weigh our options, and decide for us, but they don't know the why or the how of what happened. They don't know what I have learned or how Ian has changed. They don't know what Ian has learned or how I have changed. They evaluate us on their own criteria, based on their own biases and life experiences, those experiences full of their achievements and failures. They don't know me; they don't know Ian; and they don't know what each of us really wants. Deep down, you know?

It was strange that first evening when Ian was back at the house after he moved in all his clothes and other stuff. We did all the things we had done before, but our actions felt weirdly unfamiliar, like we were rehearsing a play, like our moves were fabricated, like we were trying too hard to be normal. Try-too-hard Lydia and Ian. Normal day-to-day activities, like filling the dishwasher, emptying the dishwasher, and refilling the dishwasher, felt like roles in a script. Instead of the clumsy dance of our initial early days together, these were prepared actions, with each of us aware of the other's role, watching to see if there was a slip-up, if one of us had forgotten our lines. I suppose that was what had to happen, and fortunately the strangeness didn't last long. Brayden is back too, and Captain and Tennille are happy to have their little buddy to play with again. So am I. I missed him more than I ever thought I would.

It sometimes seems that Love Eliza never happened, that there was just an interlude where we were both away, where we weren't together, that was never meant to be permanent. I try to figure out if I meant for him to be gone from my life forever or if I secretly hoped we would reunite, but I am not that introspective. I can't tell. Ian says he knew we would get back together again, and that he never gave up on us. Us. But I struggle with that because he did give up on me to be with Eliza, didn't he?

Although normal has fallen back into place much as before and with little fanfare, there is lots of work to do to make sure we don't fall back into the sameness of our past relationship, the sameness that didn't work. We didn't communicate properly, and we are ensuring that we keep talking now and that there are no secrets. It is hard because Ian continues to travel to and from the oilfield, and I have my own scheduling issues at the hospital. Still, hard doesn't mean impossible, and we are both willing, wanting, and desperate to do what we need to do, to be our best for each other. We make the time for each other.

As I watch Ian with Brayden and feel his love for me and our little baby, I am shocked that we almost didn't make it. We were both so stupid, so stubborn, and weakened by pride that we couldn't muster the strength to care enough to make it better. Somewhere along that continuum either of us could have been honest and said we needed more, we wanted more, and we loved the other too much to be apart. I am certain that what happened with Eliza and our inability to work through it at the time did not have to happen. We let it happen. We won't let it happen again.

Two weeks after Ian and Brayden moved back home, Harley had her babies, a little boy and a little girl. A millionaire's family all at one time. They are doing really well, and all three are home from the hospital. Cliff is beside himself with pride and happiness. I worry he will drop one of them out of sheer excitement, but Harley has a watchful eye. When we went to see them in the Health Sciences Centre, I was in awe at the sight of those tiny, perfect babies. And as I held them, one at a time and then together, I secretly compared them to the size of my pregnant tummy, and I thought perhaps there wasn't room in me for even one of those babies. I thought wrong.

I am finally done work and am taking a full year off from the hospital to be a mom. Ian left yesterday morning for Virden to meet with a client and will be home later this afternoon. He was reluctant to leave and reassures me that if I go into labour, he is only a three-hour drive away. After taking the opportunity to sleep in, I have been lazing around all morning—reading magazines, listening to music, and drinking chamomile tea. I've already been into the spare bedroom, which is the nursery now, ten times this morning, fussing with crib pads and baby hangers, but mainly enjoying being ready to bring our baby home. I feel so happy and ready. I am so, so ready.

I sit on the sofa to read a magazine, but I have a hard time focusing. I keep looking around the house and seeing things that need to be done. I start in the kitchen, taking dishes out of cupboards, wiping them out, reordering them. I take everything out of the fridge, washing the crusty cap of the ketchup bottle, wiping out the ring of soya sauce in the door, making sure everything is perfect and clean. I work in the bathrooms too, cleaning cupboards and wiping floors. It is a tight squeeze to get behind the toilet because there isn't much room back there, but I am determined to get it clean. While Captain doesn't shed, the carpet in the hall is covered with hair from Tennille, and my old vacuum won't pick it up. I take a hairbrush and get on my hands and knees, brushing the nap, making sure to get along the wall. It is a bigger job than I expect, but I stay at it until it is perfect. I have finalized my nest, and it is time for the baby to come.

I stand, hot and sweaty, and a bit dizzy from being on my hands and knees so long. And, as I bend to pick up the pile of hair I have gathered, my water breaks. Such a strange sensation, like peeing, only with no control. I wryly note that the warm liquid running down my legs onto my newly cleaned carpet is the exact same temperature as my pee. To be honest, I am not sure what it feels like to pee down my leg, but it makes sense that it would be something like this.

I call Ian on his cellphone. When he doesn't answer, I tell myself he is out of range or in a meeting, and I leave a message. I start to dial Harley's number, but stop. She has enough on her hands right now, and although Cliff would take me to the hospital if I asked, I remember that he's away again. Then I call Maggie. Again, no answer, and I leave a message. As I start to think that perhaps I should call an ambulance, Maggie phones back to say she can't pick me up. She is out in the countryside at a farm, but she has called Jesus, and he is on his way over to pick me up and take me to the hospital.

Jesus.

I clean myself as best I can and put on some clean clothes. I grab my bag, carefully packed for just such an occasion, and put it by the front door. I wait for Jesus to come.

When the doorbell rings, the dogs start barking. I go to the front of the house, and there stands Jesus in a Ramones T-shirt and with a panicked, stressed look on his face.

"Sit down, Lyd. I'll take your bag. I'll be back. You rest. I'll be back to get you."

He physically seats me in a chair on the porch and races out to the car with both Captain and Tennille following him. He is back to get my bag, which he had forgotten. The dogs are still outside, and he has forgotten about them as well. He tells me to stay sitting and is gone again.

Back in a minute, he asks if I am okay, if I need anything, should we leave right away. I ask if he will find the dogs, and he emphatically agrees that is a good idea. Back again, this time for their leashes to round them up.

"Are you ready now? Which hospital?" he asks as he pushes the dogs into the main part of the house and closes the door.

I nod, feeling that my train is headed full speed for the station of motherhood, and my lunatic friend is the engineer. I tell him, "HSC…Health Sciences Centre."

Jesus nods. "Got it."

As we walk to the car, he grips my arm hard.

"I'm making sure you don't fall," he says.

I have never fallen off the sidewalk of my house, a perilous precipice of two inches, in all the time I have lived there, but Jesus is just making sure. He explains that he has filled the back of his car with blankets and pillows so I will be comfortable.

It is a full ten minutes from my house to HSC, and there is hardly room for me in the backseat. I am stuffed in, but somehow, I still manage to get my seatbelt done up, maneuvering the buckle around tummy, pillows, and blankets. I'm not actually sure what all the linen is for, but I am apparently just along for the ride. As Jesus pulls out from the curb, I feel my first labour pain. A low, throbbing pain, like a menstrual cramp, only longer.

Jesus is driving too fast, and I ask him to slow down. Then we proceed along Portage Avenue toward the hospital at a manageable twenty kilometres per hour. Traffic is pulling out and passing us, drivers staring at our vehicle in annoyance as they pass.

Jesus helps me inside, so I can register at the desk of the emergency ward. Then he goes to park his car. I am put straight into a wheelchair as there are regulations that need to be followed. Besides, after the crazy ride with Jesus, I am happy to be in the safe hands of professionals. When he comes back, Jesus realizes he has forgotten my bag in the car and says he will go back to get it for me. He looks relieved to have something to do.

While he is gone, I am admitted into a labour room. The pains began in earnest, getting closer and closer together. Sometime during the afternoon, I am relieved to see Ian walk into the room. I can tell he is both excited and nervous as he holds my hand and talks with me. After a while though, I didn't want to talk anymore, content instead to listen to his soft voice chatting with the nurses and doctors. It is comforting, that deep voice, talking small talk.

They say that women forget the pain of childbirth the moment they see their new baby, and I believe this to be absolutely true. When the nurse places my tiny baby, our little girl in my arms, I look into her eyes, and I promise her that I will help her be all that she can be and that I will always love her. And then, just like that, she leaves my absolute control and becomes a perfect little person, all in her own right. Ian walks around from behind me and gently asks if he can hold her. When I pass our daughter to him, I see the tears roll down his cheeks.

Olivia is home and thriving. She is my everything, and I often stand in front of her crib while she sleeps, watching her breathe. Like every mother who has ever watched her child sleep, I am awed by the creation of life and the part I have played in this miracle.

Chapter 38

Harley

I am awakened from a deep, hard sleep, the kind of sleep that leaves me feeling unsure of where I am, even of who I am for one brief moment. In the second brief moment, I remember where I am, who I am, and that I am responding to the cry of a baby. My baby. Imogen is awake and hungry. I'm not sure how long she has been crying, but I seem to be hardwired to wake up whenever either or both of them are crying. Usually it is Imogen who starts the crying. She is bigger and hungrier than Asher.

Cliff is away again, on tour. I miss him so much and wish he was here. When we first got together, it never occurred to me a musician would always be away, but how does anyone know what the outcome will be when relationships first start? When I realized I was interested in Cliff, should I have stopped to think that if, when we had twins, he would often not be there to shoulder some of the load? Too late to think about that now. This is my life. Our life. And I love him and accept it.

I am still sleepy. It is dark in the bedroom, and I turn on the bedside lamp and slowly walk over to the bassinettes. I pick Imogen up and take her to my bed. I then go back and wake Asher, thinking that if I can feed him at the same time, I might manage a feeding schedule that will let me get a few hours of sleep in a row. I'm still not adept at nursing twins, and I fuss with babies and pillows until they are all in position for feeding. Imogen quickly latches on, but Asher is too sleepy, and it takes some encouragement to get him to suckle. He keeps falling asleep as soon as he has a bit of milk in his stomach. As I look down at them in the soft light of the bedroom, I am filled with such a profound love for them that it surges through me. My milk flows harder.

They are both asleep again, and I am sleepy too. I resist the urge to leave them in bed with me, to go to sleep with the little ones propped on their pillows, because I am so afraid that I will roll over on one of them. I reverse the initial process, and minutes later, I am back in bed with the light out and the babies sleeping in their bassinettes. I sleep, hard, until I am awakened again by the sound of a crying baby. And again.

In the first few days, it was particularly hard managing feeding and bathing and diaper changing. Thank goodness Cliff was around to help. He would wake up first and bring me the babies, one by one, to feed, then he would return them to their beds. He won't be home now until Tuesday, which means I have the weekend to get through on my own. I haven't been out of the house for two days, occupied and preoccupied with being a mom. The word sounds funny, coming out of my mouth, referring to me. Mom. Mommy. Momma. Mother. Ma? No, not Ma. Cliff bought groceries before he left for his tour, so I have everything I need. Well, almost everything.

Lydia was supposed to come over last week, but instead, she went into labour and is now home with her baby. I can't wait to meet Olivia, but it will be a few days yet. I am happy for her and for Ian, but I am so disappointed that I wasn't able to visit them in the hospital. Still, she promises to drop over in a day or so. By then, it will feel so good to have someone else to talk to.

The last time Lydia came over for a visit was the night after Cliff left town. I think that, as much as she wanted to see me, she was more excited to see Asher and Imogen again. The lasagna she brought with her, purchased from Superstore, was huge, but she said I could freeze some for later. I know I won't. I know I will eat it, meal after meal, until it is gone. I don't feel like cooking, but I have to eat something. Right now, the repetition of the meals suits me, suits the repetitive schedule of looking after Asher and Imogen. So much repetition that I am starting to lose track of time, of what day it is.

Cliff calls to say they have another opportunity out west, and he won't be back now until Friday. We talk for a long time, and when we hang up, I cry. I am starting to feel isolated and abandoned. It isn't his fault, but there isn't any end to the needs of the babies, and there is no break for me. When he was away before, I would spend time writing, but I don't have the attention span or the time for that. I have the television to keep me company and find myself sitting watching it between feedings.

Mom calls to see how things are going. She has called a few times since the twins were born. She wants to talk about them, about me, about how we are. At first, I was surprised, but now I welcome her calls. We have started a new relationship. Behind us, but not gone, never gone, is a mother who resented her life and her children, a lonely embittered woman who failed to nurture nineteen babies. Nineteen babies who grew up wild and unloved like weeds. Behind us is also me, the wild and unloved weed girl, a resentful misfit, aimless and angry. I honestly don't know what she is to me now. Can she ever actually be my mother? Can she ever not be my mother? I'm not sure I am completely welcoming her back into my life either, but I want to give her a chance with me. Don't look back, Harley. Ignore those footsteps you have left behind you. My head says don't trust her; my heart says I need to. My heart wins.

I ask her if she would like to come and stay with me for a few days. I explain that Cliff is on the road with the band, and I wouldn't mind some company. It will be the first time in years that I have spent more than a few hours with her. She sounds so happy that when I hang up the phone, I feel the same excitement as when I watch someone open a special gift that I have given them. Excited, but also anticipatory and invested. The thrill of the power of being able to give someone exactly what they want. Then I remind myself that Mom is not my special project. She is a hard woman who has lived a failed life. It is not my job or my duty to fix her. There is no fixing to be done. There is a difference between fixing and giving someone the opportunity to change for the better. I have a brief thought of me standing in that line, watching Lydia, then my saviour lady, now my good friend, wanting not to disappoint her, wanting her judgement of me to be a good one. She didn't fix me.

I spend the rest of the day on the merry-go-round, feeding, burping, changing, and sleep for all. Everything again. When Cliff calls again, I tell him about Mom coming. He still hasn't met her and sounds wary of her visit. He tells me to be careful. I agree. Feed, burp, change, sleep.

At 9:30 a.m., the buzzer for the lobby door rings.

"It's me. Mom. Viola."

Yes, Mom. I know who you are.

I let her in and wait for her to come up to the apartment. There is a faint knock, and when I open the door, Mom stands there, her face falsely bright, unsure of her welcome, looking like a Jehovah Witness with a stack of Watchtowers in her hand. She looks like I might send her packing. Sorry, I have all that I need. Try next door. Of course, I usher her in. She sets her red, vinyl suitcase by the door. It has a large strap and buckle tightened around it, clearly as back-up in case the zipper breaks. It doesn't look like there's much in it; thankfully, she doesn't plan on staying too long. I remember seeing that suitcase as a child, and despite being old, it looks in good shape, as if it hasn't been used much.

I tell her she will be staying in the babies' room, that their bassinettes are in my bedroom for now. She drags her suitcase to it and lifts it onto the single bed. She takes out two small gifts, one wrapped in pink tissue paper, the other in recycled birthday paper.

"I ran out," she offers simply, in case I had forgotten.

I hadn't forgotten. This is the way things have always been.

She hands them to me, and we walk to the kitchen. I place them on the table and begin making some coffee for us. We sit at the kitchen table, and I can tell she is anxious for me to open the presents. Inside are two exquisite pairs of identical moccasins, as tiny as two of my fingers. They are beaded, the tiny glass beads brightly coloured, and the stitching is even. There are tiny moose hair tufts in pink and blue around the edges. The fringe has been cut as fine as string. I can still smell smoke on them.

"These are beautiful, Mom. Where did you get them?"

She looks shyly down, then up at me, excitement, sadness, love on her face, and she tells me that they were once those of her twin sisters. She has kept them in a bottom drawer in her bedroom, unable to part with them. Her grandmother had given them to her sisters when they were born. I finger the tiny slippers, feeling in them a sense of history, of belonging, of the joining of generations, of Asher and Imogen to their great, great, great grandmother. I also feel the joining of Asher and Imogen to their grandmother.

"We'll try these on them when they wake up, Mom. And we'll take pictures for you."

Mom is here to help, and help she does. She gets rid of the left-over bits of food hiding out in the fridge and makes actual meals, each one different. All the laundry gets done, the beds and towels changed, and groceries purchased. I sleep and wake up to Mom standing over me, a baby in each arm, advising me that they are hungry. The floors are swept, the carpets vacuumed, the toilets cleaned. Her house on Park Avenue has never been so clean. In between feedings, we chat or watch television or go for walks, or I nap.

Mom has started to read one of my books, but she isn't much of a reader, and each time she picks it up, she falls asleep, dozing in her chair. Once I found her asleep, the phone book in her lap. When she woke up, I asked her what she was looking for.

"A friend named Chartrand," she answered. "We lost touch years ago. There are too many here." And then she promptly returned the book to the shelf where she found it.

I appreciate her help but am most impressed by how great she is with the twins. Everything about having a baby seems easy for Mom. Of course, that should not be such a surprise to me, given that she had nineteen of them, but I was the youngest of them all. I have never even seen Mom with a baby in her arms. As she rocks the twins, I can tell she is a natural, exactly as the doctor had said when her first baby was born.

Sometimes, when I watch her busying herself around my home, I am so angry I want to shout at her. Why couldn't you have done more for me when I was a child? Where were you to support me then? Why did I have to do everything myself? Why didn't you help me? Why did I have to pull myself up by my own bootstraps?

But I hold my tongue. My mother, whoever she was when I was growing up, was trying to be my Mom, and now she is trying to be a grandma. Dad isn't around, so here she can be anyone she wants to be. She hasn't had a drink since she arrived, and smoking means a trip down the elevator and outside, so cigarette breaks are few and far between. I have been trying to find out more about her family, her parents, her brothers and sisters, but she either avoids these questions, answers them quickly, or lies to me. When I ask where there are now, she shrugs and says she doesn't know.

Cliff calls to let me know he is going to be home tomorrow. The tour is over, and they are driving back to Winnipeg for a well-earned break. I am beside myself in anticipation, and I think it is finally time for him and Mom to meet. However, when I say that to her, she becomes antsy, says she has to leave, that she can't stay any longer. She immediately goes into her room, packs up her red suitcase, and puts it by the door.

I don't think she is ready to meet Cliff. I think this new person she is inventing may be too fragile to stand the test, the scrutiny, the judgement of someone who loves me, of someone who knows all our dirty laundry. She still needs to prove herself to me, to herself, before she can prove herself to Cliff.

She is at the door, purse in hand. She has kissed Asher and Imogen a hundred times and tells them she will see them soon. She turns to leave, but I stop her. Then I remember. "Mom! The slippers! We need the picture!" Mom comes back into the living room, and together we work the little slippers onto soft baby feet. Mom holds the twins, one in each arm, and I take a photo with the camera on my phone. We put the babies back into their beds and walk to the door again.

I cannot remember the last time I hugged my mother, so I simply say, "Hugs?"

She stops and turns toward me. I hug her, and she feels warm and soft. This does not seem familiar at all. I feel her pat me on the back twice. The moment has been ended.

"I love you, Mom."

She smiles, grunts, and says, "Ya, me too."

I watch her walk down the hall toward the elevator, pulling her suitcase behind her, the tiny wheels inadequate for its load.

Chapter 39

Maggie

Nancy is back in the picture. As much as I have tried to be non-beige, to add colour to my life, to exist with Mexican dishes on my table, I can never be as colourful as Nancy.

She blows into a room, big breasts first, big teeth second, oozing sex availability, sex for sale, whaddya got to trade then? Jesus tells me her girls are in better shape than they were. I feel jealous that he is looking, that he appreciates someone's fine work.

I feel jealous. Meaningful words. Maybe I do want what I didn't think I wanted. My own girls are small and have never entered a room first, but that was never a bad thing. Until now. Instinctively I touch the top of my blouse, pulling the edges closer together, protecting my inadequate breasts from the likes of Nancy's, big and bold, revamped, restyled, sitting up high. This is not a fair fight. My teeth are pretty good, though. Smaller than Nancy's, but they could lay waste to hers in a whiteness brawl. And healthy. Yes, I have brushed and flossed my teeth. Neither my breasts nor my teeth ooze sex, so I have no weapons with which to do battle with Nancy. Healthy teeth don't count in the kind of war I am heading into.

Each day when I go to work, travelling the perpetualness of the Manitoba prairies and eking bovine life from orchestrated gene pools, Nancy goes to The Brick, slowly drawing Jesus to her breasts. Is he even aware? I wonder what he wants. We are friends only, so I should be able to ask him that question, but I am afraid of the answer. Is there truth in the statement that men and women can never just be friends? I am beginning to believe that's true. What I know for sure is that I am capable of hiding the truth from myself, of pretending to want nothing, as long as my status quo isn't threatened. And I am starting to think that maybe I took Jesus for granted. Did I really believe he would settle for nothing more than warm comradery with non-beige me? I have been relationship lazy, and evidently, there is both a risk involved and a price to pay. I accepted our non-sexual bond as something we both wanted, and now I am about to lose my friend to a slut. Go Maggie. That felt good. I have been happy, but now that is threatened. I need to take my small, healthy, white teeth and my tiny breasts and hole up, sharpening my mental talons, determining what I want and then making sure I get it. I am not beige.

Nancy has taken a few shifts at The Brick and is generally making herself available to Jesus. I ask him about trusting her after her abrupt departure that almost bankrupted him. He says she has changed, but I think the only change in Nancy is that she has no money now. That she knows an easy mark isn't a change. She always knew one.

I am old. I have passed the demarcation point in life where I could be anything I want. Now, I must make do with what I have. I can tweak me a bit here and there, hitch me up here and pat me down there, but in the end, I am pretty much now what I am ever going to be. There is no time left to decide, late on the curve, to become a doctor or a ballerina. I have to narrow my options. I can either move up the scale of bovine reproduction, or I can create a dumbed-down version of me, taking light jobs in retail work. I can join a fitness centre for women, but I won't be winning any weightlifting contests. I can travel, of course, but where will I go? How risky will it be? Will I have adequate health insurance? I could leverage my future by practising some old and rusty skills, trying to make up for lost time, using what I already have, but is that what I really want to do? I can't help but wonder if I am at that point in life where people should be saying, "Oh, look at Margaret. Isn't she content?" What I think those people are saying is, "Oh, look at Maggie. Hasn't she given up on life." I don't remember putting that one foot on the edge of the slippery slope. Still, here I go, free-falling, away from everything I have carefully built for myself. I close my eyes. It's all downhill from here.

It is late afternoon, and I have spent most of the day driving from farm to farm. At each stop, I am offered a cup of coffee or tea with evaporated milk from a can or powdered creamer, the whitening options of those who live the rural life. Finally heading home, my nerves are jittery, and my thoughts are fast, coming out like bullets from a machine gun. They aren't connected, but there is force behind each of them, and I know I will need some musing time to put them all together. What I have determined so far is there is no time to waste, and I need to leverage my friendship with Jesus into something else, if that is what we both want. All I need is a bit more time to figure out what that is. But who will give me that time? Nancy has already blown the two-minute warning whistle, so there isn't much of it left. Come on, Maggie. The time is now.

I stop in at The Brick for a drink on my way home. I go to The Scotch Room, but it's quiet, and Nancy is tucked up at Jesus' bar-top, enraptured by another of his animated stories. He is laughing, and she is watching him, analyzing him, judging him. If Meaghan was here, she would have sent Nancy packing, then told Jesus that once bitten, twice shy. She would have asked him point blank what he was thinking, encouraging a woman who had taken all that he had and left him in financial ruin. She would have taken Nancy by the scruff of the neck and the top of her pants and heave-hoed her out the door, landing her squarely on the curb of Portage Avenue. Heave the hoe. But Meaghan isn't here anymore. I am caught in sad reverie, thinking about her, her absence, her death, our loss.

I take my drink over to the bar side and sit beside Nancy. Jesus' eye catches mine, quickly, guiltily. Busted, Jesus. What are you doing? What do you want? Let me help you figure it out. I sip my drink and listen to him talk. Nancy encourages him, but I note he is less animated, less flirtatious, with me as part of his audience. Jesus is moving toward his best behaviour, sharing eye contact with both of us, talking with us equally.

When the bar starts to get busier with the after-work crowd, Nancy offers to help him serve drinks. Jesus is about to say yes to her offer when he catches my eye, and instead says no thanks, he has it under control.

When I was a child, we called that look I gave him the hairy eyeball. Now they call it the stink-eye. I sense Nancy's back stiffen, and I know she has identified her enemy.

She swivels her bar stool slightly away from me. I swivel mine slightly toward her. The dance begins. Game. On. The battle call has been heard. Behind the bar, Jesus pours draught for customers, unaware. Or aware and not showing it. I wonder what it would be like for Jesus, simple rock 'n' roll T-shirted Jesus, to be the prize in a fight to the finish. Will this appeal to his ego, or will he be saddened by having to make a choice? I think I know him well enough. He doesn't like what is happening. He is a good man.

Nancy is not a good woman. The excesses of her life have found her, sagging her skin, yellowing her teeth, leaving pores on her nose gaping large and black, but the worst is the rot from the inside. Her despair is eating away at her. Bit by bit, hopelessness and disappointment chew away, leaving her more and more empty. She is retracing her steps now, looking for when she got old, trying to recreate her past, to give herself a second chance. This can't happen, of course, particularly not with me watching over her, keeping track of her actions. Find some other past life to redestroy, Nancy. Somewhere along the way, she ended up with none of her dreams fulfilled. Is Jesus the most likely way to happiness? Or like the rest of Nancy's life, will he be the temporary answer that will buoy her small, dense heart, buried deep beneath her newly perky breasts? Nancy doesn't care about Jesus, and it hasn't occurred to her that part of being in a relationship with someone is to bring happiness and fulfillment to them as well. She is so blinded by her own failure to achieve that she thinks only of her own needs. What can she get? What can she steal? She wants to get Jesus in her life, and she will steal him from me. Now I feel guilty for leaving him out in the open, shiny and valuable, for anybody to come along and snatch.

I order another drink. It goes down smoothly, and I feel my anxiety lessening as the scotch hits its mark. Another easy mark, and I feel my tense energy leave my body. Where does it go, all that tense energy? When millions of people return home from work, pounding back millions of decompression drinks, where does all that negative energy go, pent up all day in the name of following rules made by no one anyone knows? Is there a psychic reverse charger where you plug yourself in and the tension leaves your body to go out into the world to charge those whose strength is wavering? Or does that tension simply hover over us, waiting for the next day, for a weak moment, waiting to jump back in and continue the damaging build-up?

I watch Nancy as I sip my second drink. She laughs too loud, and she keeps checking to see if I am watching. She knows the game is on, and she waits to see if she can drive a reaction from me. I am quiet, pretending complete absorption in my own thoughts, giving her no indication that she is worth my attention. The bar has filled up, and Jesus has no time for games. Nancy orders another drink and then another. She is drinking hard, and I nurse my drink, watching her. I can outwait her, and I do. Her posture has changed, one shoulder dropping, and her words have taken on a rounded, less precise quality. She leaves her drink at the bar and goes to the bathroom. When she returns, I can tell she has reapplied her red lipstick. It is thick and forms a bloody crust around the top of her drink. I watch her as she notices it and tries to lick it away, smearing its waxy substance with her tongue. She catches my eye, and I smile. First blood has been drawn. Nancy orders another drink. Determined not to leave the battleground, I order a third drink and a glass of water.

A man around the corner of the bar sends a drink over to Nancy. Jesus delivers it, along with a nod indicating the sender. When Nancy smiles at the man, he brings his drink over beside her. Jesus watches as Nancy slurs greetings and thanks to the man, drunken fawning. She paws at his arm. I sip my water. She heads outside for a cigarette, her steps unsteady, her shoulders held too square, making eye contact with everyone on her way, placing each foot carefully. Her purse is on her chair to make sure her seat remains empty, waiting for her return. Her new friend orders her another drink, and Jesus puts it in front of the empty chair. When Nancy returns, she stumbles into her chair and exchanges words with the man. She gulps down her drink, grabs her purse, and heads for the door, her friend in hot pursuit.

Nancy can be bought, and the battle won for the price of two drinks. I leave my third drink untouched and settle up with Jesus. We look at each other, and I swear he looks relieved. Perhaps he doesn't have the strength to resist Nancy, even knowing that disaster is the only possible outcome. Does he know she will manipulate him into losing his sense of self, his pride, for her sake? Does he think she needs saving, he her saviour? I have saved him instead. I am the saviour lady. Thanks can come later. Muchas gracias.

I am up early and about to leave for work when Jesus calls and asks if he can come over for a drink this evening. At first, I want to say no because I can't tell from his voice if he is angry or upset or disappointed or indifferent, none of which matches the smile on my face when I first heard him on the other end of the line. The end of the line. Is this it? Has time finally run out?

I drive from farm to farm, my thoughts always returning to what happened last night. Nancy had embarrassed herself, of course, but I was consumed by worry that I too had stepped over a line. I was so intent on getting Nancy out of the picture, of winning the battle, that I forgot how Jesus must have felt. My emotions through the day run the gamut from those of a small, mean girl intent on getting what she wants to those of a woman who has rescued something incredibly precious from theft.

But there is something else going on in my head, something even more worrying, especially if time has run out. I realize that I love him, for all his good and bad, and that the battle in the bar was only me being terrified that I would lose him to Nancy or to someone else. I have to tell him how I feel, but how to say it? I'm not looking for a dignified way or a way that will preserve my pride in case he doesn't feel the same. I need a way that will let him know I want to spend my life with him, that I love him, really love him. I am looking for a way to tell him all that, regardless of the outcome.

When Jesus arrives, I pour him a drink, and we sit in the living room. I am so thankful for him, for his presence. I observe his long, unruly hair, his wrinkled pants, and a T-shirt so worn the name of the band is indiscernible. I want to speak first, but Jesus has come to me, and I know I need to hear him out before I can say anything. Is this the stuff of kids, or am I feeling the passion of youth at my age? If so, it is both a gift and a curse.

He clears his throat. Then he takes a long drink from his glass.

"Bit dry."

Another moment passes until he finally begins to speak. And oh, how he begins. He tells me of his love for me, of his loneliness, of his respect for me, of how he wishes I was beside him in his bed when he wakes up in the morning, wishes he could kiss my lips before going to sleep. He talks about wanting the comfort of my love and wanting to share his days with me. As I listen, I hang on every word, each a pearl in a string of possibility. They aren't the exact words I had planned to say to him, but they are pretty close. When he finally finishes, he picks up his glass and takes another long drink and then continues.

Jesus tells me his story of loneliness, of his search for love, of how he had been desperate for the type of love that other men had. He was disappointed in himself, ashamed, in fact, that he had seen Nancy as a person in whom he could invest these hopes. He talked about last night and how his own stupidity had created the situation at the bar. He said he had spent long hours after closing thinking about what he wanted and how he would get it. "There is something I want to ask you, Maggie.".

"Will you marry me, Maggie? Will you be my wife? Will you take this old guy, for better or worse, or even worse than that? Will you let me love you, care for you, help you in every way I can?" A final drink drained his glass and then he took my hand in his. "Please say yes, Margaret. My Maggie. Be my wife."

All my carefully planned words are wasted, of course. I need only one.

Chapter 40

Viola

I've been keeping in touch with Harley by calling from time to time, but I don't like to call too much in case the little ones are sleeping. It really felt good meeting Asher and Imogen, and seeing Harley doing pretty good too. She sent me a photo of the little twins wearing them slippers I gave them. I still don't know her Cliff, but she seems stuck on him, and anyways, he's the baby-daddy, so she's stuck with him too. She don't call me much, but she does call.

Aaron is coming home in a few weeks. I'm pretty nervous about it because I got used to having the quiet of the house to just me. I seen him a few times in the last bit, but gas costs money, and there ain't much of that since he and Lionel went away. Anyways, I don't like to drive if I can help it, and I never was much good at it. We ever only had one car anyway, and Aaron always had it, so I didn't get much practice. It ain't my fault he got into trouble, so why should I try too hard to make him happy? It's not like there is too much to talk about anyways. I can't be bothered seeing Lionel. He never was much good to me.

I've been trying to find some of my brothers and sisters, and I think quite a few are still around the hometown. Sometimes, I think about that little town and growing up there and what it was like to be a little kid running wild. There was a store, but there never seemed to be too much in it to buy, except for cigarettes, chips, and candy. There was a lot of candy.

Rows and rows of it laid out in little boxes at about a kid's eye level. I loved that candy so much, it made me ache just thinking about the sweetness. Sometimes I would get some money, mostly from collecting pop bottles, and go to the store. Sometimes I nicked a few pennies from Mom's purse or Dad's dresser. Mr. Rene, the owner, would give us kids a little paper bag, and we would pick what we wanted from the little boxes and put them in the bag. Even now, when I see a little brown paper bag, I think about filling it with candy. When we had enough candy to match our money, we would give the bag to Mr. Rene, and he would empty it and count it all up. If we had extra candy, sometimes he didn't make us pay, so we always had a few more in the bag than we could pay for. Mojos. Spearmint leaves. Popeye cigarettes. Licorice pipes. Jaw breakers. Green candy shoelaces. Cinnamon toothpicks. SweeTARTS. Lik-M-Aid. Big red wax lips filled with sweet water. So good. Sometimes, I put the candy in water and made pretend juice. We touched the boxes of candy with our dirty fingers, which would probably get us sent to jail now, but Mr. Rene didn't care a bit. He was just a good old guy, selling cigarettes and chips and candy. But once we was old enough to smoke, he charged us full price and no extras for free. Fair enough.

Me and Aaron drove back home a few years ago, just for a look around, and we tried to go see Mr. Rene. I thought he might be able to tell me where my family was. But the store was locked up tight, and there was a big piece of a cardboard box taped in the window saying "Closed." The sign over the door was still there. "Grattons." Rene Gratton. We never called him that though. We only ever called him Mr. Rene. The store didn't look like it had been open for a long, long time. Maybe he died. I guess people just go into the city to buy their stuff now. I don't know where the kids would go for their candy though. Makes me feel a bit sad about that because there sure wasn't much to do in that town except eat candy or smoke or drink at the tavern, and now they can't even eat candy.

I'm making a cup of tea when the phone rings. I don't get too many calls, and it makes me jump because it rings so loud, and my nerves is shot because of Aaron going to come home soon. A man's voice asks for Vi. Ain't nobody calls me Vi except for my family. I say nicely, "Vi speaking," just like a fine lady, and I wait to hear who it is.

"Vi, this is Paul. Did you used to be Vi Chartrand? This is me, Paul Chartrand."

My brother, Paul. I haven't heard from him or of him for too many years to count. The last time I saw him, he was riding his bike down the main street, a girl's bike that was way too big for him, his little legs pumping them pedals because he was too short to be able to sit hisself up on the bike seat. He was a smart one, younger than me, and I wonder what he wants. Everybody always wants something, this I know, and I need to be careful not to give him too much information.

I tell him that I was Viola Chartrand. We have some phone chit-chat, the nervous kind that can only lead to meeting up, one-on-one. He says he will come over to the house and that he is in Brandon on business. Likely on business. His business will be trying to scam something from me, that's for sure. I tell him I got no drink in the house, but he says that's okay, he just wants to meet up. He's on his way over in about a half-hour; he don't have too much time. I'm not going to dress up or clean the house because I don't want him to think we got stuff worth taking. I do rinse out the teapot because, truth told, I am kind of excited to see him. Curious as hell, too.

When I hear a knock at the front door, I run to the front room and look out the window. There is a long black car on the road, the windows dark so I can't see in. There is another knock, and I go to the front door and open it, leaving the storm door shut.

Paul stands in front of me, clear through the ratty screen, as if he were six years old, still on his bike. His skin is shiny, his hair is combed back, his sunglasses are dark, and his ironed shirt is all whitey-white under his navy suit. I don't do expensive stuff, but I know it when I sees it. He looks expensive. He looks young too, way younger than I do, or than Aaron does, and there is something clean and honest about him. I take too long to read him, and he lifts his sunglasses and peers at me quizzically. I open the door and let him in.

As we walk into the living room, he stops to untie his shiny black shoes and slip them off his feet. His shoes look thin, like they can't support a foot or a body or a life. He couldn't run fast in a shoe like that. I look around, ashamed that I haven't cleaned a bit, knowing he will leave with my dirt on him. He leans forward to hug me, but I step away, step back, just out of reach, and ask if he wants a cup of tea. He accepts, and I tell him to have a seat while I go get it.

I need to get my bearings. I just imagined that my people would all be like me, scraping together a life at the bottom of the heap, hating everyone and trusting nobody. My people don't do shiny and new and expensive. I can see how he sees me, his older sister, wearing out her life, padding around in bare feet in piles of her own filth, alone in her house, ugly and unkempt and without pride.

The kettle whistles, and I make tea. I pour it into two coffee cups, one with the phone number for Midas Muffler and the other touting the benefits of the YMCA. I note there are brown rings on the inside of both cups, but it is too late to clean up. I yell at him about taking sugar, but he says no thanks, and I carry the cups into the front room. His sunglasses are perched on top of his head, and he is perched on the edge of the chesterfield, his long legs splayed between it and the coffee table. He looks awkward and out of place. He ain't awkward, but he sure is a fish out of water. Paul Chartrand. My little baby brother. Who'd a thunk it?

We talk, but it don't flow smoothly. He asks about Aaron and the kids. I ask about how he has been doing, and I'm trying to find out how he got all that money. He's president or something of some corporation, which is like a business. He has a driver who waits in the car outside. His corporation is expanding into Brandon, and he will be in town from time to time. He's lost track of the others and never gets back home. I watch his face as he speaks. His eyes are warm, and his smile is perfect, not just teethwise, but genuinely caring. There is no wariness or weariness on his face. He has a wife and a few kids, almost grown, and lives in Winnipeg. He starts to ask about each of my brood, but each has a long and sordid story, and with nineteen of them, we could be at it for a while. I give him a quick rundown, leaving out the worst bits. I land on Harley, the youngest, and tell him about her, her books, her babies, her happy life, and my recent visit. I try to play down the hardship of my life. The clouds pass over the sunlight in his eyes when I mention her little twins, and he asks if I remember our twins. He was just a little guy then, but he still remembers that sad time. I feel my heart harden at the painful memory, and I watch his face soften at the thought of his long dead sisters. We are light years apart.

He finishes his tea, and says he has a meeting to attend. He promises to call again. I watch him tie his shoes. He ties them like a little boy, wrapping rabbit ears around each other. I want to cry, watching my baby brother put on his shoes. He reaches for a hug this time, and I let him touch me. He turns to go, and as he walks down the sidewalk to the road, I see a man step out of the car, and open the back door for Paul. Paul didn't steal anything from the house as far as I can tell.

I feel kind of shaky, like I can't quite get back to me, to who I am. I have another cup of tea and think back on Paul and the rest of them, trying to remember what they was really like, you know, as people, and not just as snatches of memories. I think about my mom and dad, but not for long. Then I think about each of my brothers and sisters. I never knew them as adults, and as children, their memories is distorted, out of context to my adult's perspective. They is my family, sure, but they is strangers, and I probably couldn't have more than a cup of tea with any of them without running out of things to say. Besides, where would I start? There is life-times of experiences between all of us, more differences than sameness, and I don't think there is enough time left in life to figure all that out. Anyways, I can't be bothered. Paul won't be back, I'm pretty sure, and with Aaron coming home, that's definitely a good thing. Aaron don't have much patience for fancy people.

The phone rings again, and the loud jangle makes me jump. It's Stony Mountain. Aaron is getting out in six days. He'll be coming home. My nerves settle at that news, and I look around, thinking I should spruce the place up a bit, get things ready for him getting home. It's been a long time.

Chapter 41

Harley

I keep thinking about Mom when she stayed with me in Winnipeg. She had been energized during our visit, but as I watched her walk away from me down that long hallway and head back to her life, I saw how old she had become. It wasn't her slow step or greyed, bent head. It was an image of her nearing the end of her life, waiting to catch up with the coffin. I didn't sense she had a lot left to receive, and she'd never had a lot to give.

At first, I was filled with love and optimism that we could have a relationship. For a few weeks after she left, she called from time to time, checking to see if I was okay, how the babies were, how I was doing with Cliff away. But slowly, the calls came less frequently, and I haven't heard from her for a long time now. When I call, she doesn't answer the phone. I hate that I have been so easily discarded. I wanted to matter in the eyes of my mom, and for a while there, I think I really did.

Dad is out. My brother isn't, and from what I have heard, Lionel won't be out for a while yet. Dad is back home in Brandon, drinking and smoking and fighting. I don't think he is dealing drugs anymore, although I don't know for sure. What I do know is the dealing was Lionel's influence. Dad simply doesn't have any entrepreneurial spirit or business acumen or even an industrious bone in his body. He would have been a worker bee in the distribution of illegal drugs, not the queen bee. In fact, he has always looked for reasons to let others do the hard work, preferring that his role in any story be small. He had the sex. Mom had the babies. The babies raised themselves.

I have been feeling kind of despondent about Mom. It felt good to have a grandma for Asher and Imogen, but Cliff warned me not to hope it would last. I knew that when Dad got home, he would once again consume Mom's thoughts, emotions, and time, and it would be too easy for her to simply revert back to being a follower. She can't support. She can't sustain. And now, she is following in Dad's footsteps, taking the easy way, following someone who is already taking the path of least resistance.

I worry about doing better, about being a better mother and nurturer. I am terrified I am not adequate for this job, whether I have the ability to change the direction of something or someone simply by putting my foot down in the flow of it and seeing it move toward something new. Who can empower me to put that foot down, to make that change, to raise my children in love? Cliff tells me I am strong, I am good. But is that in spite of or because of my parents? And does it matter either way?

Who put their foot down in the flow of my life when I was headed off in a wrong direction, knowing too much of nothing at all? Of course, I know there are many who redirected me, and all of them family, although not the family I ever expected.

Lydia, imperfectly perfect, with her own burdens, who loves everything with too much passion, driving all her bargains hard and with her shoulder against the wheel. Lydia is the one who first stomped her foot down and changed the flow of my life. Nothing is easy for her; everything happens with extreme energy, the hardest work, but somehow when she found me, she was exactly what I needed when I needed it. She was a reluctant resource, sulking about the commitment before rejoicing in its possibilities. I remember the days of the old Volvo, replaced now by a fancy SUV. Lydia and the dogs and a newly found Harley piled in, heading off toward whatever needed doing. I simply became part of what she had to offer, not part of any plan she had.

She also pulled Meaghan in, invited her into her life, gave her everything she had, but not one bit more or one bit less. Then she left both of us to our own, to flourish, to succeed.

Wanting to protect her friend, Meaghan was at first suspicious of me and my intentions. Then, slowly but surely, she saw me for who and what I could be. I still remember that click on the line when she hung up on me and how that was the start of the rest of my life. She was strong and determined; she lived on her own terms; and she taught us more about life than she ever knew.

And then along came Orval. Lonely, unfulfilled Orval. We were two outcasts, smoking cigarettes together, huddled against the world, sharing our kindnesses and our stories seven minutes at a time. His gift to me was me, an opportunity to become something more, someone intent on living beyond my situation by sharing stories that would connect me with those who had been waiting patiently for me to arrive.

Jesus came into our lives as a friend who needed a family, and who became part of this family of friends, weaving himself into everyone's life with his simple ways and incredible stories of his own and those of others. By inviting me in, he helped me find a new purpose and allowed me to show him who he truly was, but it was Meaghan who stomped her foot down and changed the flow of his life.

Margaret watched Lydia and aspired to a richer life so that Maggie could inch toward a fuller and more satisfying version of herself. Her gifts are her words and her experiences, although it is her understanding of and love for Jesus that endears her most to all of us. And then there is Cliff—strong, sensitive, funny, and so full of love, trying to do the right thing every step of the way. Cliff and Harley, lovers and parents, learning together, leaning on each other, and leaning on those around them.

No, Mom. No, Viola. You are not part of this family, my family, so you don't get to claim credit for me, for my happiness, for my ability to pull myself up by my own bootstraps. My strength comes from the people who have gone out of their way to stand in the way when things go sideways, who will block the wind, stop the flow, and pull the load. It doesn't come from those who live small lives with their focus on what they can get next or what their entitlements are or on giving the smallest amount possible.

Your role has been filled by Lydia, she who is a giver, not a taker, who has given me the gift of personal responsibility. There are no entitlements in her life. She has worked for everything she has and has shared that everything with the people around her. Adversity isn't even in her vocabulary. She and Ian have something special, something they almost lost, and I think they appreciate it more because of that. I often think back to those early days, sitting in her porch, paralyzed by the uncertainty of my youth, with no resources, in a strange city, unmissed by my family far away, unsure of which forks in the road took me to where I was. How did I get from there to where I am today? I still want to make Lydia proud of me.

No, I did not get to where I am on my own, and I will not continue on my own. There is a full life and a deep love on which to thrive here in the company of friends, past and present, lessons to be learned in the gift of family, then and now, and I am excited about the possibility and opportunity in the road ahead, in the paths we take, in the flow of our lives.

The house is quiet, and Asher and Imogen aren't due to wake for at least an hour. Asher and Imogen who got the start I should have had, who got the mother and father I always wanted, who are already beyond my control. They are my reason to be more, to be better, to be.

I stand and move to the table by the window. The light from outside is bright and warm and full of promise. As I turn on my computer and open it to a new page, there are words already in my head, in my heart, aching to be brought forth from the void, to see the light of day.

I start to type. There is a story I want to tell …

Here is the world.
Beautiful and terrible things will happen.
Don't be afraid.

CPSIA information can be obtained
at www.ICGtesting.com
Printed in the USA
LVHW041532120623
749513LV00006B/607